T0033212

PRAISE FOR

SIX DAYS in ROME

"Francesca Giacco is a stunning writer, and *Six Days in Rome* is a brilliant transporting experience—a novel about belonging, with heart and heat; a gorgeous and literary holiday."
—Lisa Taddeo, *#1 New York Times* bestselling author of *Three Women* and *Animal*

"Sometimes it takes a three-thousand-year-old city to feel brand new. *Six Days in Rome* unfolds with all the crisp wonderment of a two-star hotel map. Sensorial as hell, it acknowledges the major landmarks and thoroughfares, but knows you have to get lost in the invisible, the unrendered, to find what you didn't know you were looking for. An ode to funky wine labels, good taste, and true inspiration, Francesca Giacco has penned a stunningly cool and stylish debut."
—Paul Beatty, Man Booker Prize–winning author of *The Sellout*

"If Sally Rooney and Frances Mayes co-wrote a novel in an Airbnb near the Spanish Steps, it might read something like *Six Days in Rome*. Smart, keenly observed, and deeply felt, this is a book for anyone who's ever journeyed abroad to find themselves."
—David Ebershoff, *New York Times* bestselling author of *The Danish Girl* and *The 19th Wife*

"Giacco's debut is an intimate, entertaining, clear-eyed evocation of a disillusioned young female artist's coming of age amongst the ruins of Rome and, like her heart-broken narrator, very good company."

—Elissa Schappell, Author of *Blueprints for Building Better Girls*

"*Six Days in Rome* is a masterful debut—a literary travelogue that maps both the internal and external, capturing the intimate fire-works of heartbreak and the endless question of identity, alongside the sumptuous backdrop of Rome. Francesca Giacco has written a novel as artful as it is affecting." —Adrienne Brodeur, Author of *Wild Game: My Mother, Her Lover, and Me*

"Giacco's rendering of collecting pieces of a shattered heart is relatable and encouraging...But an even greater draw is the feeling that just under a week in Italy really is included in the cover price, through descriptions of pistachio gelato drowned in olive oil, jasmine snaking up a crumbled Roman column, and exchanging the deep love of a partner for the rough kiss of an espresso-drinking stranger." —*Glamour*

"In this sensual novel of rage, heartbreak, and desire, a young artist named Emilia travels to Rome to reckon with the end of a relationship. When an encounter with an American expat sparks a new connection, Emilia begins to see herself in a new light—both as a woman and as an artist." —*Harper's Bazaar*

"Elegant...Upscale escapism." —*Kirkus*

"Sensual and deliberately paced...Giacco revels in her setting, providing rich descriptions of the streets, food, and people Emilia encounters...Sumptuously written." —*Publishers Weekly*

"Writing—and travel writing in particular—should transport a reader. Surprisingly few authors can successfully do it. Francesca Giacco pulls it off in her debut novel...Passion, exploration, and reflection [pair] with evocative descriptions of pasta, glorious wines, magnificent museums, and architectural wonders." —*Air Mail*

"Part *Eat Pray Love*, part *Heartburn*, part family saga, Giacco's debut novel takes readers on a luscious journey rich in description and emotional resonance...Readers will want to linger in this world created by a promising new writer." —*Booklist*

"Makes just as much sense of the ancient city at the heart of the book as it does love and heartbreak...may inspire you to take a solo journey, even if it's only one of self-discovery." —*The List*

"Francesca Giacco's exceptional use of language in *Six Days in Rome* creates an immensely nuanced protagonist in Emilia...Sensational sensory descriptions capture what it feels like to experience Rome's famous and off-the-beaten-path sights in the sultry July heat, as well as the city's sounds, touch, smells, and particularly its tastes...Giacco's prose keeps us turning the page...for the intimacy she creates between us and Emilia so that we become enraptured in her nuanced journey and, ultimately, deeply care about where she's been...and where she might be going."

—*Martha's Vineyard Times*

"[A] contemplative, quite moving account of a heartbroken young artist's overseas trip."

—The Film Stage

SIX DAYS in ROME

A NOVEL

FRANCESCA GIACCO

GRAND
CENTRAL

New York. Boston

This book is a work of fiction. Names, characters, places, and incidents are the product of the author's imagination or are used fictitiously. Any resemblance to actual events, locales, or persons, living or dead, is coincidental.

Copyright © 2022 by Francesca Giacco

Reading group guide copyright © 2022 by Francesca Giacco and Hachette Book Group, Inc.

Cover design by Tree Abraham. Cover image © Georgios Kritsotakis/Shutterstock. Cover copyright © 2023 by Hachette Book Group, Inc.

Hachette Book Group supports the right to free expression and the value of copyright. The purpose of copyright is to encourage writers and artists to produce the creative works that enrich our culture.

The scanning, uploading, and distribution of this book without permission is a theft of the author's intellectual property. If you would like permission to use material from the book (other than for review purposes), please contact permissions@hbgusa.com. Thank you for your support of the author's rights.

Grand Central Publishing
Hachette Book Group
1290 Avenue of the Americas, New York, NY 10104
grandcentralpublishing.com
twitter.com/grandcentralpub

Originally published in hardcover and ebook by Grand Central Publishing in May 2022
First trade paperback edition: May 2023

Grand Central Publishing is a division of Hachette Book Group, Inc. The Grand Central Publishing name and logo is a trademark of Hachette Book Group, Inc.

The publisher is not responsible for websites (or their content) that are not owned by the publisher.

The Hachette Speakers Bureau provides a wide range of authors for speaking events. To find out more, go to hachettespeakersbureau.com or email HachetteSpeakers@hbgusa.com.

Grand Central Publishing books may be purchased in bulk for business, educational, or promotional use. For information, please contact your local bookseller or the Hachette Book Group Special Markets Department at special.markets@hbgusa.com.

Print book interior design by Abby Reilly

Library of Congress Control Number: 2021053685

ISBNs: 978-1-5387-0643-5 (trade paperback), 978-1-5387-0644-2 (ebook)

Printed in the United States of America

LSC-C

Printing 3, 2023

For my parents,
who taught me that imagination is precious

One does not love in order to dominate and conquer life—life being just a silent sequence of woes, interrupted, but not mitigated, by ephemeral sparks of distressing exaltation.

Miracles were rare, but they did happen—the approaching step of her Beloved seemed to be one.

—Anna Banti, "La Signorina"

How can I begin anything new with all of yesterday in me?

—Leonard Cohen, *Beautiful Losers*

SIX DAYS in ROME

PROLOGUE

VIA GIULIA

MY NAME IS EVERYWHERE here.

It's given to thin, dead-end streets, out-of-the-way piazzas, churches in need of repair. I see it used to advertise perfume on the side of a bus and sprayed in hot-pink paint on the side of an ancient building, a declaration of hate or love.

I've never been Em. Or Emma. Or Emily. Or anything but Emilia.

No nicknames, abbreviations, or shortcuts. Even at times when it would have been easy to settle for any of those alternatives, I've insisted, corrected people's pronunciation, written in the right spelling on class rosters and preprinted name tags. It's always mattered to me. I'm unwilling to compromise.

I follow one of my namesake streets, shaded by laundry hanging from balconies. A church bell rings somewhere.

The sun is relentless, the heat inescapable. It is the middle of the afternoon, the middle of summer. The bougainvillea will continue to weave its way around doorframes and windows and climb the walls for months. Walls that must have always been that Roman shade of orange. That color I've never seen any-where else.

I'm here for just a few days, alone. The trip was planned months ago, for and with someone else. But he's gone now, in a way that's finally starting to feel comfortable or natural or at least not a constant source of pain. He's gone and I'm very much not.

I move at my own pace. My face is still, my mouth relaxed, just short of a smile. The soles of my sandals slap the stone beneath me too loudly, even when I try to take lighter steps. I hear lunch dishes being washed behind closed windows and cracked-open doors.

There are no tourist attractions in this part of the city, no famous fountains or recognizable relics. No remarkable view from anywhere. It is the sliver of time in the afternoon when everyone sleeps. I am walking just to walk, the sharp incline stretching the backs of my legs. The sun hits my bare arms, the base of my neck in a way I know will tan, not burn.

A group of monks passes to my left, speaking softly, taking deep drags of their cigarettes. Two of the five look up to smile at me. I purse my lips in chaste response, wondering how much they must be sweating under their robes, that unyielding black polyester. Their designer sunglasses and expensive watches catch the light.

My past-tense love, the man who's not here but should be, was raised Roman Catholic. Once an altar boy. Still wears and maybe believes in the golden saint on a chain around his neck. He claimed to have briefly, decades ago, considered the seminary. Months earlier, while looking over my shoulder as I bought our plane tickets, he mused out loud: "I love seeing priests and nuns in Rome. They always look so happy, like they just won the lottery." His hand enclosed my shoulder. "Comforting, isn't it? That kind of certainty." Then, after a sip of wine: "No, it's better than the lottery. It's like getting tenure. Everlasting tenure, forever and ever, amen."

I imagine what these monks might say if I told them about him, if any of them would hear my lapsed confession.

A stream of water, likely from one of the faucets or fountains I see everywhere, winds its way through the stones under my feet. Downhill now, moving effortlessly. I envy its gravity. The only rule it needs to follow.

It's either the time of day or some wrong turn I've taken, but I'm suddenly surrounded by people. I was expecting the shade and quiet of Via Giulia, but it's nowhere to be found. Tour guides hold neon flags and yell into clipped-on microphones. Men speaking Italian as a third or fourth language point at laminated maps. Perched on a low wall, her back to the river, a woman in a long, dirty skirt plays "Hotel California" for tourists on an electric guitar. Her bare feet dangle.

An older Italian couple catches my eye and doesn't let me go. The man approaches me slowly, warily, but with purpose. Like I'm his best worst option.

"*Quale strada per la Fontana di Trevi?*" they ask me in unison, their faces as wide and hopeful as open windows.

They think I'm one of them, that I know this city, or at least that I speak their language. Like any American abroad looking to blend in, I feel a jolt of pride.

This has been happening a lot, often enough that I've looked up my response in Italian and practiced my pronunciation in the mirror of the rental apartment. *Mi dispiace, non parlo italiano.* Or, if I'm feeling confident: *Non parlo molto bene l'italiano.*

But now, when it matters, I freeze. I shrug my shoulders, let them down. My face blooms red and I turn away, leaving them to search for someone else.

Crossing the Tiber, no shelter from the sun. I pick up my pace toward the thick shade of the trees in Trastevere, weaving around groups of people, held still by all that surrounds them.

I hear a few familiar seconds of Tom Waits from a car window before the light changes and it's gone. His low growl, a voice I've heard many times: both slow and sad on this recording and light, laughing at one of my dad's jokes, midcigarette on the terrace at my parents' house. *"The night does funny things inside a man,"* he sings.

I close my eyes for a moment. I see a dark bar, mercifully cool in the middle of a heat wave, pint glasses slick with condensation, me sitting beside a man who knows every word of this song. A body starting to become familiar, whose bad singing voice and furrowed brow I'm starting to love.

Tom Waits, that song, that man, that bar: all parts of a subtle chorus of memory. A web of songs and poems and late nights and early mornings that twist and change and never quite disappear. They're fossils, tokens. Badges of honor, or not.

Aside from ordering a drink or asking for more olive oil or mumbling *scusi* every time my elbow brushes a person passing by, when is the next time I'll truly speak to someone else?

THURSDAY

MAYBE ALL ROMAN BRIDES are serene. This one is.

I watch her from the café, at one of the outdoor tables that's still catching the last of the early evening sun, in the middle of the island in the middle of the river. I can see details that someone walking by might miss, like having good seats at a play. Her dress flashes with cheap sequins or crystals, scattered across the waist and skirt like an afterthought. The fabric is gathered between her shoulder blades, pinching. The light hits her square in the face, but she doesn't even squint. Her gaze is distant, focused on something that's invisible to me.

The stone paving this piazza is sloped, a defiant, imperfect tilt toward the river on one side. This café seems built into the dip, old books wedged under table legs to compensate. The church is at the center of the square, flat on its own thick foundation, a nonnegotiable.

A child, maybe hers, chases one of the groomsmen around the square in a makeshift game of tag. Her mother, or soon-to-be mother-in-law, talks loudly on a cell phone, too quickly and far away for me to try to understand.

There's none of the hushed drama that comes with American weddings, no pageantry, no nerves. The mood is calm and still, in deference to the higher power at work here—if not God, then maybe just familiarity, the inevitability of two compatible or similar people being together. Making promises, eyes shining, in front of a select few.

The groom is lingering by the door, not giving her the reverence we've been taught that brides deserve. He shows no signs of becoming overwhelmed or tearing up when seeing her in a white dress. Even the thought of something that choreographed or contrived feels laughable here, watching them. He's seen her before, will see her again. The white dress, what it purports to mean, pales against what these ancient walls are holding up, what they've kept out and let through. There doesn't even seem to be a photographer.

The untouchable look on her face, as if she were floating just an inch above the rest of us: it's familiar. Her gaze like those of the saints I'm starting to see immortalized in frescoes and mosaics all over this city. Eyes focused far away, sure of some delicious secret.

I've been to Rome once before, but years ago and never alone. My parents brought my brother and me when he was eight and I was twelve. We stayed in an apartment by the Spanish Steps, furnished with hanging tapestries and thick rugs and delicate, antique furniture. The wooden beams that framed the doorways and held up the ceiling were from the owner's family house in Puglia. I remember being fascinated by that, how pieces of one home could be used to support another.

One day, there was a guided tour of the Vatican: giggling at Swiss guards, running through the gardens, a few minutes in the Sistine Chapel, necks stretched, before being ushered out. I sped through the museum, doing a quick scan of each room, picking my favorite piece before moving on, while my brother listened intently to descriptions of brushstrokes and marble quarries, patronages and papal states, the artist's connection to the church and all it meant. He got as close as possible, his face sometimes only inches from a painting or sculpture.

A breeze slips its way across my skin, still damp with my sweat and water from a fountain I passed on my walk here, a wolf's head carved out of stone. I let it fill my hands, splashed it on my arms and face, threw the rest on the back of my neck so it dripped between my shoulder blades, flowed down my spine. Something I'd only ever seen old Italian men do in movies.

There are empty tables behind and in front of me now, all of us keeping some distance. Even with the air, light, time of day being what it is. No one is speaking English. The glasses in everyone's hands glow red and orange with Cappelletti, Aperol, and Campari. A mother gives her baby an orange-slice garnish to chew on.

I sip an Averna, on ice with a lemon peel, my third of the day. These cocktails, their variations and what they mean, were a big part of my pre-Rome education. He made samples, playing bartender in my kitchen. Measuring out vermouth and splashing soda like an amateur chemist. I was schooled on the differences between a spritz and an Americano. A classic Negroni and a sbagliato. How delicately his tongue hit the back of his teeth at the end of that satisfying, foreign word.

His hands moved. His voice rose and fell, eyes studying my face, maybe imagining what it might look like in Italy. How it might change.

It's not surprising, that I miss him a little more each time a new drink arrives. It's hard to see an empty chair and not imagine him in it, stretching his long legs out, head tilted back a bit to feel the last of the sun on his face, his flat fingers flipping the pages of a menu.

He was present in every decision I made for this trip: the apartment, the restaurants, the day trip to Pompeii, which he'd never seen. We chose the dates to align with his birthday. Late July, even though it was, as he said, the worst time to be in Rome. I thought of what he might order for a late lunch, the hint of a smile as he read a book under a tree in the Borghese, maybe his hand on mine after we stopped for a drink and watched day turn to night, and other things I didn't even know to anticipate, that would have been surprises.

And there was the untold potential of what I might say or do or encourage, what possibilities might present themselves, to make him more devoted, convinced he'd come to the right city with the right person. I've heard time away changes relationships, gives them longevity, maybe offers a life raft. The freedom of a strange place, to be someone else, to try on whatever feels like it might fit.

The postcards I bought earlier are fanned out on the table. A ritual almost every time I go somewhere worth chronicling: write to a few people, trying to capture what I see, how being in a particular place makes me feel.

I only buy a certain breed of postcard. No "Ciao from Rome" in red, green, and white lettering. No lettering of any kind, actually. No Colosseum or Forum or any other obvious monuments. No gladiators. This eliminates a lot. The ones that meet my criteria are usually more expensive, €3.00 instead of 1.50. All chosen with their recipients in mind, in hopes the cards might live magnetized to their refrigerators, pressed between the pages of a book, or tucked away with worn ticket stubs and dusty photos and other things to keep.

One shows the Piazza Navona at night, fountains at full blast and lit with an eye for drama. Gods and horses and waves sculpted midcrash, all illuminated from below. The always-crowded square is empty, which seems impossible. No packs of tourists or restaurant hosts trolling for customers or men selling cheap toys and counterfeit handbags. Resting everything on old sheets, ready at any moment to snatch it all up and run.

Another: jasmine wrapping its way around the ancient column of a ruin, hit hard with afternoon light. And, for effect, an old woman looking out the window of an adjacent, equally crumbling building. She stares directly at whoever is taking the photograph, as if to say, *So what?*

The one in my hands right now: the Bocca della Verità, staring dead ahead with blank eyes, its gaping mouth meant to swallow the hand of any liar. Where did that story come from?

I drain the last of my Averna, turn the statue's wide eyes over, and write to my parents.

I'm here. Back in Rome. The beautiful mess, as Mom calls it.

I used to think you only took the two of us to the Bocca della Verità for a laugh, some *Roman Holiday* reenactment.

Maybe you did. Do you remember how relieved Jack was when he made it out unscathed? I loved that look on his face. Like he'd won a race.

The pictures you took, the two of us side by side, made up the Christmas card that year, the year I was thirteen. For so long, it was the only picture of myself I liked. It still might be my favorite.

I know you might not really understand why I'm here. Maybe I have to come back every fifteen years or so, to make sure the place hasn't crumbled, to drink good wine and see the pope. Sounds like one of Dad's lyrics.

I love you both. I'm grateful you showed me this city first.

The words barely fit. I make my handwriting smaller as I realize how close I'm coming to the end. The sentences are cramped, a little slanted. The last few drift over to where I've written my parents' address in Hudson. Not the artfully spaced, just-spare-enough message I'd seen in my mind before I started.

Everything about this seems a little wrong, or at least odd. It's been months since I've seen them: an unseasonably warm dinner at their house, a night that still makes me shudder when I think of its details. Weeks since we've spoken: clipped conversations with my mother, nothing from him at all. I'm not sure what I'm trying to prove, sending something like this. Maybe the fact that I can rewrite history, select my memories and discard others, if that's what I decide I want.

It can be exhausting, the consideration I give whenever I write or draw or do basically anything. You could call it perfectionism or commitment, but that suggests usefulness or efficiency. Even what

I just wrote: it looks sentimental, pointless almost. Too carefully balanced, with no hint of how I actually feel now, sitting here.

I slip my feet out of my sandals and rest them on the stone, something I wouldn't dream of doing at home. But here it's all smooth cobblestones and dull asphalt, worn down by slow, poetic, vague decay, instead of once-white New York sidewalks gone gray with thousands of footsteps, decades of dog shit, endless wilting bags of garbage.

The Bocca della Verità, if it had any magic at all, would have known to grab me, even twenty years ago. It would have seen what kind of liar I am. Not pathological, more creative than deceptive. Why say I read two books last week, when I can make it three? Yes, I saw that movie or met that person, ate at that restaurant, shared that opinion. A few embellishments, a catchy line of dialogue, invented in the moment. Something to make a story memorable. At worst, the lies I tell are some embarrassing combination of laziness and impatience. But also the occasional flicker of imagination. There's comfort in it, knowing I can reliably become more than I am.

Another drink arrives, though I didn't order one. Deep red, alive with carbonation, a blackberry resting on ice cubes. An older man to my left points at the drink, the tip of his finger within poking distance of the rim of the glass. He's alone at the table next to mine, but sitting only a few inches away, close enough to put his arm around me if he wanted.

"The blackberry," he says in slow Italian. "That's what they give when they like you."

Now I know the word for blackberry, by process of elimination. *La mora.* I pop it into my mouth, smile in the man's direction and say nothing.

The church doors open and cheers spill out from inside. Bride and groom walk quickly to a waiting car. His hand is around her waist, pulling a little. Finally, a bit of life behind her eyes, a fraction of something to lose.

I imagine an early communal dinner somewhere, maybe followed by a party for the adults. Cold red wine sweating in water glasses, children falling asleep on laps. A small band, someone's brother playing guitar.

The screen of my phone flashes a particular shade of blue, which it only ever does for one reason. For one person.

E,

How strange, me writing to you on my birthday, asking for a gift.

I wonder if you're in Rome. I hope you are.

But what I'm asking for, and don't deserve: will you please tell me you're okay?

M.

I should have known. This day can't possibly pass without some word from him, some nudge, some challenge. I stare at his words until the screen goes dark, then remind myself where I am. A tree bending precariously toward the river. Late light streaming through its thin leaves, making them almost translucent.

The sun setting on Michael's birthday, though he has six more hours of it than I do. We'd planned all of it this way, his birthday being our first day, waking up to Rome, to a whole new year. My hands shake a little until I trap them between my knees. Take a deep breath, stare into the light until it hurts a little.

What could I possibly say in response? That I'm delirious, with lack of sleep, with the beauty and current of this place, and wish he were next to me? With such force it almost aches? That I don't know exactly where I am or why? Why this café, this table, watching this wedding, right now?

I've always been so careful of what I say to him, and how. It's hard to write to a writer, though he'd tell me it shouldn't be, that I'm overthinking, that whatever I say is fine because it's me saying it.

I didn't sleep on the plane. I never do. If I take a pill or let an edible dissolve under my tongue, I hallucinate, instead of drifting off like I'm supposed to. If I drink enough cheap red wine to sedate myself, all I get is an exhausted hangover. My body fights all of it, like it might resist anesthesia or a blindfold.

The man next to me slept from takeoff to landing. All eight hours and twenty minutes. He was one of those, the kind of person who's out as soon as the landing gear folds in on itself. A sound and sensation I've always found soothing, though never so much as to put me to sleep. His mouth stayed open for the whole flight, gaping in my direction with no air seeming to flow in or out. His expression so open and empty I wanted to slap him awake.

When I did finally fall asleep, it was in the taxi from Termini to the apartment I'd rented for six days in Monti. Well, technically, Michael had chosen the place and paid the deposit, after a meticulous online search. We needed a quiet street, high ceilings, a decent kitchen, a big enough bed. In this neighborhood, never that one. Most important, a balcony. He never asked for his money back. I never offered.

"Signorina! Signorina?" The driver woke me in time to see a few seconds of the Colosseum. I tilted my head upward, leaning into the turn of the car, then weakly met his eyes in gratitude. An odd, but charming gesture. Something that almost surely gets him a bigger tip. One of the carabinieri guarding the barricade, thousands of years of history behind him, yawned into the hand not gripping his machine gun.

This trip was supposed to be important, maybe even monumental. There were certain touchstones I planned on passing, checking them off in my mind like mile markers in a race. Him seeing me paralyzed by jet lag, needing a shower, battling no sleep, a foreign language, maybe a lost suitcase, and loving me anyway, being glad he came. The two of us bickering over where to go when, whether to window shop along Via Condotti or walk the twenty minutes to the modern art museum. A verbal tic or pointless worry or slowing pace that would charm, then irritate, then charm him again. Things I'd been told were harbingers of intimacy, a word I pretend to cringe at but secretly worship like some powerful, unknowable deity.

Being in Rome, this was supposed to be different.

I've walked the length of London Bridge in the deep cold of a December night, wind blowing my mind blank. I've stretched my legs in the grass by the Canal Saint-Martin, sipping lukewarm rosé from a plastic cup, catching the last of the late summer. I've looked past orange trees flowering, Alhambra looming, exhaled hookah smoke drifting by.

All of it alone. All of it practice, I'd thought, for now. Though, if I'm being generous or optimistic or simply open, this time could be a different kind of practice. An experiment in self-sufficiency, instead of waiting for something to happen, for someone or some circumstance to tell me what to do. I could, maybe, fill all this absence with something that matters.

I'm surrounded by devotion, passing small altars everywhere. From carved-out sanctuaries housing statues to prayers spray-painted on bus stop shelters. So many Virgins behind plexiglass, in alcoves between clothing stores and specialty food markets. Her ever-plaintive looks upward, immortalized in tile on the sides of buildings. Coins scattered at her feet, arrangements left hastily in water bottles. The flowers are either dead or fake, dyed unnatural colors like the magenta or cerulean from a box of crayons. I walk in decadent loops, turning whenever the mood strikes, when a street seems more inviting, stopping when I get too hot or tired or just feel like it. Over and over, when given a choice, I take the quieter path. Holding someone's hand would feel oppressive.

I fought jet lag with churches all afternoon, going into every one I saw. No matter how grand or abandoned looking, open or closed. The hot and cold, light then dark, helped keep me awake. The last one I found, twenty slow steps from the rental apartment, sucked all the warmth from my body. The heat, making me feel dumb and desperate moments earlier, was just a memory, suddenly absurd.

There are more than nine hundred churches in Rome.

All the frescoes and murals and windows are puzzles to parse. It's usually clear who's most important: Jesus, Mary, various apostles.

Painted in the midst of their most meaningful, devout moments, set in glass in poses to inspire awe and piety. The women in these scenes are usually off to the side, bearing witness to whatever miracle is happening at the center. The young female martyrs stand out among them, painted to glow from within. That much holier, within an already chosen group.

Even their names have the air of permanence, demanding respect. Agnes, Cecilia, Perpetua, Catherine. They were sold into slavery, whipped with heavy metal chains, burned with boiling animal fat, dragged naked through the streets of the city. They starved themselves. Their throats were slit. Through it all, they placidly believed.

I lit a candle for someone with each stop, starting with the obvious: my parents, their parents, my brother Jack, close friends, then lapsed friends, and, when I exhausted them, people I've lost track of completely. These meditations grew increasingly random, wishing happiness or even just peace for people from across my life, who might not be able to pick me out of a crowd. Sometimes I couldn't even remember their names, just a detail about a face or something they said or whether they made me feel nervous or hopeful or safe.

In the Basilica di Sant'Agostino, which looked boarded up and abandoned until I found a side door, I lit a short, unremarkable votive for a high school friend's now ex-boyfriend, who was kinder to me than he needed to be. When I tagged along on their dates, he was curious what I thought about the movie we'd just seen or the music that was playing. Always looking me in the eye when I answered his questions. At parties, if my red plastic cup was empty, he'd fill it.

He wore aviator sunglasses with yellow lenses, which would make most people look sick but gave him an odd, approachable air instead. I remember being in the back of his car after school, when he'd drive the winding country roads in Hudson, accelerating before hills so his little Honda Civic would go airborne for a few terrifying seconds. My friend screamed with laughter in the passenger seat, a natural thrill seeker. I was silent in the back, nails gripping the velour of the cushions, grasping for stability that wasn't there. It was one of the first times I felt truly afraid. Not of monsters under my bed or bumps in the night, but true fear. Like I could die because someone felt in control but wasn't.

At Santa Maria in Cosmedin, surrounded by symmetrical arches and perfectly aligned windows, it was a thin taper for a girl who lived next door to us when I was little, who was at our house after school and almost every weekend. She loved watching my mother cook, was hypnotized by the sight of her whisking an egg for breakfast or crushing garlic in a mortar and pestle. We played in the yard, making up stories, transforming the bent branch of a tree into a throne, taking turns being queen. For laughs, Dad would pick us up and sit us on top of the refrigerator, our little legs dangling from what seemed like a dangerous height.

I saw her years later in New York and she asked me to be in her wedding, even though we hadn't spoken in over a decade. We met at a shabby Midtown restaurant, next door to a theater, and shared a bottle of the cheapest champagne on the menu, watching tourists wait in the standby line for an eight p.m. show. All I remember about her fiancé was the distinct impression he was older and rich, and that both those things were important. It was going to be an

Armenian wedding, she told me. Which meant she would wear a golden crown during the ceremony.

It was called off just a few weeks later, before I had the chance to buy a dress. I made an effort to choose a new candle for her, one whose wick was still waxy and untouched. My euro coin rattled when I dropped it in the collection box.

I'm not praying for these people, exactly. But it's not enough for me to just walk in and out of these churches, stare at adorned ceilings and walls, wonder at the curves in sculptures. It serves as a reminder, maybe. That my life is big and varied and will continue to change and grow. That I will never stop meeting people, gathering up their details, so many that I can afford to forget.

I pass the Bocca della Verità on the way out, looking much smaller than I remember. A long line of tourists waits for photos. Maybe, years ago, we'd come early in the morning or during lunch because, in my memory, we had the whole courtyard to ourselves. Jack sizing up the statue, me striking the right kind of pose. My parents saying what they knew would make us laugh for the picture.

"Flowers *and* wine? You're forgiven!"

This is how Michael and I met, a little more than two years ago. With his quick line and my smile in response. On the commuter train leaving the city, sometime between Grand Central and Mamaroneck, him asking if the seat next to mine was free— then occupied by a fistful of eight-dollar tulips and two bottles of cheap Italian red, a strip of cardboard to keep them from knocking together.

I was on my way to see married friends in the suburbs, regale them with exaggerated tales of the single life, get drunk by their fireplace, sleep fitfully in the spare bedroom of their starter house.

He looked at my things, then looked at me, thinking of what to say. Delivering it with a natural kind of confidence. He wore it like a skin.

I don't think I responded the way he'd expected. I didn't blush or laugh nervously or playfully protest that I had nothing to apologize for and how dare he suggest otherwise. I looked up, matched his assertion with calm.

"I should hope so," I said, moving everything so he could sit.

I found it hard to look away from him. Gray around the temples, in a careless way. A mouth always just short of a smile. Big, kind, green, incisive eyes. That sort of line wouldn't have worked if he didn't look the way he did. He asked, and my mind and body instinctually answered. I had very little choice.

He told me he was a writer. I told him I was an artist, which, at that time, was halfway true.

"I'd love to see your work," he said.

"Would you?" I made every effort to seem lightly amused, instead of eager and hungry for more of him, which I was. I've never been much of a flirt.

But it worked. By the time I left the train at Cos Cob, he'd taken my number, insisted we make a date.

I quickly learned he was just Michael, had no nickname, accepted no substitutes, same as me. He always keeps a tab open when ordering a drink. He pets dogs on the street, but ignores children. He sleeps ;with his knees pulled into his chest, never snores. A vain, exacting dresser. Keeper of strong, well-researched opinions.

Someone deeply private and disarmingly funny. Someone I was desperate to impress.

The apartment I'm renting on Via Clementina for these six days is owned by a woman in her forties. Her hair is stringy, pulled back carelessly, and her eyes are tired. She inhaled deeply after opening the front door, needing the extra breath to explain the differences between the garbage and recycling, apologize for the temperamental elevator. But the pants she wears are delicately patterned, cuffed just right to draw attention to kitten heels, thin ankles. Her cheekbones are high and sharp.

Out of pride, I tell her it's fine if she speaks Italian, that I understand, no problem. She tries to talk slowly for me, but forgets halfway through and speeds up.

She has lived in Rome since university and owns this place, which she rents to travelers and tourists, and one two floors down, which she shares with her husband and two sons. I ask how old they are, attempting to be polite in my clumsy Italian, and suddenly she's telling me, in equal parts Italian and thickly accented English, that her sons are twins. One is loving and sweet and never causes any problems. The other is horrible. He stays out late at night, does something else, having to do with a car. She mimes hands on a steering wheel, making a sharp turn. Or maybe they're both awful and she only wishes she could have had a perfect child. It's hard to tell, barely understanding every other word. Syllables and phrases sound almost decipherable, like they could fit together and mean something, then slip behind my eyes.

She says something about not being able to marry her sons off, hooking her index fingers together to indicate a successful match, while showing me how to lock the front door. She watches me turn the key three full times before she's satisfied. "There have been problems," she says, ominously and in clear English. I do my best to assure her I can twist and then push when I feel the door give way. Reading the exhaustion on my face, she finally leaves. The key is heavy and wide in my hand, with teeth and indentations. It hangs from a Colosseum key chain that was once covered in blue glitter but now has only a few sparkles left.

I tried to learn Italian before this trip, enough to be proficient in the ways I imagined would matter. I had visions of myself flawlessly ordering pasta or asking for a table for two, holding my own in casual conversations at cafés, self-sufficient, remarkably relaxed.

I spent too much money on the Pimsleur method, sat in front of my computer, repeating phrases, translating back and forth, talking to no one. I've always been a good student.

Italian appeals to me: a wilder, freer language, with all its z's, malleable sentence structure, and the relish taken in not just pronouncing every syllable but stringing together as many as possible. Full of possibility, especially when compared with the rules and precision that come with French, which I learned as a child. My mother only answering my questions if I asked them in her fluid first language.

It was important to her that Jack and I not only learn French, but never lose it. Even now, when she picks up the phone or I meet her somewhere or walk into their kitchen in the morning, it's a toss-up which language we'll speak. But it's worked; my fluency has never wavered. Dad has picked up bits and pieces over the years, but if the three of us speak at what's become our natural pace and complexity, it's lost to him.

I know enough simple Italian vocabulary and remedial grammar to recognize parts of what I hear now, but too little to fully understand or reproduce almost any of it. Like seeing water rushing in front of me, frighteningly fast, quick and cold, wanting desperately to dive in.

My suitcase tips over as soon as I let go of the handle. The bed is wide, freshly made with white sheets, a little turquoise accent pillow. When deciding on this apartment, we looked at photos of the bedroom, light streaming in sideways through the window, a small framed photo of an anonymous saint centered above the headboard, and shared a smile.

It would be so easy to sleep. Even the thought of it is delicious.

Dad would say, "A nap is a rookie mistake." Not to give in, that he's learned the hard way. All those night flights, crossing so many time zones.

I hear it as clearly as if he were sitting beside me, which he always does at family dinners. Dad next to me, Mom across, and Jack next to her. It's never been discussed or formally decided, just the natural order of things. We all take our places.

I shower instead. There is a half-used tub of olive oil soap, black and thick, on the ledge of the bathtub. Its label is peeling unevenly, stuck on at an angle by hand. Maybe leftover from whoever booked this place last, or here as some sort of amenity. I scoop three fingers into it. It's waxy and tough at first, then blends with my wet skin, then disappears. A hint of brine, then lemon, then nothing at all.

The steam from the shower escapes through an open window, so the mirror is clear and honest when I step in front of it.

I ask my reflection, out loud, "Who are you today?"

A question my dad has been answering and asking me forever.

When I was little and he woke me up for school, he'd ask himself in my mirror and make up stories and faces that made me laugh.

One morning, he was the captain of an Arctic ship, looking for penguins, cutting through all that ice with an army of hair dryers like the one under my mother's sink. A week later, he was a boy ballerina, flexing and pointing his bare feet at the foot of my bed as my eyes adjusted to daylight.

Some days I'd tell him I was a veterinarian. Others, an explorer or a Greek goddess, depending on the book I was reading or what I'd been learning in school. He took every idea seriously, asking clarifying questions in a sober tone. He always wanted detail—exactly which animals I'd be saving and why, what my next expedition was, or who I'd turned into a tree because their worship wasn't sufficient. That sense of possibility was contagious, no wrong answers.

The older I got, the more honest he became.

"I'm my own guru today. Meditated for two hours outside, nothing but me and the frost. I don't think it's helping."

"Who are you today, honey? You need to come see us soon. Your mom would like it. She paints twenty hours a day now, seems like."

From the studio, a week before his new album was scheduled to wrap: *"Today I'm finished, a pathetic old man who will never think or write anything true again. What more do I even have to say?"*

Once, in tears, from an echoing hotel bathroom: *"I'm a lonely fucking sap today. She'll never forgive me this time."*

He'd call me when I was in college, late at night or too early in the morning, from Toronto or Prague or Melbourne on tour, and ask that same question, sounding far away but no less compelled to hear my answer.

I sometimes reassure him, never flatter or lie. Maybe that's why he keeps asking and listening and answering.

Water drips from the ends of my hair onto the tile floor. They're perfect white, accented with deep blue brushstrokes, a pattern of dots and curves that's probably been repeated for hundreds of years. The grout between them is scrubbed clean.

Today I am alone. I am in a beautiful place. I am honest, with nothing to hide. I am better off.

Dinner is at eight.

Monti is busy, wide awake after a late-afternoon nap, with a drink in its hand. Doors to all the bars are open, and people move their stools outside into the street to watch others passing by. The restaurant is twenty minutes away, if I walk with purpose, like I'm in a hurry. I check my phone to confirm the right general direction, then put it away.

The dipping sun transforms the deep orange of a government building into sherbet, pastel and sweet. On a balcony above my head, a man waves a broom back and forth to clear a cobweb.

I can't see the ambulance, but I can hear it. Two tones, high and low, repeat themselves over and over. Simple and direct, different from home. Jack has always said he's comforted by the sound of an ambulance, probably because he's not in one when it drives by.

It's likely speeding down one of the wider, paved streets that runs from the Tiber toward Termini and Piazza della Reppublica, cutting through shopping centers and ancient ruins equally, not discriminating.

I turn off this small square, down a road that seems to get thinner and emptier the longer I follow it. An old woman smokes silently in an open doorway, but, other than her, there's no one. She stares at the building across the street, which has been gutted for what looks like a while. Parts of the façade and most of the staircase inside are completely gone, suggesting a job that started with fervor, only to be abandoned halfway through. Two bags of concrete lean against each other in the shadows. A cardboard sign, possibly explaining what's happened or will happen, flaps in the light breeze. Enough of the ceiling is missing in the right places, so I can look up through it and see the sky losing its blue.

Sure enough, this street shrinks into a dead end. So narrow that a small Fiat has realized it too late and gotten stuck. A little crowd starts to gather on either side, yelling out unsolicited advice, casually invested in the outcome: whether the driver will cut right or left, if the police need to be called. People at a nearby café sit at small tables, lopsided by the old stones that make up the street, and watch while they drink and smoke and talk.

Piazza Navona is on the way to the restaurant. I'm not sure exactly where, but I can sense it's close. The crowds are getting thicker, more frenetic. People are walking with more urgency in the same direction, knowing they're about to see something they can check off their lists.

And, with a slight left, there it is. All this space suddenly, an exhale. Butter-yellow buildings, with their faded blue windows. Some apartments have flower boxes, some are bare. If it were a little darker, I'd be able to see inside.

Spectacular things in Rome can just happen like this, with no warning. Around a nondescript corner, a gorgeous slap in the face. Even though I remember posing for a family photo on this very spot, perfectly centered to capture the obelisk, the curve of Sant'Agnese's dome and the light from all three fountains, I still marvel at it all, like Michael said I would.

I purposely walk through people's cell phone videos, but try to stay out of their pictures. The fountains' lights come on, turning the water swimming-pool blue. Some god or warrior chokes a fish with his bare hand, the muscles of his forearms rippling just right. An octopus curls itself at another's feet. A horse kicks its front legs up, a ferocious or terrified look in its eye. The four rivers of the fountain converge, and I'm close enough to feel the spray in my hair.

I reach for my phone to check that I'm still walking in the right direction, and it's vibrating with a call from Jack.

"*Ciao, Emilia,*" he greets me, with a cartoonish Italian accent. "*Come stai?*"

It's early afternoon in New York. He'll be sitting on the sixty-second floor of a glass tower, in his very cold office, drinking the green tea his assistant buys in bulk, making any number of million-dollar decisions with one side of his brain while he checks in on me with the other.

"I'm not even going to try to match that." I laugh at him. "I'm fine. A little jet lagged, but I made it here alive."

"Where are you? It sounds loud."

"Piazza Navona. Do you remember coming here, years ago? A lot of people around, but it's a gorgeous night."

Taking a trip like this isn't something he'd ever do, but at least he doesn't question my doing it.

"This will be good for you, getting away." He says this with certainty, as if it could be proven. "You'll eat and drink well, in a beautiful place. You'll feel better."

I wish he'd be able to hear me if I were to tell him it's not that simple. But, for him, I think it might be. Maybe it's the same part of him that makes it easy to take risks with other people's money, or go cliff-diving for the first time without hesitation, or avoid bad or unpleasant news so thoroughly it's as if it never existed.

Instead, I just say, "I hope you're right."

A few minutes from the piazza, I see an English-language book-store, its name lit up in purple neon I can see from the street. It's a small storefront that takes advantage of its depth, like a railroad apartment. Extending further and further like a paperback-lined tunnel. A few people browse; most are listening to a reading that's finishing up in the back room.

I'm startled by a mirror, propped up on my left between book-cases, the glass chipped and covered in fingerprints. I turn and see my sharp reflection, a face betraying nothing. I look like a stranger.

When I left Michael that first day and got off the train in Connecticut, I didn't tell my friends about him, even though he'd given me an anecdote they would have loved. The novelty of meet-ing someone on the commuter rail on a Friday afternoon, coupled with the comfort in knowing they'd never have to rely on chance to meet someone ever again.

When they asked if I was seeing anyone at the moment, I gave my typical, self-deprecating answer and bought his first book from the shop in Grand Central as soon as I stepped off the train. It's set in Beirut, a city I've always wanted to visit, just before war between

Lebanon and Israel in the eighties. A man, estranged from his Lebanese family, politically unmoored and feeling hopeless, meets a French woman who teaches at the university. For a time, it seems she might be able to offer the happiness and security he's been seeking, could possibly save him from a life in which he's barely present. They make certain corners of the city their own, debate the impending conflict in smoky bars, have transcendent sex in her cramped apartment near the sea.

That first book changed who he was to me, what he could be. All before we'd spoken for longer than ten minutes.

I read the rest in a fever: his next two books, then every published story or essay or review I could find. Consuming them one after another, worried the feeling would fade. That summer, whenever I was in the park or at the beach or spending a long weekend somewhere, one of his books was with me. I lay on a blanket in the grass or on the warm stone by the pool, eagerly flipping pages, hearing half of my friends' conversations or whatever else was happening around me.

The joy and hunger those books gave me then. The sense of possibility, of being with or even just around this brilliant person, who could write a heartbreakingly perfect sentence just as easily as whisper something delicious and filthy in my ear or touch my wrist in a way that made me feel understood. It makes me a little sad now, to know I'll never read any of them ever again.

Later, when he recommended other books and movies and poems to me, I pursued and consumed them all the same way: captivated, possessed even. Reading and seeing what he thought I should was all I wanted to do.

I never deluded myself into thinking this was normal, this way he seemed to perceive some deep part of me. It felt thrilling, but individual, even targeted.

His books are full of little details I thought only women could recognize or remember. One of his characters, after a fight with her lover, studies her face in a bathroom mirror. She leans over the sink, her face inches from the glass. Fingers tracing her forehead lines, smoothing her eyebrows, filling the divot above her lip. As she walks back to him in the bedroom, he notices the ritual has left red marks on the points of her elbows: indents that underscore the pressure of her concentration. Thinking of identical marks I'd seen on my own arms before, the sting of bone pressed against marble, I wrote in the margin, *He clearly pays attention.*

He did tell me once that the reason we love someone is because we share their adjectives.

I look for his books on these shelves, as I do in every bookstore. Scanning the names on the spines until I reach the *S*'s, between Salter and Saroyan, and then the combination of letters that always makes my throat feel tight, even now. This shop carries all four, even has two copies of his second novel, which was by far the most successful. But I'm looking for the latest one, published a few months ago.

My whole body vibrates with anticipatory pain, possibly rage when I open it to the dedication page. I know what I'll find, but I look anyway. The book, which he finished a month before I met him, is written for her: a woman I assumed was past tense, but is, in fact, present. The woman who, when I asked, exactly once, if he was involved with anyone else, went unmentioned.

I don't know exactly why I do this. Maybe it's to build up a tolerance, to prove I can handle, even accept, this new reality. Maybe it's to ensure I come to thoroughly hate him.

This could be New York—the curated selection, the well-read English speakers hanging on an author's every word. But the fading light, the rustle of other people's voices, even my fingers on the cool stone wall, the faint smell of foreign sweat in the air: it's all just different enough to remind me I'm somewhere else.

The reservation I didn't cancel is in ten minutes. Michael's birthday dinner.

This is perverse, what I'm doing. Most people would think so. Maybe even I do. A sensible person would let any feeling of responsibility lapse, possibly call the restaurant to cancel, but more likely just not show. Leave the table for some happy, still-intact couple to enjoy. I'm hoping sitting down, eating, and drinking there is a way to be near him and take something from him at the same time.

Michael chose a restaurant he'd heard a lot about, had always wanted to try. I made the reservation exactly three months ago, as soon as the date became available. It's odd to finally be standing at the doorway I'd seen in so many photos, hailed as a must-visit, framed just so, then posted by so many people. The man guarding the entrance holds a clipboard, looking impatient and bored at once.

I give Michael's last name, which happens to be Italian, but concentrate too hard on saying it perfectly and fumble the vowels at the end. He finds it quickly on his list anyway. I try to tell him that at one point there was another person, but now I'm here alone, navigating past and present verbs. He smiles in a way that confirms he's not listening.

The restaurant is full and loud and warm. Old wooden beams,

walls and floor made from the same stone, too-white lights, a nickel bar. A thin path, made even more so by a few tables for two along the wall, leads to a small dining room. This place also operates as a salumeria and specialty shop, encouraging people to buy some element of what they've just eaten to bring home with them. Aged pork haunches and shoulders hang from the ceiling and rest on top of shining steel meat slicers, curved where they've been shaved down over and over. Different shades and sizes of cheese are lined up alongside jars of capers and truffle salt and preserved lemons, all for sale at a steep markup, on shelves that reach to the ceiling. There's a single barstool off to the left, so I claim it.

I've never understood people who are made nervous by eating alone or don't know how to pass the time when a friend is late to meet them for a drink, how those few solitary minutes spent waiting at a bar can feel panicked and endless. For me, it's potential— things tend to happen when I sit at the bar. Usually just clumsy attempts at conversation or pickup lines concealed as compliments, but occasionally people will surprise me, tell me something interesting, something that actually matters. It happens often enough for me to feel a lift of expectation whenever I sit alone with a book or start to sketch something on a napkin.

The restaurant around the corner from my old apartment was Italian when I found it, then turned French for a few months before eventually going back. Through every change, a side of mushrooms stayed on the menu, always prepared the same way. Sautéed in the pan until they sweated and shrank to their most concentrated and rich, then cloaked in a sauce that inspired obsession—anchovies dissolved in good olive oil, the pucker of white wine, some other element that always escaped me. I craved it, tried to recreate it in my own kitchen, but always fell short somehow. There were months I forgot it existed. Others I'd go eat it twice in one week. I soaked torn pieces of focaccia in whatever was leftover, all punctuated with sips of cheap red wine.

One night, the mushrooms arrived with an extra plate, even though I was alone. The guy sitting next to me at the bar looked up from his phone screen, took out one of his headphones. I waited. He could keep staring straight ahead or he could turn his head, say something.

I thought for sure that he would, or at least smile at the mix-up, the assumption that we were together. But there was nothing. His pasta was set down in front of him shortly after. He ate it quickly, paid, and left. I became suddenly aware of eating inches away from someone pretending I wasn't there, feeling more awkward with each bite, in a way I hadn't before.

The restaurant's wall of windows looked north on Second Avenue, east on Seventh Street. The glass so fogged that all I could picture were the muted white and orange of Walk and Don't Walk. The second truly cold night of the year.

Another frigid night, at a dark bar in Paris, where Charlie Parker records are always playing. Hidden on a side street behind a famous brasserie, its door marked with a small sign, stamped with the outline of a flower. The bartenders all wear the same white jacket and have worked there for at least twenty years. I heard one of them gently mocking me as he checked a glass for water stains, holding it up to the dim light.

"Here I am at Rosebud," he said, as me, in an accented English falsetto. "Drinking my martini and drawing pictures in the dark."

I shot back with something in French, playing up my accent: not quite Parisian, but, thanks to my mother, still far more precise than he was expecting. We had a laugh. I stayed longer than planned, kept someone waiting.

Killing time in London, waiting for a friend to leave her office and meet me at a pub. It was early summer, the heavy door open to the noisy street. I'd been at the Tate Modern all afternoon, was making notes about Lucian Freud and Celia Paul, Rodin and Camille Claudel. Artists and their women, reduced to muses, wasting away on pedestals. I'd stood in front of huge, crisp photographs of glaciers at varying degrees of disappearance, unsure of what to do with my helplessness. Endured the high-decibel screams of children running laps through an exhibit that threw their rainbow shadows on blank walls.

Sitting at the pub, I let myself write whatever came to mind, not allowing my pen to leave paper until I'd filled a page. A usually reliable way to figure out what I actually think about something. My other hand rested on a glass of syrupy red wine, filled to the brim.

The man, more of a boy, sitting next to me had weaponized his attention to the point I could feel his eyes following my handwriting as it moved down the length of the notebook. Distracted enough to finally look up, I wanted to dismiss him with a glance, but found I couldn't. He looked younger than my brother, with a soft jawline and smooth forehead.

He'd been dragged, he said, out for a drink with his friend and her boyfriend, pointing out the back of a blond head, a hand clinging to the arm of someone tall and broad, her face tilted up at him like a flower toward the sun. "How can you write in a place like this?" he asked, with disbelief and a little admiration.

"I'm not really *writing*," I said. "Just getting some thoughts down before I forget."

"Still. That kind of focus." His eyes on my open notebook. "Sorry, I hope I'm not bothering you." Phrased carefully to be polite, while making it difficult for me to deny him.

"You're not." And that was, to my surprise, mostly true. I got the sense he needed gentleness, more care than I would typically give someone in this situation. He spoke fast and at me, with an eager-ness that hadn't been discouraged out of him yet. Every few minutes, the couple he'd come with would look over and roll their eyes.

He'd gone to Saint Andrews, overlapping one year with Jack. When I mentioned my brother (tall, dark hair, economics major, American, obviously), he said the name sounded familiar but didn't think they'd ever met.

"I wasn't much for socializing that last year," he said. "Was dealing with a lot."

I had no desire to know more, to take this bait, but he was determined. Despite how quickly he was drinking, his posh accent stayed put. He ordered another beer. "I got tangled up in something very messy, acted badly. Acted unforgivably, some might say."

The pub grew even more crowded with people leaving their offices for the weekend, reaching over both my shoulders for drinks or waving above my head for the bartender's attention. I felt not quite trapped, but enclosed.

"I'm sure whatever it was couldn't have been unforgivable." I was trying to be kind, nothing more, but it was all the encourage-ment he needed.

"A girl I knew, my friend's sister, she was young to be there. Only sixteen. Some kind of math prodigy."

I forgot my wine and my notebook and studied his face. A nervous half smile that betrayed his guilt or shame or whatever it was, mixed with the clear pleasure in having someone to tell. His index finger circling the mouth of the glass, over and over. Refusal to break eye contact with someone who was listening, a new and invested audience. I wanted to leave him and wherever this was going behind, while also wanting to know what he was about to tell me.

"I found out one of the professors was sleeping with her. Well, she told me, actually. Felt she could confide in me, ask for help." His tone, the way he chose and spoke those particular words, told me everything. "She was all mixed up, thought she was in love with him while knowing it was wrong at the same time." He shook his head at the naïveté, safe in the conviction he'd never be so clueless, so vulnerable.

I could picture him, at the moment he got that news. Seeing it as a call to action. His concerned brow, a paunch to his stomach, hair starting to recede. How many chances does a man like him get to feel like a hero?

"He was young, though, to be teaching. Not one of the old bearded men, not much older than us." His self-protection, for whatever was to come.

"The lines were blurred, then," I said. "Sounds like a complex situation." I enjoy feeling like an authority in anything, even common sense. "That must have been difficult, not knowing what to do." My glass was too full to lift, so I leaned down for a sip. Cheap and sweet.

"Right, I really didn't know. So, I told my advisor, someone I trusted like a friend. And it got out immediately. Everyone suddenly knew." He paused for effect. "Which is not what I wanted."

"Did he lose his job?"

"It never really got that far."

"What do you mean?"

"The next day, the day after I told someone, he killed himself. Jumped off a bridge."

I tried not to let my face betray what I was actually feeling: surprise, embarrassment, sadness for him. I attempted comfort instead.

"You were only trying to look out for someone. I hope you don't feel this is your fault. It's not."

My friend called, suggesting dinner somewhere else. I said I was sorry, that I had to go, and asked him if he was okay until he said he was. I left him there, looking hurt and staring into another drink.

Scanning this bar, filled with pairs of excited tourists and blasé Romans, I wonder about him, hope he feels forgiven and maybe not so lonely.

Here, the conversation that surrounds me matches the volume of the music, instead of one drowning the other out. These voices are buoyant, lifted by the nights these people are embarking on, or already having. The crowd is a relief, knowing that I've made a good, or at least an interesting choice.

The bar is dotted with wine glasses, ringed with stains and sediment like the trunks of trees. Bowls of pasta filled with different shades of tomato red and egg-yolk yellow. Squat glasses of sparkling water. Every few moments, a bubble makes a mad dash for the surface.

A small, framed image of Jesus hangs above the espresso machine. Crown of thorns, streams of blood like sweat, pleading upward expression.

The menu is made up of many laminated, double-sided pages,

fitted in a three-ring binder that reminds me of school. Too many options, some marked with stars, suggesting that there are good and bad decisions to be made. There isn't just salsiccia or prosciutto, but multiple variations of each, served alone or with different cheeses. The permutations could be limitless. I see dishes up and down the bar that I can't match to the words on the menu. One couple pours wine from a bottle with no label, just the anonymous dark green of the glass. The light passes through it. What's inside is already half-gone.

A waiter passes by, his swinging arm missing me by an inch or two. Each muscle in his face is defined to the point of exaggeration, forming its own divots and contours and borders. He's just short of handsome, perfect for a line drawing. Quickly, strategically capturing a face or object or feeling, pen not leaving paper until I've finished. The kind of exercise I'm always reminding myself to do, something between practice and personal challenge. One of my favorites, done a year ago: Jack early on one of the rare mornings he woke up at our parents' house, drinking coffee, still wearing his glasses, taking an absentminded bite of toast. Once he realized what I was doing, he made me tear it up.

I order sparkling water, stumbling over *frizzante*, and a glass of prosecco. It's nice to hear the sound of my own voice.

The wine is rosy caramel in the glass, ribbons of bubbles curling and curling. The bartender points to the bottle with one hand while pouring with the other. "Franciacorta," he tells me. Then, after sizing me up, he continues in English: "Better than prosecco. It's like champagne, but made in Italy." This is the second time I've ordered one drink and a bartender has given me something else, something I like more.

I taste salt and lemon, clinging to one another. Carbonation lights up the back of my throat and I stifle the beginnings of a cough, the way I would if someone had passed me a joint. The bottle disappears behind the bar.

The first time I met Michael for a drink, I ordered prosecco, drank three glasses quickly because I was so nervous. It was early June. I was late, ran from the subway, slowing down a block before the bar so I wouldn't be out of breath or show any signs of effort. He looked surprised when he saw me, though we'd met before, that night on the train. The whole time I knew him, he always wore some version of that look when I met him at a restaurant or turned to his half of the bed in the morning or stood waiting on the other side of the door when he opened it. Some mix of recognition and disbelief.

That first night was the beginning of an avalanche, or that's how I see it now. Unstoppable and, in a way, beautiful, if you don't mind destruction. After leaving the bar, we walked his dog, a husky named Beau, up and down Greenwich Street, past the same restaurants and boutiques three or four times. Making a turn on North Moore, finding our way back on Hudson.

"I wouldn't have pictured you with a dog," I told him. "A fish maybe. Or a couple of plants."

"I didn't pick him," he said, steering Beau away from a pizza crust on the sidewalk. "A remnant of another life. He's cute, though, right?"

Each detail or joke or story we told fell into its place. Every little leap I took was met. I sensed him studying my face, my walk. What to say to me, how I might respond.

Even though he's older, has seen more of life in so many ways, his excitement and enthusiasm that night matched mine. For what I had to say, all the opinions we surprisingly shared, where we'd both been and wanted to go—it shocked me, the strong suspicion I'd been with him, in that room before.

He pulled books off his shelves for me, flipping to certain stories he'd read so often the pages fell open exactly where he wanted them to. I sat on the floor, my back against the wall, bare legs stretched satisfyingly long, throwing a tennis ball for Beau. He brought it back each time, nudged my hand with his cold nose.

Michael looked at me from where he stood by the bookshelf. Even though the lights were dim, it was easy to read the hunger on his face. The gratitude, too.

I wanted to please him, yes, but I also wanted to please myself.

A couple to my left splits a plate of mortadella, spotted like a leopard, luxurious slices layered and folding in on themselves.

One line on the menu stands out: anchovies with bread and two types of butter—my Italian isn't good enough to determine what they are. I see an order of them pass me by, on the way to a table. It's the kind of thing Michael loves to order in a restaurant, anything that might give a less adventurous eater pause. The hidden gems, he'd say. At one of our earlier dinners together, he'd ordered rabbit terrine for us to share. I mirrored him, spreading it casually over buttered toast, and took a bite without hesitation. Ignored the little bones.

If he were here, he'd have to talk me into the anchovies. So I order them on my own, regretting it a little as the bartender turns his back.

The restaurant's soundtrack is one horrible cover after another, all interpreted in different, conflicting styles. "Dancing Queen" as bossa nova, "Man in the Mirror" with a soft acoustic guitar, "Don't Stop Believin'" turned reggae, nothing matching or making sense. They're interrupted by one original, the most recent single from a once-popular singer in the US. She hasn't released any new music in years. This song is supposed to be the beginning of her comeback.

Dad has always rolled his eyes at her voice. "She sounds constantly on the verge of tears," he says. "How is that even possible?"

I'd tell him, "Your voice isn't for everyone, you know." And it's true. Dad's voice is slow and ponderous and very deep. In some cases, he growls more than he sings. His lyrics are more widely adored. They've been worshipped and analyzed and tattooed on forearms and wistfully quoted by thousands, maybe millions of people.

To that, he'd shrug his shoulders. "I've never claimed to be a populist," he'd say.

I feel around for my pen, pull a postcard at random from my bag. It's printed with a photo of the Appian Way at night, arches of a gate in ruins, the old stones of the road lit to look like they're shimmering.

I planned on waiting to write this one, giving myself time to formulate something perfect and eviscerating. But it's the card I picked, so I put it all down in a rush, rewarding myself with a long sip of wine, popping the bubbles between my tongue and the roof of my mouth, when I finish.

Michael,

All roads lead to Rome, right? Waiting to board the flight here, I looked up what that actually means. How, in every town the Romans conquered, they'd build a road that pointed in the capital's direction. How even now, after the empire was won and lost so many different times, all those reminders are still there.

Funny how some things just stubbornly remain. No matter what.

I don't want to hear from you. I don't want you at all.

My pen hangs in the air for a moment, wanting to finish with *What a fucking coward you are.* Instead, I sign with my first initial. A simple loop, cascading into another, as if what I'd written above was of no consequence, caused me no pain.

I tear off one of the stamps I bought earlier, printed with the new pope's face, smiling like he actually means it. Given the other options—the Italian flag, a dead politician's profile—there was no question what I'd choose. And I'm always charmed whenever the supposedly pure mixes with real life and instincts and vices. Like the calendars I've seen at every newsstand I've passed: a handsome priest for each month of the year, as if they're New York City firefighters. It's in the air here—this fervent belief in beauty, worship of sex, trust in the divine.

I let the stamp rest on my tongue, then press the pope's face into the top right corner of the card, enjoying the sight of his calm next to what I've just written, in slow, self-consciously perfect script. Michael loves my handwriting. That always gave me a certain level of satisfaction, similar to knowing I could reliably make him hard with the sound of my voice.

The anchovies arrive, fillets that glitter, fanned in a half circle that traces the curve of the plate. Two pats of butter in the middle, one pale yellow yuzu and the other deep beige vanilla. Bread surrounds it all, focaccia with whole olives and fat halves of figs baked in, such abandon it's almost obscene.

I tear the plate apart and put it together again: ripping off pieces of different flavors of bread, spreading them with one of the two kinds of butter and always a thick piece of anchovy. I smear some of the butter on Michael's postcard in the process. All of it comes together, my focus like an assembly line, purposeful and gluttonous at once. The flavors shouldn't make sense, but do: sharp salt and creamy sugar, dank oil and bright citrus. I eat one piece immediately after another, like an animal.

The couple sitting next to me, at the corner of the bar, is drinking Gaja, a Barbaresco. I don't know much about wine, but I'd recognize that label anywhere. As with so many quietly expensive things, it's deceptive in its simplicity. No clever branding or illustration meant to catch the eye—just thick navy letters, basic font, on a plain white label. A drop skims its way down, leaving a pale violet trail in its wake.

I want to ask them about it, or somehow show them I understand what it is to know and drink something like that. I rehearse the Italian in my mind before speaking it, something trite and harmless like "I love that wine" or "What a wonderful choice," if only I could remember the word for choice, but the woman catches my eye before I'm sure.

Instead, it just comes out: *"Molto bene."* And I point at the bottle, like a fool.

The man reaches for my pointing hand and grasps it, shakes it. He's Giuseppe. His wife, on the stool next to him, is Elena. Their English isn't bad and they're eager for this chance to use it. He motions to the bartender and I can tell he's asking for another glass.

"No, no," I insist, shaking my head and smiling at him. But he ignores me. As does the bartender, who is already pouring.

So I decide to tell them my parents' Gaja story, which, between them, has become apocryphal. As so much of their shared history is. For me, it's more of a party trick.

This was before I was born, soon after they were married. I speak slowly, to be sure Giuseppe and Elena understand.

Dad had either tried a glass of Gaja somewhere by chance or just knew it was appreciated by people who knew wine. He'd bought a bottle, for their anniversary or her birthday or some other occasion that needed a dose of attention, and hid it in the back of a closet, maybe wrapped in a sweater or tucked inside an old boot, depending on which of my parents was telling the story.

Then he went away on his first European tour. But I don't tell this couple that. Nothing that might invite questions (like why my mother didn't join him) or force me to tell the full truth. Sometimes I'm in the mood to share all of that with strangers, receive their surprise and excitement, watch their faces change, size me up all over again. Not tonight. Instead, I say he was on a business trip, which is essentially true.

While he was gone, my mother had some friends over. They ordered pizza. My parents had just moved into their first house in Hudson and there was hardly any furniture. Maybe a thrift store couch and some folding chairs, pillows on the floor.

I remember that house in fuzzy, distant ways. The first place I ever lived, one I constantly investigated and used to hide myself.

We moved away, back to the city for my parents, when I was six, not long after Jack was born.

When asked, they'll say Dad was traveling more then and it was easier to be centrally located. Maybe something about their kids getting more culture, a joke about proximity to better restaurants. And they were right for a while, until it all felt wrong. Too much had changed. The city was too loud for my mom, held too many distractions for my dad. I have memories of screaming and slammed doors, but mostly silences. When they later moved back to Hudson, the new house was bigger, on its own stretch of land, with a view. My parents had more information, experience, and money. All of which helps to make a life, or improve the one that's already there.

By the time the pizza showed up that night, my mother and her friends had finished the wine people had brought with them, and all the other alcohol in the house was already gone. Any reinforcements were a few miles down a twisting road, no husbands or boyfriends to send on a beer run.

Giuseppe and Elena start to pick up on where this is going. The wine is in front of me, and I use this pause in the story to finally pick up the glass. My nose nears the edge, not too close, smelling a wisp of clove cigarette and a hint of balsamic vinegar, the expensive kind, kept in the back of the cabinet for drizzling only. I swirl the wine counterclockwise, as I've been taught. A small sip. It rests on my tongue. I hold it there. It tastes like nothing and then suddenly blooms.

I can't imagine my mother searching the house for something to drink, checking every likely or unlikely place before somehow finding the wine in the closet. The woman I know, if the wine had run out, would have shrugged her shoulders, given a cursory glance to the pantry or refrigerator, and made coffee instead—or used it as an excuse to end the night early. Who knows what she was like before, all the particular ways in which she's changed.

But they both insist it happened this way. She didn't know anything about wine, had no idea of the bottle's value or why it was hidden away. I set it all up, each detail where it needs to be.

Whenever I hear or tell this story, I always wonder what my mom and her friends talked about that night, or any night back then. Was she her usual brand of calm, floating above everyone's jokes and stories and moods? Gathering the right group of people together, sitting back and watching them mix? Or did she have more brash moments then, favoring one friend over another, studying the ripples of her attention as they expanded? No doubt she worked with the secrets she possessed about everyone, trusted confidant that she was and is.

When I'm around her and her friends now, on visits home or around holidays, there's a knowingness, a code to whatever they say. They laugh off the fact that they worry about everything, roll their eyes at their husbands, reference their consistent sleep deprivation, make casual mention of summer houses or Christmas ski trips. While their circumstances are different now, I don't think any of them have actually changed that much. The ones who liked to pick at old wounds and turn things serious, the ones who carried tarot cards always and spoke reverently about the moon, the ones who stayed in the kitchen washing dishes while everyone else ate dessert—they're all essentially the same. The glimmers of my mother's warmth and wariness and practicality are brighter when she's with them: all clues, suggestions of what remains, what's always been there.

So my mother and her friends drank a four-hundred-dollar bottle of wine with pepperoni pizza and a family-size bag of potato chips. There might have been ice cream. I add in my own little details for effect sometimes. Giuseppe and Elena's eyes grow wide. Their hands move to partially conceal a laugh.

When he came back, Dad asked her, "How was it?" Incredulous, impressed even. And how could he not be?

"Delicious," she answered. Without apology or regret.

I play the end like a punch line, as I've seen both my parents do countless times. The result is mostly satisfying, a little disappointing, maybe. It makes my mother sound different than she is, more unapologetic, maybe even careless or callous. But there are elements I recognize. A give-and-take I've seen slide from one extreme to another my whole life. How my dad pays, how my mom collects.

And now they share a bottle of Gaja on their anniversary every year. That's a touch I know to be true, having seen it myself over and over. Depending on where Dad is playing or recording, it might not happen on the actual day, but the sentiment is always recognized.

He makes a show of buying the bottle, putting it in a place of prominence: the island in the kitchen, the bench that faces the front door. Subtlety has never been his strong suit; it didn't matter whether it was planning a sincere display of affection for my mother or an attempt to cover up the letters and photos and phone calls from other women. One year, he put a bottle in the middle of the staircase, to be sure she'd see it, and she almost kicked it over.

Elena and Giuseppe love this idea of tradition, and I wonder if this bottle they've ordered means anything significant, or if this is just their average Thursday night. I feel a little guilty, and lucky to be intruding.

Giuseppe pours more wine, ripe cherry red, for each of us. "To your parents," he says.

And I can tell by the way he touches her glass with his that they've been together for years, have children, share a home, fight to make their life together work.

My pasta, rigatoni alla gricia, arrives: salty, creamy, spiked with black pepper, dusted with pecorino, just sour enough. The pork cheek crunches slightly, charred in the pan until it's almost sweet. Elena ordered the same thing, told me it's what I should get, and now watches me take my first bite, a beatific smile forming on her face when I close my eyes to savor the taste.

"I have an unpopular opinion." A man, sitting to my right, is tapping me on the shoulder, talking too loudly in my ear. "Gricia is the best Roman pasta. Agree? Disagree?"

Elena and Giuseppe are watching, so I don't want to be rude and essentially ignore him, which is what I would do in New York. A short, uninviting laugh, a smile that's more of a wince, my back unequivocally turned. But that's not an option here.

"I agree. This is delicious." I look at him with eyes that have nothing behind them, no hint of warmth in my voice, hoping he'll get the picture. He doesn't.

In the time it takes for me to answer his question, Giuseppe and Elena are paying their check, standing up, saying goodbye. I feel a quick pinch of sadness that surprises me. I thought I still had the chance to learn more about them, to at least get beyond some silly story about my parents and a bottle of wine, hoping for the kind of conversation that doesn't really teach you anything, but still makes you feel less alone. Now the tide has shifted, taking them out, and it's too late for me to swim against it.

Elena hugs me as they leave. They probably think I'm grateful for attention from this man, spared from what they think is a dull conversation with older, married people. I wish I could tell them otherwise.

"Let me guess, you live in New York or LA. Or maybe London. A fellow expat?"

I tell him I live near Madison Square Park, that I've lived in or near New York City my whole life.

He wants to tell me all about who he was when he lived in New York, how much money he had, the number of stories in his townhouse, his famous friends, an affair he says ended in him dissolving his hedge fund to save a female employee's reputation, but reeks of sexual harassment to me. He introduces himself as Craig.

Now he lives here in Rome, where he apparently advises startups on how to keep themselves afloat. He mocks the Italian work ethic, or lack thereof. How he tries to instill basic accountability and productivity in people he claims have no interest in either. He brags about the suits he's bought, the best in the world.

Since he's here and Giuseppe and Elena are gone, I try to make the best of things, see if I can make him squirm. For no other reason than him sitting here, existing, twirling his fork, serves as a not-very-subtle reminder that most of the men I meet are boring and just short of desperate. I don't want to be confronted with what I've lost, how hard it will be to find again. I ask Craig how old he is.

He says he's forty-two. He must be lying.

"I won't ask how old you are. I know that's rude, but obviously you're young and obviously you're beautiful."

He tells me this with some urgency, like something important depends upon me understanding how much closer he is to death than I am.

I don't have the energy to say I'm only ten years younger, that plenty of people wouldn't consider that young at all.

"You must deal with men like me constantly, talking your ear off in bars, wasting your time."

Just to fuck with him, I say, "And most of them are terrible in bed, too."

Instead of taking this opportunity to fall all over himself, thrilled that I've brought up sex unprovoked, as I predicted, he insists upon the value of giving myself up and offering my body to another person, how careful I must be, how this is such a great and precious thing. An odd approach.

Michael and I didn't have sex that first night. We circled one another for hours, never coming close enough. He said goodbye quietly, hand lingering on the small of my back, his breath in my ear. The smell of him was clear for a precious minute, then faded.

Leaving his apartment, I was skittish and jumpy in a way I can only describe as unconsummated. I sent him a text.

I really wanted to kiss you.

Shocked at my own transparency, how little I cared.
He replied instantly.

And yet you didn't.

When we did sleep together, it was unexpected, no time to plan or prepare. A few days after our drinks and walk, he called me and mentioned his apartment was being painted. He'd decamped to an anonymous hotel around the corner to escape the fumes.

"It's lonely here," he said.

He barely even had to touch me. When he did, he knew just how. It's dangerous for a man to understand so much, to have that kind of power. One finger pressing inside of me, then two, then three, with such certainty it was contagious.

Early the next morning, I gave details to a friend—his hand in my hair, the specific, masterful ways he went down on me, the shape of his cock, a delicate kiss on my cheek—over the phone in the back of a cab, not caring what the driver heard or thought. They were the first of so many things I'd say and share and try to figure out, evidence of how challenging and consuming he was. But I want many stories, not just this one.

Craig seems to be having an excellent time, meaningful even. His hand brushes my arm at first, then, gaining courage, rests above my elbow. At one point, he grabs my shoulder, to steady himself and make a point at the same time. He studies my face closely, with something approaching sincerity.

"Can I ask you something?" Before I can answer, he continues, "And if you ever want me to fuck off and leave you alone, just say that. Just say, 'Fuck off, Craig. I want to be left alone.' You promise you'll tell me?"

I can't believe it, but I reassure him. "No, it's fine. Ask me your questions, Craig."

This feels close to charity. Does he see it that way? It makes so little sense, how some men just don't care what the tone or trajectory of a night or an hour might be, as long as it carries the chance of them getting laid.

"So you're an artist?" he asks, without giving me any time to respond. "That's amazing. I didn't think people could be artists anymore."

"What do you mean? You don't need permission. You just make art, if that's what you want to do."

I watch him formulate a careful answer, the deep lines of his forehead, sleeves of an expensive white shirt rolled to the elbows, the nervous way he keeps touching his ear, a crooked tooth.

"Do real people even pay for art these days? What about galleries? Can you get anyone to pay attention to you if you're not Jeff Koons?"

Like I'm any kind of authority on the subject. An artist who hasn't sold a real painting in over a year, who relies on an algorithm to shill drawings that were supposed to be a side project, who recently gave up the lease on her studio because trying to make anything new surrounded by her unsold, agonized-over work got too depressing. But I roll my eyes, challenging him directly in a way men like him seem to love. "Have you heard of the internet?"

"The internet!" He yelps it almost, clearly thrilled he can now categorize me as smart, quick. "That's good. That's very good."

What does Craig look for? How does he settle on someone, decide to try? Is it just proximity, a perceived level of difficulty, or is there a standard? If there is, he's decided I meet it, that I'm worth the effort. Worth the machinations of a man who is in no way remarkable, but moves through life with certainty: that he'll ultimately be rewarded with the right kind of recognition, amount of money, sort of woman. Maybe it's been there all his life, a low drumbeat moving him forward. So steady he doesn't even hear it anymore.

Another drink? He does that thing I can't stand, two fingers in the air. How hard is it to get someone's attention without gesturing at them like a dog?

"Okay, here's a question." He points to my glass, which I've drained of the Chianti he ordered, and the bartender refills it. "When you think about your work, the art you make, the people who appreciate it, does it make you proud?"

Especially maddening about Michael: the way he slowly, incrementally made himself essential. When there was something to tell, he was suddenly the person I wanted to tell it to.

"I'm a perfectionist. It takes a lot for me to be satisfied with something. But yes, sometimes." I take a sip. "Occasionally."

Craig forces a toast, tipping his head, tucking his chin a bit so his eyes meet mine. "To perfection."

It all comes back to power. I always wanted it, almost never had it. And even when I did, when Michael would look at me like I'd given him some precious, impossible gift, I never kept it for long.

It's after eleven, but I'm not tired, not at all.

I've turned down Craig's invitation to be his guest at some club. A place he's told me is built into a ruin on the perimeter, just past the largest Aurelian gate. He knows the owner, who happens to be a famous Italian film director. It's far, but don't worry, he'll call us a taxi.

I come back from the bathroom and find that he's gone, as I'd hoped. But he's also moved all my glasses of wine from his tab back to mine.

There are still people forming a line at the door when I leave the restaurant, studying the menu, looking through the glass. To my right, this little street is brightly lit. People linger in front of a gelateria. Music shakes the doorframe of a hookah bar. In the other direction, a young couple wanders between streetlamps, dodging the light, their voices low. I follow them without deciding to.

They walk slowly, his hand tracing the plateau at the base of her neck, playing with the strap of her silk dress, coming to rest on her lower back. His eyes watch what his hand is doing. She stabs at a cup of gelato with a pink plastic spoon.

His casual worship. Does she appreciate it? I didn't, when I had it.

They turn down a tiny alley, an afterthought, covered by an arch that connects two buildings. Someone has lit short candles in the divots between cobblestones, casting shadows on curving walls. Garbage overflows from dumpsters that line both sides of the passageway. In candlelight, they look like tanks. Graffiti traces the width of the arch, indecipherable.

Why take the time to turn something more beautiful or different or distinctive than it has to be? A question that could be posed to this entire city.

I'm always drawn to details like this, though it's hard to know if this attention is natural or if I've been taught to notice. When I was six or seven, my mom brought me along on one of her monthly visits to MoMA, a schedule she's kept religiously, then and now.

A new exhibition had just opened, *Matisse in Morocco*. The line to enter the gallery was long, but we got in right away. It wasn't clear how or why, but I remember being thrilled.

The room was warm and smelled stale with sweat, the museum's air-conditioning no match for the size of the crowd and the heat of the city in August. To distract myself, I started skipping from one painting to another, making zigzags across the room. The sooner we finished, the sooner I could go to the park or the zoo or whatever else she'd promised. But Mom was insistent I look closely. "Slow down, Emilia," she kept saying. "Slow. Down."

She kept two fingers linked around the flesh of my arm and made me look at each painting for at least a minute before moving on to the next. And eventually, thanks to her, I started to see.

Using color and energy and light, Matisse had created something personal. Close to paradise, I thought then. A window opening onto a broad landscape, rolling hills and the tops of trees painted deep blue, because he wanted them to be. The dome of a mosque shining not just white in the sun, but pink and yellow, too. A passageway set apart in green, to look all the more inviting. He gave the same attention to his model's brightly patterned shoes, kicked off onto the floor, as he did to three goldfish, striped different shades of orange and outgrowing their bowl.

Matisse made up his own Tangier, based on nothing more than what he saw and how it made him feel. It belonged to him, whatever it was that gave such life to those paintings, but I loved it, too. I wanted it for myself.

We're alone now, the couple and I. I fall back so they don't sense me, one step for every four of theirs. Not quite close enough to hear what they're saying, what language they're speaking, even with the echo from the walls. Their shared tone is low and warm, thick with the comfort that comes from trusting the person beside you.

I still worry I'm walking too close, observing something that's not mine, something I have no right to. I am desperately avoiding even the chance of them turning around, giving me some kind of accusatory, disparaging look. I don't think I could bear it, not right now. Just let me watch.

He dips his half-eaten supplì into the peak of her gelato, bites into it with gusto. She screams in mock horror, playfully nudges his shoulder with hers.

Michael was never any good at concealing his moods. I watched him closely, more sure than not that I'd be able to predict what he'd do or say—to meet his excitement or petulance accordingly or fight against it, if I wanted to.

So after more than a year and a half together, when he finally told me he was married, that he had been for nine years, my reaction differed from the lie I told my friends. To them, it was a whiplash kind of story, sudden and destructive. The type that makes you feel safe and superior when you hear it because it's not happening to you. The unsettling fact that whatever connects two people can transform from belief to betrayal in the turn of a phrase. But if I'm being truthful now, I wasn't totally shocked.

The specifics were a surprise—meeting her in Portugal, the life they'd had in San Francisco, her job as a professor of rhetoric (whatever that is) at Berkeley, how they'd lived apart for the last two years while she was in Argentina conducting research for a book of her own, and the fact she was now, I imagine, coming back, expecting to resume their life together—but the overwhelming feeling that his real life was a secret, that I'd seen only a sliver of him, was almost welcome. My instinct, which I'd denied and smothered until it was softer than a whisper, had been right.

Michael had a wistful tone to his voice when he spoke about her that night, a little smile even, despite probably trying not to. He couldn't help it. It made me want to rip his throat out.

But it was all a confirmation of something I knew for certain, something rotten creeping in. Not too long before, he'd opened the door to me while he was finishing a phone call with his mother. He gave me that contented, comfortable smile as he spoke to her, maybe even a benign eye roll at whatever she might have been saying. But I knew instinctually that his mother had no idea who I was. I would never meet her.

He told me he'd realized he needed to give his marriage another chance, a real chance. He was careful to point out he never explicitly said he was single or divorced. Always so exact, with one foot on the high road. But I knew what he was really saying, how being with me made him realize he needed something else.

Yes, he'd been hungry for me and all my moods and experience and details. But he was equally evasive when I tried to delve deeper into his. And I didn't ask for clarity. I took his silence, his attention, and translated it to mean what I wanted.

We sat across from each other at his salvaged-wood kitchen table, leaning forward in our chairs as if agreeing to a truce or terms of disarmament. Which, in a way, we were.

"And I do care for you, very much."

"Oh, you care for me? That's nice."

"Emilia, please. This isn't easy for me."

"Really? What can I do to make it easier?"

"Try to have an actual conversation, maybe. Talk to me."

"I guess I just don't really see what there is to talk about. I thought this was a relationship, but to you, it's a litmus test."

"I know it's hard to understand."

"It's not. I get it. Completely. I'm so fucking sick of you equating inexperience with ignorance." I tend to get eloquent when I'm enraged. It can be a double-edged sword.

I should have said what I actually meant, instead of trying to be clever. Like, *I love you. I would do anything for you. How could you do this, so simply lie to me, prefer someone else? How is there enough of you for that?*

I knew men could be deceptive, turn cold even. I usually looked for ones who seemed incapable of it, who were too transient or self-involved or focused elsewhere to truly impinge on my life or cause me much pain. The bartenders and the actors, the photographer perpetually off on assignment, the business school students from France and Argentina in town on visas that would, eventually, expire. The former Marine turned hedge fund manager, who wore a Rolex Submariner on one wrist and a beaded friendship bracelet, made for him by his six-year-old daughter, on the other. And, inevitably, the musicians. I always grew bored or impatient with them the fastest.

But never true heartbreak. Though I'd seen it secondhand so many times, to the point it made me question my own tolerance of pain once it finally happened to me.

Some of my friends have weathered true devastation—men who would never be ready to marry them, relationships that ended in draws after eight or nine years, multiple miscarriages, partners who'd died of sudden illnesses—but were able to recover their lives, even move on shockingly quickly. They've dealt with my kind of superficial hurt but haven't lingered. So a man I loved lied to me, chose someone else. Big fucking deal.

And yes, I knew I didn't have all of Michael, knew that something would eventually come crashing through, clarifying everything.

The confirmation of my foolishness, I'd been patiently waiting for that.

When the couple turns into a bar, I give it a minute before I follow. Leaning against the wall, looking like I could be waiting for someone or deciding whether or not to smoke.

I look through the snug doorway, to the warm light inside. Big iron gates have been thrown open on either side, like those used to protect an ancient castle or a well-fortified prison.

Two men nearby are circling one another in the street. Their voices rise quickly in a way that makes the muscles in my neck catch and tighten. A few seconds pass before I realize they're sparring, just playing at fighting. Like children, with too-short attention spans.

I'm starting to realize how physical Italians are, always touching whoever they're talking to or fiddling with a lighter or resting their weight on the side window of a car that's been parked haphazardly in the street. Constantly using or involving their bodies. There's a word for it: familiar. Whenever there's a lull or empty moment, they fill it with some kind of contact.

I wish I knew how to draw potential, to confine and then let loose what that urgency looks like. That quiver we hold in our limbs, our chests, the arches of our feet, the part of us always ready to spring into action. Every time I try, it's never quite right, closer to impatience or nerves or need.

The bar is designed to resemble someone's kitschy living room: mismatched furniture, bad art hanging crooked on the stone walls, a neon Cynar sign all lit up, its artichoke shaded and glowing. Crossing the threshold, I get the self-conscious feeling I've entered a conversation halfway through. Or it might just be a side effect of walking into a room like this alone.

Tables have been pushed against the wall, their tops painted to look like slices of oranges, lemons, and limes. Chairs are stacked so high they lean, all to make room for an impromptu dance floor. I sit at the bar, on the stool closest to the door. The bartender sees me coming and makes a show of pulling himself back behind the bar with momentum leftover from dancing. I order an amaro, which I've always found isn't so much a digestif as an excuse to keep drinking. He lifts the largest bottle of Montenegro I've ever seen, shaped like some kind of missile, and pours it into a shallow glass. Thick and syrupy and sweet. I'm supposed to sip it, but I don't. The couple I followed has found a table in the back. They sit, watching people dance, his hand on top of hers.

A few men my age linger at the bar, turned around on their stools to face the rest of the room, cigarettes between fingers. I constantly see people rolling them or clutching pouches of tobacco or delicately separating one paper from the rest. Something to occupy everyone's hands.

In the bathroom mirror, my face is mine, and also not, covered in a thin veil of something wrong, something I can't pinpoint. I try the usual solutions, smoothing my hair, wiping the shadow of mascara from under my eyes, but none of it works. This sort of disconnection would usually frustrate me, slicing through whatever else was happening with the sharpness of insecurity, second-guessing. But I'm too drunk and far away from anyone who matters to care.

I wordlessly join the circle that's formed in the center of the room, which always seems to happen when a group of people collectively decides to dance. Whether they're in a dark middle school gym or under an extravagantly lit wedding tent or happening upon a warm, crowded bar in Rome. We twist, or try to. My waist goes one way, my hips and legs another. Over and over, like a pepper grinder. Opposing forces. I focus on making my palms so flat my fingers curl up, slice the air, kick my shoes off to make a point.

Two girls twirl next to each other in a corner. One of them practiced, someone who's taken dance classes. She chooses a point with every turn and her eyes catch on it. The other is smiling at nothing, lost in herself.

Then I'm on the ground, my knee turned out and already throbbing with pain. There are a few gasps when it happens, but then everyone, almost immediately, is back to dancing.

A man comes in from outside, splits the crowd with authority, like he might own the place. He fits his arm around my waist, lifts, leads me to a chair, makes sure I sit down.

I haven't seen or spoken to Michael in thirty-nine days. More than a month separating me from our last, gutting conversation. I do wonder about his timing, breaking up with me just before coming here. A year and ten months of stringing me along was fine, but taking this trip, that was just dishonest enough, apparently.

I wonder where he's spending his birthday. Mexico maybe, somewhere seemingly simple or predictable, a place he could just as easily make his own. But no cocktail with an umbrella in it or anything like that. Far too common, undignified even. He's likely letting the sun dry his skin on some beach after swimming with his wife. His fucking *wife*.

The doors hang open, music flowing out. In the street, people are dancing to it, leaning over tables, sharing drinks and cigarettes and joints. A dog licks the last bit of tomato sauce from his owner's bowl of pasta, left for him on the ground. It could be midnight or four a.m. I wouldn't be surprised either way. The air is the same temperature as my skin, as cool as it's going to get.

The man pushes a glass of water into my hand, closes my fingers around it. I drink slowly, watching everyone else move.

"You need to be careful," he tells me.

"I know, I'm sorry." I rub my bare knee, skin unbroken, for emphasis. It will definitely bruise. *Mi dispiace*, I remind myself.

He fetches some ice from behind the bar, wraps it in a napkin, holds it against my leg until I take it from him. My hand touches his for the briefest moment.

"*Grazie,*" I say.

He likes my accent, tells me it's better than it needs to be, for an American. For a few seconds, I consider what it might be like to sleep with him, whether he'd be tentative or experienced, focused or playful, selfish or not. Would it be a cure? Or at least an effective anesthetic? Dulling the memory of one person with the presence of another?

When his back is turned, I slip out into the street instead. I walk past the people gathered outside, toward what I'm hoping is the river. Someone breaks a glass, then curses, in an apartment above my head. All the windows I see are open.

Months ago, I was at my parents' house, lying on the kitchen floor with the dog. Dad had been asleep for an hour, maybe more. Jack was in the Cotswolds with his fiancée's family, part of a compromise they were making. One holiday with our family, the next with hers. Though he was away more often than not.

It was one of the quiet nights between Christmas and New Year's Eve. Mom was reading emails on her laptop, shopping the holiday sales. She asked me whether I liked this coat, these boots. I'd lift my head, say yes or no, my hand still scratching behind the dog's ears, knowing she'd whine if I stopped.

Mom was quiet for a minute or two. Clicking something, typing a few words, sipping the tea she'd made for both of us.

"I hope you're standing up for yourself," she said in a soft voice, clearly bracing herself for how I might react but risking the fallout anyway.

I looked at her, unsure how her train of thought had traveled from laughing at the dog and evaluating lengths of hemlines to this. "What are you talking about?"

"I get the feeling that maybe you've accepted less than you deserve."

My instinct was to fight her, or act offended or put off, or at least question where this feeling came from. Instead I just looked at her, as neutrally as possible, though I desperately wanted to cry.

She turned back to whatever she was doing at the computer, slowly tapping away.

"I just hope you're looking for someone who's kind." Kindness was always paramount to her, which made me wonder about the different ways my father didn't show his. She'd never met Michael, but I'd mentioned him enough that I'm sure she thought she had all the necessary information.

"I am, Mom." I answered her in a tone I hoped would put an end to this.

"Believe me, there's nothing sexy or redeeming about someone difficult. Life is hard enough."

My mom's brand of parenting has rarely been about emulating how she's lived her life, and almost always veers toward precautionary tales instead: me learning from her missteps, lost opportunities, many concessions. Her telling me what I knew was true but would, in all likelihood, still ignore.

I think for a few seconds about calling a car or looking for a taxi stand, but the night is calm and I'm drunk enough that the walk back seems the better, more poetic choice.

I don't want to lie by omission. Or delude myself into forgetting what actually was, forgetting that final night, the one I'm ashamed of but also knew was inevitable.

I'd been in his neighborhood for hours, ordering drink after drink with no pause to taste or reconsider. A means to an end, sitting by a bare, swept-out fireplace at the bar around the corner from his building. A place we'd been together more nights than I could remember, cozy in the winter, out of place and depressing in the summer, as it was then. Most places would fill a fireplace with plants or candles, something to camouflage. This one sat empty, as I did.

I knew from experience when the overnight doorman would be off duty, took the elevator up as I'd done so many times before. I threw my fist against his door over and over, hard, for what seemed like a very long time. My knuckles were swirled navy and deep purple for days after, a constant reminder.

For a few horrifying, exhilarating seconds: the possibility that she could be there. Her, standing innocent and victorious on the other side of the door, hovering behind him, wiping sleep from her eyes, wondering who could be knocking so loudly and at such an hour.

But no, it was just him.

"If you weren't married, if she didn't exist, would you be with me? Would you want to be?" I asked him this through tears, taking all the deep-down pathetic things I was never supposed to say out loud and using them as fuel.

It was so important, so crucial, that some part of him, even the smallest part, still wanted me, that everything I'd felt hadn't been an apparition. I needed to hear him say it, because I didn't believe anything I told myself anymore. I didn't realize, as I do now, that whether he did or not was irrelevant.

"I can't honestly answer that." He touched my wet face. "She does exist. I can't give you what you want."

"You could. You so easily could." I knew I was being petulant, giving away any pride I still had. I didn't care.

"I'm sorry. You know how I feel about you." I didn't, not at all, but I took that sentence and warmed myself with it. "If my life were different." He pushed the hair off his forehead, exhausted. "I don't know."

A wonderful, terrible moment—it wasn't yes, wasn't no. Even if I didn't get him, I got distant, cloudy affirmation. And that wasn't nothing. You could even say it was a kindness.

I don't remember when I left, or how. Since then it's been silence. Until today.

———————

The Tiber is a welcome sight. I grip a lamppost for a moment, extra stability, and stare at Saint Peter's. Lit to glow, to suggest it never sleeps, gears of faith forever turning. I feel a weight could slowly be lifting, so gradually it seems there's no movement at all.

The longer I was with him, the more uncertain I became, transforming myself accordingly. I adopted so much of what he loved and hated and rejected and valued, became some version of myself that existed in relation to him.

But it was for good reason, or it seemed that way at the time. What was the harm in feeling unsure or adrift for a minute when my reward was his acceptance, respect, even admiration?

For him to say, "I love that about you" or "I couldn't put it better," or just wordlessly hold my gaze in response to something: it all felt unquestionably worth it.

The surrounding layers may have changed, but I was still myself at the core, always. And now there's no need to watch what I say or wait for the sweetness of someone else's approval. No more wondering what he'll think, how he'll assess.

Wandering like this feels tenuous: with him in just the corner of my mind, not pervading it, knowing he can't be sure of where I am, that he'll never know anything about me again if I don't tell him. I'm sure, innately, of how important it is to ignore him, not let him in.

I crave a time when I'll go hours, days, weeks without thinking of him. I'll never forget his existence entirely, that's impossible, but there's hope that he'll fade to a distant mistake, one I'll eventually acknowledge only with a laugh and shake of my head. Someone who wanted more, when he already had so much. I'll simplify him as selfish, and then forget again for a while.

A friend of mine preaches that there's something to learn from every relationship, no matter how seemingly pointless. That's bullshit, in this case. What is there to learn? That I was blind, even willfully so?

I follow wide, well-lit streets, passing falafel shops and pizza stands catering to drunk tourists, looking up only briefly at Piazza Venezia, bright white and close to empty. The sight of Trajan's Forum means I'm close to home. Home for now. Lit like it's an art installation or even an amusement park, encouraging everyone who looks at it to consider the beauty in decay. Columns somehow still standing, cats stalking shadows between blocks of marble, weeds growing wherever they can. The napkin that once held the ice for my knee is soaked. I wring it out on the ground, throw it away.

I know, for a fact, that I'll think of him in an hour or two, in the bed we were supposed to share. His fingers and tongue and cock inside me as I touch myself to sleep. I look forward to it, in spite of everything. The certainty is a comfort.

The men selling selfie sticks and key chains give me a half-hearted sales pitch, but I stare straight ahead. No amount of alcohol will rob me of the ability to ignore something I wish weren't there. A New Yorker's gift, or something.

A massive brick building cuts between the traffic of Via Nazionale and the quiet shelter of Monti like the bow of a ship. According to the map on my phone, it's the Villa Aldobrandini, once a palace, now a museum devoted to some cardinal's art collection. I say the name aloud, sounding it out. There's a garden beyond this wall, described by someone's blog as a "leafy escape," a place to stop and sit after a day of sightseeing. A light, hot rain has started to fall.

Passing by, I reach up to touch the feet of a statue built into the wall, the joints of her toes worn down by years of superstitious fingers. Just because I can. The stone is porous, rough against my skin.

There's a saint for every occasion, every illness, every catastrophe. Genevieve saved Paris when she diverted Attila's Huns away from the city, just by praying. The Virgin Mary has, supposedly, protected countless cities from wars, invasions, natural disasters. Not to mention everything she does for women: defense against infertility, strength during childbirth, the ability to endure it all. When Saint Catherine's followers tried to smuggle her severed head out of Rome, she performed a posthumous miracle. The soldiers, searching the bag that held her remains, found rose petals instead.

I've never understood any of them: the selflessness and certainty, the tolerance for pain, relinquishing all their free will, ultimately their lives, for some vague, protective cloud of faith. But maybe I should be thinking about it differently, how they sought and held on to power. How their names are still, more than a thousand years later, whispered in prayer.

A mint-green Vespa misses me by inches, making no effort to swerve or slow down, accelerating into a turn at the bottom of the hill. Someone clings to the driver, their two helmets bowed together. My heart beats so hard and fast I feel it in my ears, the crown of my head.

Emilia was a saint, but not a martyr. She lived a long life, died a natural death.

FRIDAY

ROME DOESN'T KNOW WHAT to do with a woman alone.

All the Italian women and girls I see walk side by side with men or huddle in clusters with their families or roam around in identical-looking packs. Their voices high, tremulous with what could be excitement or insistence or exasperation. They speak far too fast for me to understand, with their own idioms and shortcuts. If I were here with someone, I doubt I'd be this curious.

The fact that I'm alone is likely more noticeable at night. The lack of a man, or anyone who might help to explain me, stands out, poses a question. But now, as I turn a quiet corner, away from the Piazza della Madonna dei Monti and in search of coffee, my solitude doesn't seem to matter much. It's close to nine. Everyone is distracted by the day ahead, doing their shopping or visiting or whatever it is Italians do in the time before lunch. I'm awake naturally, with no alarm and earlier than I expected, spared by jet lag somehow. The lack of a hangover, of any kind of cloudiness or weight, is a miracle. The space between my shoulder blades feels light with expectation.

The curve of Nero's Domus Aurea is just visible between roof-tops. This easy access to ruins and churches and the Palatine Hill was the reasoning behind renting an apartment in Monti. This way, we would be surrounded by history, able to run into it, instead of planning visits to monuments, standing in line at the Forum, digging up fossils for ourselves.

I avoid the cafés in the piazzas, with their set tables and white cloth and unfurled umbrellas. In Italy, you drink your coffee stand-ing up, Michael told me. Quickly, at a counter. No complicated orders, no special requests. You take what they give you.

The richness of his life, of everything he knew, was never-ending to me, new depths to plumb always.

There were enough moments of note that he could forget and remember them regularly. Offhanded mentions of meeting Hunter S. Thompson in a tiny bar in San Sebastián, or staying too late at an Upper East Side party where Cindy Sherman was playing the piano. Showing me a personally signed copy of *Gravity's Rainbow*, how strangely loose Pynchon's signature was. Michael flipped a few pages and read the first line with reverence. *A screaming comes across the sky.*

To me, it was a particular kind of knowledge, his proximity to what was interesting and rarefied. Or fame, if that's the right word. But either way, his markers of cool and competency were different from the ones I grew up seeing and learning. There was still mess and selfishness and addiction and general bad behavior, of course, but with a veneer of intelligence, a shine.

Michael subscribed to the idea that true genius is often solitary, rarely pretty, and almost never given its due, let alone cheered for. Making me less and more starry-eyed, all at once. I've always liked someone who knows the rules, no matter what they happen to be.

And it was reciprocal, that fascination. He wanted to know everything about me. The questions he asked, the details he remembered, how closely he listened. It all made me feel smart and interesting and worthy of his attention and care, to the point that I wanted to make him feel proud, whatever that took.

Having the father I do probably helped. I don't remember exactly how I told Michael who he was, but we hadn't known each other long.

"You're kidding," he said. "What a childhood that must have been." It was a line meant to show this new information didn't sway him in any way, that he wasn't so easily seduced by celebrity. But afterward I could sense him searching me for traces; the music I liked now took on new meaning, my gray-green eyes, a depth in the way I spoke.

They met once, if you could call it that. Dad had come into the city to see an old friend of his play piano and sing standards at Bemelmans. He'd reserved a room upstairs, planned to make a night of it.

"Come by if you want, honey," said his voicemail. "Martinis on me."

I could have said maybe, or "I'll try, but no promises." I could have declined the invitation altogether, not even mentioned it to Michael.

But I wanted them to meet, wanted to see what could happen when one part of my life stood face-to-face with another. When two men who demanded so much of me, took everything I happily gave, looked each other in the eye.

It usually took some convincing to get Michael above Fourteenth Street, but that night he paid for the taxi. The bar was warm and loud, painted walls swimming with color and gleaming gold. The man at the door was about to explain the cover charge, until he saw Dad wave us over.

Michael's spine straightened, his stride grew purposeful, cutting a path through the crowd. People often don't realize how tall Dad is until they see him in person.

I introduced them quickly, over the hum of the bass and the rattle of drinks being shaken behind us.

"A pleasure," Michael said. He was attempting to be casual. Respectful, but not obsequious. But I saw it how my dad must have—a classic case of trying too hard. This was nothing new, watching someone meet him for the first time: the obvious effort to act natural, the restraint in every smile, every syllable. I'd figured Michael would be immune to it, but apparently not.

If Dad remembered who this person was to me, he showed no signs of it, just a hint of a faraway smile. Applause for his friend and the band when it was called for. A bit of small talk between songs. *Oh, you're a writer? That's wonderful. What are you working on these days?*

Was it possible Dad raised an eyebrow when Michael's back was turned? As if to say, *This is the kind of man you choose?*

Could I have seen that?

But no, I told myself. They shook hands, smiled. We had a drink. We left. That was it.

The linen dress I'm wearing now—white, thin straps, as loose and light as possible—is already becoming heavy with the heat. Clinging to my ribs, the backs of my thighs. The bruise from my fall last night is impressive, the point of impact a blot on the inside of my knee, rays of muddy purple fanning out.

The place I choose is on a corner, hidden from Via Panisperna, with doors open on each of the two streets it occupies. Air passes in and out, fluttering the edge of an old campaign poster, *Forza Italia!* printed in a fading red, beneath Berlusconi's practiced, demonic grin. His forehead flat, shiny, completely free of lines. The linoleum floor has just been swept clean: dirt from the street, empty sugar packets, and half an orange peel linger in a dustpan, left unemptied in the corner.

A few older Roman men stand at the scratched counter, the glass beneath offering a view of simple pastries and assembled panini, waiting for the press. The espresso machine and analog cash register are manned by a teenager on his cell phone, tapping out a text message, studying the screen through the hair that falls in his face.

"Buongiorno." The first words I'll speak today—a fresh opportunity. *"Un caffè, per favore."*

With a nod of the boy's head, his back turned, a few quick movements, it appears, with two sips of seltzer in a glass to match. I drink one coffee, then another, then another. I think he's the first person not to answer me in English since I arrived. Granted, he's not answering me in any language at all, but this still means progress. Instead of attempting *un altro* and possibly breaking this spell, I smile at the empty cup and he fills it again, sliding a new, clean one to precisely the right place, flicking his wrist to grind the beans. He can measure the espresso by sight, by weight. His fingers remember the exact pressure needed to encourage the aging machine. Everyone who walks in and out knows him by name, stops for a handshake or a nod of the head.

One of the men's cell phones rings every few minutes, the tone imitating church bells after a wedding or baptism or some other ceremony signifying hope. Each time, he answers with a whispered "*Pronto?*" His hand cups the side of his mouth.

I drink each espresso almost immediately, as they do, and singe the tip of my tongue, the back of my throat. The men standing on either side of me act as if I'm not there, likely continuing the conversation where they left off yesterday morning.

They've formed their own hierarchy, a daily drama. The ringleader—at least I see him that way—asks exuberant, maybe teasing questions of the boy behind the bar, shakes a passerby's hand with authority, answers one of his friend's outbursts with noticeable coolness. He wears a pale yellow shirt and gives me a little bow before drinking his coffee in one shot.

Newspapers hang like clean laundry from clips in the shade underneath the bar. No one feels the need to comment on my order, ask me where I'm from, or say anything at all. If I came back every morning for a week or a month, what more would I notice or learn?

To my left, a man with a thick, well-cared-for mustache attacks a crossword puzzle, one hand flattening the newspaper against the counter, the other poised in midair, fingers curled around a pen, ready to strike.

When I was six or seven, when Jack was starting to walk and talk, Dad was back with us. Or at least staying long enough that I remember him checking my homework and helping me memorize poems. I was starting to listen to audiobooks in the car to and from school or turned up loud on the stereo at home. He let me take the CD out of the case and place it delicately in the tray, my finger carefully looped through the hole in the middle to avoid any scratch. I watched him nod and close his eyes at certain parts of *The Velveteen Rabbit* or *The Giving Tree*, trying to decipher what was so special, so worthy of his silences.

For science class that year, I did a project on seeds. I picked them out of lemons with my fingers, sifted through the mess of a ripe tomato, and dug out avocado pits with spoons: each type rinsed, separated, and organized in an empty egg carton.

The night before it was due, I sat on the stairs above the kitchen, out of sight, watching my parents drink with their friends. Dad had played a show, so he was drinking bourbon. The color and smell of it meant peace to me then. As he talked and laughed and listened, he sliced the seeds from one strawberry at a time, like a surgeon with the edge of a butter knife, and dropped each one in the egg carton, in the correct spot.

The boy behind the counter yells to a woman walking by. Before she can wave him off, he catches up to her, holding all the café's knives like a bouquet, and hands them over to be sharpened.

There is a twitch in my fingers and I want to reach for a sketchpad I don't have. Though it doesn't matter, because I'm also missing my pen, forgotten on the bedside table in the apartment in my rush to get out the door.

I put my fingerprint to my phone instead, make a few notes about the hair on his forearms, the thin line between his eyebrows, the different lengths and shapes and angles of those knives. All with the intention of recreating this scene later, unlikely as it may be that I'll actually do it. These few random words and incomplete phrases are a poor substitute anyway. "An artist without a pen," I say, under my breath and to no one.

Even at RISD, when drawing and painting conceptually or from a photograph was reinforced as a necessary skill, I lost interest unless I could see something clearly, whether actually in front of me or just in my mind.

Michael kept a notebook with him always, would never dream of being caught by inspiration unprepared. I take a breath and the thought vanishes. I'm slowly getting better at this, forcing unwanted visions of him from my mind, through inhales and exhales.

I should know better, though. Capturing the world this way is something that has reliably made me happy, certain, like I'm doing what I'm supposed to. I remember the exact day I discovered how to make a sphere look round on the page. Sketching hands that looked stick-like, then extraterrestrial, then more and more detailed and real, like they could actually belong to someone. Years later, in my always-freezing studio in Providence, I'd work on two paintings at a time, waiting for one to dry while I worked on the other.

Proximity to pen and paper is especially important now, because I draw and color and caption for money. Actual money, not a studio rapidly filling with canvases people nod at and praise and rarely buy. It's still surprising that I'm able to make a living from it, but I really do. Like basically everything else, it doesn't look or feel the way I thought it would.

It started with friends asking me to draw their tattoos. Words of significance and stanzas of poems written in tight, exact script. Sometimes little objects or images: a pomegranate, Jeanne Moreau's face copied from the *Elevator to the Gallows* poster, the outline of the state of Indiana.

I've done illustrations for baby shower invitations and place cards for weddings and dinner parties—angular capital *A*'s and *M*'s, decadent *C*'s and languorous *S*'s.

After seeing how much people seemed to like getting exactly what they asked for, I spent less time on the wall-sized abstract paintings and bright, too-honest portraits that crowded the un-ventilated space I rented in Queens, and started to illustrate my own life. Or, more accurately, I isolate and satirize it in a way that allows women my age to see and laugh at themselves just enough. I advertise and sell my drawings, though they really sell themselves at this point.

Girls with long limbs and slim faces and fashionably full eye-brows and lips, but also messy hair, flat chests, a bit of paunch to stomachs that peek out over the tops of too-tight jeans. The kinds of bodies that suggest a regular gym routine but also don't shy away from dessert or wine or a slice of pizza late at night. In short, relatable.

Or: relatable for a certain kind of woman, no older than thirty-five, living in a big city on either coast, who equally values her own self-worth and what other people think, who fights and loses against the impulse to chronicle and share every worthwhile or photogenic thing she does.

Eventually, I started making note of things that stuck in my mind, what made me laugh or made me crazy, brought life to them, and things began to change.

I write captions, either rambling or succinct. Sometimes, it's two sides of a conversation, the script growing bigger and wilder as a misunderstanding grows. Or it's a transcription of whatever a girl is typing on her phone or laptop to a friend or a guy she likes or a coworker who's testing her patience.

Somehow, the collision of my sense of humor and endless appe-tite to evaluate, judge, and try to understand people has made me successful. As a sort of wayward, accidental anthropologist. My top sellers, in no particular order:

1. Words that sound like caring, but are actually camouflage. The ideal cloak for someone who never misses an opportunity to talk about herself: predictable refrains of "I know exactly what you mean" or "I went through something so similar." I draw the words like weapons, shot as if they were arrows into the flesh of a story or confession, wounding whatever point our heroine was trying to make.

2. The paradox inherent in being either invisible or offensively tempting to a married man. This one observes him through binoculars, in his natural habitat: a hotel bar. The paragraph-long caption, stretched to fit the corner of the page, is meant to be read in a hushed tone, as if watching him from a safe distance while on safari: "All too common in this part of the world, the married man's behavior confounds. Note his ring hand in plain view as a telltale defense mechanism, his visible bristle when you take the seat next to his, how he won't ask a single question or look your way, for fear of who knows what."

3. The crooked towers of lies propping up self-aggrandizing statements like "I'm just *so* busy" or "If not this week, then next" or "Things are crazy right now!"

4. The cruelty of a woman's inner voice: its relentless, one-sided diatribe when she looks in the mirror. We see the back of her head, her hair twisted into a neat chignon. Shoulders down and still, she stands in an elegant, simple black dress, barefoot on a clean tile floor. The dress cuts a slim V, revealing the pleasing curve of her back. But her reflection is warped: from the fog

of the mirror, her own self-loathing, a combination of the two. Hair a mess, dress strained and wrinkled and too tight. Her hands grip the edges of the sink, one eye bulging just a little.

5. The futility of going back and forth, trying to make plans with someone you don't really want to see, until the two of you finally die, excuses carved on both tombstones.

It's not particularly difficult to come up with ideas or bring them to life. I am trying to capture something amusing and always just ugly enough. People click and tap and share and, often, buy.

All of this is fueled by the internet: a social media account I update at least every week with a new drawing or idea, all of which lead anyone who's interested to a website I use to sell prints of everything I've ever posted.

That's not accounting for the other, random things I add so people can feel like they know me. I upload time-lapsed videos of myself drawing something new, so whoever cares can see how thick black lines, followed by shaded gray, then premeditated blots of color, can become something larger, something that makes them smile or laugh or get out their credit card.

Personality, I've learned, is highly important when convincing people to care about how you see the world. It's strange for someone who gravitates toward privacy, values space. The idea that doing something that feels unnatural is immediately considered valuable, some kind of lesson, growth in the right direction. We should always be seeking them out, these opportunities to feel uncomfortable.

Consciously or not, more personal pieces of my life started to find their way in.

A leak in my then apartment, a dirt-cheap East Village walk-up, became a recurring character in almost everything I drew, lingering on the periphery: a wavering brown-water voice from the depths of that tenement. I painted him a friendly copper color. His edges were wavy and nonthreatening.

I thought the place was a steal, when in fact it was exactly as advertised. There were freezing drafts in the winter and trash that rotted in the summer, filling the alley and lingering in the airshaft. Neighbors who passed out or nodded off and left their sinks and bathtubs running, water pooling in my ceiling and blowing bubbles on the off-white walls. Leaving me with the stain.

Once I gave up trying to get my upstairs neighbors evicted and begging the super to add an extra coat of paint, I decided to embrace it. He (I don't know why I determined the stain was male, but he was) became a constant, strangely comforting presence— one that would one day become a story, proof of the fact that I had a comically rough start on my own.

So, he made his way into what I drew: there in the background as someone stuffs her face with takeout or lies about being en route to a party while sitting on the couch in a towel, almost as a guardian angel. Most of the time, I imagined him trying to impart some wisdom or assure that things would get better. They just had to.

Whenever I complained, Dad wouldn't hear it, saying something along the lines of "You get what you pay for." I'd refused any money from him after graduation, was waiting to see how long I could hold out. Or "proving some kind of point," as he put it. Defeat was certain, but it felt important to delay as long as possible.

It was Michael who persuaded me to start selling my personality in tandem, showing more of myself and what caught my eye.

He held my phone to record a quick drawing of a waiter at

Lucien, scribbled on the paper that covered the table, inspired by a red wine stain that became his bow tie. Shaky videos I took through taxi windows of dogs being walked by identical-looking owners, quick zooms in on each for emphasis. The way I narrated *A Streetcar Named Desire* from the couch. My feet resting on his lap, him laughing at my Blanche DuBois. It was implicitly understood that I was never to film Michael, or use his voice for my account in any way, which makes more sense now.

"Why not put it out there, how delightfully strange you are?" He said it with confidence, as if all of this was a logical next step. "People will connect with you and what you're doing. They'll see themselves." He checked the screen of his phone, midthought. "That's all people want anyway."

He was right, of course. For someone who claimed to be both contemptuous of social media and too old to understand it, he had an undeniable instinct for what people wanted to see.

The timing was right, too. People were starting to pay attention to the less pretty parts of an online persona, which, ostensibly, would make them feel better about their own lives. Other illustrators were drawing themselves eating cake out of the garbage or attempting to pee in public bathrooms while wearing jumpsuits. I had to seek out the right balance of attitude and sincerity, which took a little while.

Yes, I live in Manhattan, dress well when I have to or want to, see the new museum exhibits, and meet friends at the right kinds of restaurants. But I also draw attention to the large bowls of pasta I eat in bed, the stretches of days and nights I don't leave the apartment or put on real clothes, my devotion to both Tony Soprano and reruns of Julia Child's cooking show.

At first, a small but passionate following started to like and comment and share. I'm still not sure how they found me. After a few weeks, a few of them bought drawings and hung them in their entryways or next to vanity mirrors. The photos they sent me showed simple frames, low lighting, creamy white or pink or dove-gray walls. The hands holding the prints had fingers stacked with status rings, wrists heavy with Love bracelets and Tank watches. Not long after, it became a flood.

Now, at least one hundred people buy my prints every month, nail them to their walls, post pictures, and show them to the world. They tag me in those photos. I share them back, and on and on it goes. Everyone mutually appreciating and affirming one another—them on my work, me on their good taste. Or, maybe more realistically, it's just a circle jerk, all printed on acid-free paper, everything numbered and signed.

Occasionally, I'll add links to a larger abstract painting or a portrait I've done and kept, all priced higher. Sometimes they sell. Sometimes they languish for weeks and I take them down.

I buy stacks of cardboard mailing envelopes, the kind that don't bend, and keep them in the corner of a closet. Everyone at the post office on East Twenty-Third Street knows to clear counter space when they see me coming.

Maybe this kind of connection should feel good. Sometimes it does. Others, it makes me, what I'm capable of, feel small.

All of this has led to other things: illustrating new collections for the Indian and Russian editions of *Vogue*, women in thick coats and fur hats for the Bergdorf's Christmas catalog. Cinched waists and red lips, an embellished, snow-covered vision of the street signs at the intersection of Fifty-Seventh and Fifth.

Sometimes, I'm just asked for whimsy—drawings of baguettes and cupcakes and full, crisp heads of lettuce, touched with pastels, for a cooking website. Or very serious-looking caricatures of artists and architects for thick design magazines that almost no one reads, published as passion projects by people who hop from Miami to Venice to Dubai and wherever else. All confections, stripped of any self-deprecation or point of view, but they pay my bills.

The kid is back behind the counter, turning slightly pink. He can tell I'm watching him. I order a little sandwich to distract us both. He takes a few seconds to choose the best one.

It's been so long since I sketched something just to capture it, get it down before it fades. Because the light was good or I knew I could draw his cut-short fingernails just right. Or I wanted to preserve the men's conversation, the current of people moving past somehow. My wishful thinking about blending in. I make a few more little notes, trying not to let him know I'm still studying his face.

Is this how these six days are going to unfold? Circling strangers, overhearing hints of their lives, imagining what the rest might resemble? Wanting to know them? Not being able to?

I think of the piles of clothes and shoes I've left on the floor of the apartment, those bits of myself I've chosen to bring here. The time, just four days from now, when I'll put everything back, zip it easily. Packing a suitcase, whether I'm going somewhere or returning home, always gives me peace. The calm of everything in its place. Schedule, order, security. I'm not sure where it comes from, this resistance to existing in the moment. Certainly not genetics.

I make an effort to feel the smooth leather of my sandals against the soles of my feet, study the pink of my nails against the finger-sized handle of the espresso cup. The low throb of my head-ache doesn't shed any light on whether I've had too much caffeine or not enough.

A fly floats midair, suspended and still, above a bowl of ripe lemons on the bar. The boy is twisting the top off a bottle of blood-orange soda, then changing the channel on the little TV. On a soccer field in Spain, a player crosses himself before making a penalty kick, and misses.

I pass three men repairing the buzzer in the entryway of an apartment building. Or talking about how they might eventually repair it, pointing at hanging wires, looking at their phones.

The entrance is easily twelve feet high, thick, painted deep forest green and marked with a brass lion head, midroar. The actual door is cut out and much smaller, requires a step up and over. I can see it leads to a narrow, open-air hallway with natural light at the end. Maybe there are orange trees in the courtyard beyond, jasmine creeping up a wall.

Entrances and exits are open here, a luxury. Warmed by the Mediterranean, cool tile floors, high ceilings, a reverent sort of quiet. I guess Romans never really need to insulate themselves.

Barriers are precious, though: shelter from sun, cold, the noise of the street, demands of other people. I'm usually seeking out that separation, but I left all the windows open in the apartment when I left this morning, the sheets still tangled, pillow dented by the weight of my head.

One of the wires sparks in a workman's hand, prompting a few obscenities that cut through the stillness. This building, each one in this little piazza, must be expensive, forbiddingly so. People will always pay for silence, for peace.

Doorways in Rome, even to buildings like this one, are surprisingly unassuming. In New York, a doorman would guard that quiet lobby, watching over ice-cube-fed orchids, a chaise longue with strategically placed pillows that no one ever sits on. Entrances here are closer to the anonymous, indistinguishably elegant buildings I've walked by in Paris, all Haussmannian with wrought iron and beige stone. Massive doors locked by six-digit codes, buttons that glow a cool blue at night.

It's hypnotic, to wonder what they're concealing, simple vestibules or twisted staircases. I imagine it could keep me entertained for hours, dreaming up the lives led inside.

This door is wedged open by a cooler that probably holds their lunch, topped by a radio, its antenna starting to pick up "Chain of Fools" at a low volume, dimmed a bit by static.

I recognize it from the first few seconds. A series of notes I've learned and memorized and anticipated. It's one of those songs I'll always know every word of, no matter how much time passes without hearing it. The sexy, slightly messy guitar lick at the beginning. That *chain-chain-chain*, deep and steady from Aretha's backup singers, sounding like a not-so-vague threat. But my memory of it is happy, uncomplicated.

When he was little, Jack loved anything soul or Motown. He danced however he could, spinning around, kicking and high-fiving the air, his face transformed by simple joy. "Chain of Fools" was, for whatever reason, his favorite. We'd play it in the car every morning, dropping him off at preschool first, then me at the bigger school down the road. He moved as much as his car seat would allow, his chubby legs kicking in perfect time. Always exact, even then.

The postcard I bought for him shows the Tiber high and calm, the bridge stretching out from the Castel Sant'Angelo, dotted with statues of apostles throwing shade on the water. The picture must have been taken from a boat, down below looking up.

Hi Jack,

I keep seeing fried zucchini blossoms on menus and thinking of you.

When we were in Rome as a family years ago, Jack was intrigued by the idea of eating flowers, wondered how they'd taste, the petals peeking out from a deep golden cocoon. He looked for them at every restaurant, finally found and ordered them for dinner one night. Not wanting to lose face, he finished all three, even though they were filled with anchovy paste and thick basil leaves. My parents and I kept waiting for him to give up and ask for pizza or spaghetti with butter and cheese instead, knowing that even at eight, he never would.

While thinking of what to write next, I draw a curlicue vine around the border of the card, dotted with zucchini flowers for emphasis. I wish I had the greens and yellows that this calls for, but he'll get the point.

Maybe I'll sit down and have some myself, after I put this in the mailbox. I was told it's better to send mail from the Vatican, that their post office is faster because it's smaller, maybe less bureaucracy, though that seems unlikely. You loved it when we visited, jumping from the edge of a sidewalk back onto the bridge, thrilled you could be in two different countries so easily.

Today I'm drinking water from fountains and taking lots of pictures and hiking up a hill to get the best view of the city. I'm not sure what's next, but that's okay, I think.

Give Violet my love. I miss you.

I didn't think women were named Violet anymore. That was my first thought when Jack told me about her. The name gave me pause, visions of someone quiet or conventional, hair in a tight braid, bad perfume.

"She's not uptight, just British," he said. "Be nice."

And he was right. Not uptight, but always guarded, which proved more interesting.

To a casual observer, Violet is kind and interested and comfortable around me, strikes the appropriate balance of ease and respect around my parents. But she warrants a closer look.

Last November, Jack ran the marathon, his first one.

I assumed my parents would want to wait for him at the finish, in a comfortable spot, but they came up with a plan to see him three separate times along the route—at miles eight, seventeen, and twenty-five.

As we moved between the second and last stops, the subway stalled. My dad is rarely rattled, but, in those few moments, he was. His soft suede loafers tapped the filthy floor in nervous time. We were losing valuable minutes. Jack could be passing us by and we'd have no way of knowing.

Mom looked at her watch, touched him softly on the shoulder. "We have enough time. He's still in Brooklyn. We'll catch him, don't worry."

He insisted on a cab instead.

Dad sat in front, still nervous, checking the street signs as we passed, the driver's speed, refreshing the app on his phone to see how fast Jack was running. When we were stopped at a light or behind a slow-moving truck, he'd say, "Shouldn't we have taken Park?" Or, "How can there still be so much traffic in this city? They should pass a law."

I sat between Violet and my mom in the back, watching him. But I wasn't the only one. Violet observed him clinically, as if this behavior was especially surprising to her.

We lined up on Central Park South, screaming as he ran by, leaning over the barricade. My parents lost themselves in a kind of enthusiasm I didn't know they had. Jack finished in less than four hours, meeting his goal.

Later, we celebrated, everyone high on the proximity to accomplishment. A casual place, with long tables, corresponding benches bolted to the floor. Pitchers of beer, his friends making jokes and toasts, making sure my mom and I had seats at the table. Dad held court at the bar, telling stories, giving Jack's friends shit and egging them on every time an attractive woman walked through the door.

Jack was proud and happy, a beer in one hand and water in the other. He seemed invincible until he crashed hard just after eight, sinking into a booth. He kissed the top of Violet's head and murmured something about a taxi home, knowing his exhaustion would be met by someone who could hold him up, someone who knew how.

She's always been careful, but I've had a few glimpses into how she actually feels, who she is beneath all that effort and constraint.

The night she lost her job was mild, an early Friday evening at the end of March. The air was light and warm, the kind of weather that opened windows for the first time in five months. People sat outside at restaurants and on the steps of their buildings, but cautiously—as if the shift was too soon, too fragile to be fully trusted. The change in seasons, even from cold to warm, from short days to long ones, always plays with my mood. So I was happy to see Jack's call, a distraction.

"I need some help," he said.

He gave me the broad strokes: Violet had been fired and they were out with friends, trying to turn the whole thing into a party. Freedom from eighty-hour workweeks, constant emails, unreasonable clients. He asked me to join, which was really asking for backup, something he almost never does, for any reason. And they happened to be three blocks from my apartment.

Violet rarely drinks, and almost never to excess. I don't think I've ever seen her wearing something that wasn't tailored.

That night, she was leaning over the bar, tipping forward so much her feet left the ground. The blunt edges of her hair dangerously close to touching a pool of spilled drink.

A friend was telling her that getting fired today was actually auspicious. There was a new moon in Aries—a shift that paves the way for rebirth and new beginnings. This moment was hers for the taking, apparently.

Violet greeted me with a limp hug, her arms heavy behind my neck for a moment. I kept my hands on her shoulders to steady her.

"I don't know what astrology says, but maybe this *is* a blessing," I said. "A chance to do something new, less intense. Jack's told me how hard it's been on you, how stressful." She raised an eyebrow at that. "I know taking a different sort of path has helped me. Not all that pressure is always necessary, or even healthy, you know?"

"You're right!" she squealed at a level I didn't know she was capable of. "Fuck being in the office all night. Fuck constant sexual harassment. Fuck people always underestimating me."

I knocked my glass against hers. "Freedom! Right?"

"Exactly." Her stare focused, narrowed at me. "Except I actually live in the real world, where people have to work. Not all of us can follow our bliss. Only some have that privilege."

From a distance, she still looked perfect, but I could see her makeup settling in the lines at the corners of her eyes, looking at me with what I always suspected was there.

I woke up to a long, apologetic message from her the next morning, confessing that she couldn't remember exactly what she'd said, but knew it was hurtful. That I didn't deserve it, whatever it was. But I knew her real regret was that the veil fell, even briefly.

I stay close to the radio, listening to the song until it fades into the next, remembering Jack's little laugh. Wondering if he's awake right now, running past Chelsea Piers or in a car to an early-morning meeting, or still asleep, his blackout shades stretching from floor to ceiling, erasing any light.

A woman passes by in a rush, flanked by her two sons. They might be twins. The tops of both their heads reach her hips, the perfect height to just grasp her hands.

She carries small, matching suitcases, one on each shoulder, maybe leading the boys to the train or idling car that will take them all out of the city, away from the heat. They wear ironed white shirts, navy blue shorts, dark brown hair shining, just brushed.

Jack's is the same color, that nutty, deep brown I wish I had. I remember the lick of hair he had at the base of his neck when he was little, how it would curl slightly when he needed a trim. How I'd pull it sometimes when he got on my nerves or wasn't doing what I wanted, because I knew it would hurt. He wasn't the type to overreact or be easily annoyed by something, but that was always effective.

Life continues to happen around me, just slower. Languorous, maybe. People are still going to work, still traveling from one end of this city to another to buy food or go to the doctor or buy a new lightbulb to replace the one that blew last night while they were trying to finish a chapter of a book or chop a clove of garlic. An old woman curses a bus that closes its glass door and drives away without her. Her voice is low and sure and vicious.

No one knows me here, and with that, certain things seem possible. Like I'm capable of strength or abandon on this side of the ocean that would be laughable at home. I'm someone else, waiting for something new to happen.

A man slows to a stop on a scooter, wearing a full suit, his pant leg rising just enough to show loafers, no socks. The sinew of his ankle. I wonder if his life resembles what it looks like to me. A job that pays well and demands little. Friends who defer to and adore him. Parents who are proud. Later tonight, he'll drive to, eat with, gaze at a woman he loves but doesn't care to truly know.

The Palatine Hill rises up over my right shoulder, dotted with nothing but ruins that now look like caves. The stone pines lean to one side or another, branches curved like snakes midslither. I see the river with relief, proof that I've been walking in the right direction.

Michael would talk about the traffic in Italy, how pedestrians have no right of way, no rights at all, really. Like taking your life in your hands, he said.

Now, crossing the Lungotevere in a nervous dash, I see what he meant. Cars and mopeds and squat, rattling trucks all accelerating and weaving around each other and laying on their horns: I can only describe it as chaos. It's a word that means something to me.

I remember the moment I first heard it. Mom was reading to me from Edith Hamilton's *Mythology*, one of her favorite books when she was young. It was the creation myth that night, the story of how the world and mankind came to be. Right after the story of Demeter and Persephone, which would become the one I asked for over and over.

She was explaining how the Greeks made sense of their origins, what they told themselves about the beginning of the world. I memorized the phrasing exactly. I've flipped through the book many times since, searching sentences for the word.

Long before the gods appeared, in the dim past, uncounted ages ago, there was only the formless confusion of Chaos brooded over by unbroken darkness.

I made her stop reading then, mystified by the way "chaos" sounded. I could usually spell a word out in my head, but this series of syllables was a riddle. It was possible there was a *K*, maybe a *U*, but I couldn't be sure. She showed it to me on the page, and what I saw made no sense. It was discouraging and thrilling at the same time, knowing, even then, the world could be so nonsensical and also so surprising.

I forget what kind of learner that makes me: visual or auditory or something else entirely. When Dad tells this story, it's whatever will make me, and him by extension, sound the most impressive. He never misses a chance to tell people I learned to read when I was four.

I asked Mom what the word meant. "When there's no order, that's chaos," she said, after taking a few moments to settle on an answer. "I guess it's what happens when no one follows the rules. When no one listens. It's a scary thing, not knowing what people will do."

Chaos gave birth to Night, the book said. Death, too.

For months after, the word became my fixation. Visions of epic, theatrical disaster. A tornado touching down, lifting up our house as if it were a toy, scattering us to different corners of the world. The tame, worn-down mountains that ran along the Hudson coming to life, crushing our town, the earth cracking open beneath them like the shell of an egg. I drew black clouds and withered trees and orange, yellow, red flames. I darted around corners, pretending I could turn men to stone with a glance.

I used the word whenever I could, would find ways to fit it into school projects or drawings or the little monologues I'd make up for my parents' friends at dinner parties. I wrote it into stories and lots of poems, my favorite medium then. I'd recently been set free by learning that poetry didn't have to rhyme, that some of the best poems didn't.

I stuck whatever I wrote to the door of the refrigerator with tape—marring the stainless steel finish with magnets was never an option. That's where Dad found four lines he loved, in my careful block letters, written on a page torn from the back of Mom's address book—it was the only paper I could find, in a hurry to get the words down before they left my mind.

A mountain isn't perfect
Pieces glitter on the ground
Love isn't always beautiful
But chaos makes it real

A few weeks later, he played a demo of a new song for my mother and me before dinner. His guitar was slow, but sure. He sang the chorus with conviction, more than usual. The knowledge that his words were irrefutably true.

"Perfect" is no mountain
It's a shapeless, dazzling gleam
And real love ain't the tender moments
It's the chaos in between

Even at seven, I could tell the difference between a rough recording like this and the more polished, perfect ones on his albums. I could tell the difference, however small, between my words and his.

It was the song that took him from admired but mostly unknown folk singer to legend, rock star, household name. In the years since, it's become his most successful and recognizable, by far. The last time I checked, it had been covered by over a hundred different artists. Probably more than that now. It's signified crescendos and moments of awakening in movies and TV shows. The lyrics are widely considered to be some of the most beautiful in an already poetic, powerful body of work. He even re-recorded it when he turned fifty, with the idea that both versions should be compared. His original described heartbreak, yes, but still with an undercurrent of hope, a lightness in his melody, synonymous with youth and unlimited second chances—in contrast with this slower, deeper arrangement, his voice lower and more exact. Everything more final.

He attributes the lines to me in every interview. Sometimes it's serious credit being given, others it's described as a remarkable anomaly, something close to a fluke. "From the mouths of babes," he's said more than once. But he dedicates the song to me in liner notes and almost every time he plays it live. What more can I really ask for, or reasonably expect?

The winter of my second or third year of college, Dad came to town and took me out to dinner. One of the French restaurants that passes for upscale in Providence, late on a weeknight. White tablecloths that looked yellow in the low light. Votives resting in shallow pools of water, wax floating instead of sticking.

The place was full when we arrived, but had gradually emptied. The walls were close. I was off balance, thanks to the confidence that came from a dozen months on my own and a few glasses of the most expensive Côtes du Rhône on the menu.

He told me that, over the years, he's written more than eighty-seven verses of the song, turning them back into poems. That my words continue to inspire him, to this day. He even recited one on the spot, from memory:

"Perfect" is no mountain
With all its peaks and streams
It's a shapeless and dazzling gleam,
Never once pristine
And real love ain't those tender moments,
Or a finely scripted scene
No, my little darling,
It's the chaos in between

It was understood that this fact alone should be taken as the highest of compliments, but I made note of the nerves in his voice, despite the wine, when he gave it. I sat back in my chair, giving him the reception he wanted and needed, knowing that "little darling" is something he's only ever called my mother.

It's an urge I've never lost: wanting to be confused and upended by something. Being drawn to the outline of a concept or word or feeling, wanting to ascribe shape or color to it, despite not quite knowing what "it" is. That's what he took, more than my word choice or how I saw chaos on a page. And now my attempts at understanding any or all of that have become a love song. Or, more accurately, a rejection-of-love song.

A year ago, he played a small show at a dive in the West Village, one of the places that had given him a chance and some stage time when he was young and starting out. It was a gesture, a home-coming of sorts. A way for him to stay relevant and aware of his roots and also humble, possibly. Not a retrospective. There's never been mention of a farewell tour.

Tickets were outrageously expensive and sold out almost imme-diately. They were resold online for even more. Mom and Jack and

I had a table to ourselves, near the back and out of the way, which was always our preference. Dad still insisted, after all these years, that we made him nervous.

He took two encores that night, which might sound excessive but the crowd demanded it. He saved "Chaos" for last, as he so often does. People screamed with recognition of the first few chords, then went silent with reverence, not wanting to miss a word.

When he sang my lines, his eyes were closed tight with concentration. It was almost like they never belonged to me at all.

The river is low. The usual waterline, marked by moss and dirt and time, is plain to see. Shells have been pulled out and left on risers next to makeshift boat shelters. On paths paved to follow and contain the current, men in sweatshirts and short shorts run by in groups of two and three, taking advantage of the cooler morning air. I lean over the railing and watch them, my chin resting on my folded hands. The sun is already finding its way through my hair, starting to touch skin that's almost always hidden.

Vendors are setting up on the slim footbridge that connects the base of the Palatine to Trastevere, laying out miniature monuments in neat grids. A man dressed as a gladiator waits to pose for photos.

The bridge empties into a dirty piazza where teenagers drink after dark. Empty wine bottles from last night, stone benches dotted with cigarette burns. The leftover butts, some covered in lipstick, line the steps, fill in the cracks. I climb up, despite the sweet, sour urine smell, to read the engraving that blesses or endows this spot, but whatever's carved into the stone is too worn to make out.

Tourists move slowly, both wanting to wander and looking wary of getting too lost. Giving up control is hard, even when it's what you insist you want, what you fly thousands of miles to be able to do.

In the wake of the breakup, after the bruise on my hand faded, I did what I usually do, what's typically worked in the aftermath of relationships over the years.

I stayed in religiously during the week, drew and painted and put prints in envelopes late into the night, matching them to cardboard so they wouldn't bend. I caught up on neglected work and looked for new projects, new clients, contacted any acquaintance or chance meeting who had ever shown an interest. I sent inquiring, sometimes shameless emails, searching for commissions, occasionally shooting for the moon. I made lists of how to shill what I'd already done or find new applications for what already existed.

Dishes piled up. Water glasses stacked high, inside each other like nesting dolls in the sink. All signs of mending myself, rebuilding a sense of worth that had recently been swept away.

On the weekends, I was out, drinking and eating things I loved, looking for what was rich and expensive and surprising. I sat at the bar of a favorite restaurant, looked at the trees shedding their flowers and turning green and full in Gramercy Park, and ordered a thirty-five-dollar glass of something limited and rare from an aging bottle suspended behind a pane of glass. With the flip of a switch, the bartender siphoned off just enough without disturbing the value or taste of what was left over. No need for restraint without consequences.

Fridays and Saturdays, I surrounded myself with people: friends always, strangers sometimes. The one-night stands ebbed and flowed with my mood and who I was lucky enough, or not, to meet.

We'd kiss hard and soft in the corner of a bar, showing off for one another in little, practiced, convincing ways. His thumb on my lip, my hand on his belt, then below. I'd break away, check the bathroom mirror (whether it was dirty or candlelit or covered in stickers or graffiti), gasping for someone I'd erase from my life hours later, while he called a car. I'd lock my door behind him the next morning or afternoon and feel, with that click, that I'd accomplished something.

None of this adds up to a revolutionary way to leave someone in the past, but at least it had always been reliably effective. Until Michael, of course. What was so different? What had changed?

For a time, I couldn't talk about him or what had happened to anyone, including myself. It wasn't possible for me to say he was an asshole or a liar or a selfish piece of shit. I couldn't even manage admitting that I didn't deserve to be lied to. Instead, I'd double down, finding a way to assert that what he'd said or not said wasn't even a lie at all. A misunderstanding, maybe. Unfortunate, but not malicious.

I knew that if I brought him up, even in passing, it would end with me steadfastly defending him, clutching at reasons why what happened wasn't his fault or how the situation wasn't as bad as it actually was. First I made excuses for him to my well-meaning friends who were ready and willing to participate in that long-held female ritual of eviscerating an ex, listing all the ways the woman in question is better off without him. And then, once they'd had enough, I did the same inside my own mind.

I'll still do it, if I don't catch myself.

I can't even smell the piss anymore. And anyway, the shade is worth it.

I meant to leave my phone in the apartment all day, but the

vibration in my bag reminds me it's there. I don't want any kind of reminders or notifications—relating to my own life or anyone else's. No emails or requests for anything, no feed full of carefully filtered photos. No destination weddings, no beach vacations in Maine or Greece, no chic outfits or anniversary dinners or beautiful views.

It could mean many things, that vibration. It could be him, writing again, not able to stand the silence. I reach for it, hoping to turn the screen over to find that blue box, evidence of desperation that I can stretch out and luxuriate in—like cool sheets or a hot bath.

But it's nothing important, which, deep down, I knew.

This was a deal I made with myself before coming here: no communicating with anyone from my real life, within reason. The idea was to double down on solitude, in hopes it might teach me something. That maybe, with no outside interference, I could start to see more clearly.

Dad was asked about us in an interview once, the fact that he has two children who have "distinguished themselves," but outside music.

"My son and daughter are beautiful, talented people," he told whoever was asking. "I support them in everything they do, every way I can." A drag on a cigarette. "I am immensely proud."

The interviewer had done his research, decided to delve deeper.

"Your son is considered something of a prodigy on Wall Street. He took two million dollars in start-up money and turned it into three hundred million in two years." Dad's lips curl into a fraction of a smile and I know he's thinking, *If you heard Jack sing and play guitar, you'd be talking about something else.*

"And your daughter, an accomplished social media artist." Dad bristled very slightly at that, and I don't really blame him. I would have preferred "accomplished artist with a following on social media." Though that probably wasn't accurate. But it could have been worse. He could have said influencer.

A massive abstract painting I made at RISD still hangs centered above my parents' fireplace. Lavenders, pinks, four shades of blue, a shock of chartreuse, one corner flecked with gray. I finished it on a February afternoon, already dark at 3:30. I sat on the concrete floor of my studio, the blanket from my bed wrapped around my shoulders, held the brush's bristles back and released them like a slingshot.

That painting was three months of my life, at a time when everything took that long. Now almost all of what I do is quick, simple, efficient. Maybe because it all comes from the surface, no exploration, little work involved.

I've learned it's so important for people to feel like they know you, like we could all be friends, if given the chance. The correct details, deployed in just the right way.

And it goes beyond Michael's insistence that I create a persona, inject parts of who I am into what I make. Beyond the sound of my laugh as I film myself describing the art on my walls like a museum docent or someone seeing my fingers wrapped around a pen, if my nail polish is chipped. Even if I took a chance and drew or wrote something especially personal, I'd just be taking something of mine and making it theirs. If Dad's songs have taught me anything, it's that. How strangers, people who know nothing about you, will consume your most vulnerable thoughts and feelings and make it all about them. Even when you're trying to be coy or opaque, people will understand enough, and take what they want.

I've always loved having a secret. And the strength required for keeping it. Is that what Michael was doing? Did he enjoy it, in some way? Making a fool out of me?

It's easy to understand why Trastevere is the neighborhood so many people recommended, said was their favorite. It's as if what we expect and hope Rome to be was bottled, then spilled along this side of the river.

I pass a few cafés that could be my mother's sorts of places. Unassuming, off the busy streets, suggestive of food and drinks done simply, but well. It seems almost possible that I could bump into her, which sometimes happens at home.

There's a French place she loves, near Union Square. A little dirty, entirely reliable and trend-averse. They've been making the same food the same way for years. It's where my mother goes to have what, to her, is the perfect meal: an omelet and a glass of wine. That's what she ordered one night when I was walking home and saw her through the window. I leaned on the heavy door until it opened and sat with her for an hour. We didn't talk much, as I remember, but the shared silence was enough.

Whenever Michael would tell me about the meat-and-cheese shop, some magical place he'd discovered in this neighborhood, he would inhale deeply at the memory, like he needed his lungs full to even attempt to describe it.

This place was the best kind of salumeria, he said. Every part of every kind of animal you could want, cured for any number of months or years. Smooth or spicy or bright olive oil, perfect cheeses. Wine from tiny, family-run vineyards, varietals you'd never find in New York, all sold for close to nothing. Bottles clustered on narrow shelves, prices written hastily with a waxed pencil. What he loved and remembered the most was the ricotta, made from goat's milk.

"The goats, Emilia," he told me. "This family has been raising these goats for centuries."

"It sounds incredible," I answered. "Cheese made from immortal goats. I can't wait to try it. Have they been studied?"

"What?"

Then my stupid joke landed and he rolled his eyes in that harmless, comforting way he had. I loved the way he took himself, and all the things he held dear, so seriously, and I also loved making tiny, affectionate holes in that enthusiasm.

The shop doesn't look like much from the street: two narrow entrances, a small awning to mark its territory against the bustling restaurant next door.

On my left, a waiter is clearing a table after an early lunch. Noticing a few errant crumbs, he blows hard against the tablecloth, scattering them between the cobblestones.

I'm almost sad Michael is missing this, but also enamored with the thought of seeing such a detail and never telling him. It's the kind of thing he would have noticed, smiled at, appreciated.

I keep reaching for him, a twitch from a phantom limb. But every time I resist writing to him about the waiter blowing crumbs off a table or the beams in the apartment or the woman wordlessly watching the passersby from her third-floor window, distracted from her flower boxes, there's a small burst of strength. The power in withholding, the possibility of him wondering what I'm doing and imagining what fills my days here. Silence makes a point, more than anything I could possibly say. Keeping these things from him is freedom, somehow.

I've come this far. Let's see how long I can last.

Inside the shop, it's dark and hot and close to empty. The lazy ceiling fan makes no difference, spinning slowly enough to see all three blades. Wide floorboards, rough and unfinished. I follow the worn paths people have taken over and over: to the back corner, along the wall, stopping by the bucket of cured olives for a taste.

A man and woman weave around one another behind the counter, answering questions and slicing meats and weighing cheese. Pecorino of all different ages, legs of prosciutto, creamy ricotta in plastic tubs, the labels long boiled off. I want different tastes, textures. The espresso is making my stomach feel cavernous, giving me license to get anything, and as much of it as I want.

I ask for *un pochino* of pale pink prosciutto, blood-red soppressata, another kind of salami I've never seen before, so aged the slices are starting to shrivel in on themselves. All sliced thin, separated by strips of plastic wrap. The man, smiling at my Italian, cuts a small wedge of pecorino dotted with peppercorns, then a little more and a little more, until I finally settle for the whole chunk. The most expensive Parmesan, aged for twenty-four months, costs a fraction of what it would in New York. I ask for a generous slice of that, the color of a good suntan.

The man scoops a full ladle of fresh ricotta onto a sheet of wax paper, folds it expertly into a kind of bowl that stands level and doesn't leak, almost like a paper boat. He secures it with one piece of tape, a magic trick, and tells me to eat it soon and keep it out of the heat.

Sixteen euros. That's all, for everything. He places each item in a bag with a degree of care I find touching.

Michael's plan was to come here the day we left, buy all the cheese we could fit in our suitcases, have it vacuum-packed to transport home. I see the sealing machine, in a corner next to an old cash register.

Now that I'm here, the sour reminder of Parmesan lingering on my tongue, I don't know if I'd want to take it home, wrapping the sealed cheeses in T-shirts, declaring them at customs, being careful to list everything on a form. Later: letting them sit in the fridge, rationing carefully, determining the best moment to grate some over pasta or crumble the rest onto a cheese board I'd serve to friends. This is the cheese from Rome, I'd tell them. And they'd fall all over themselves telling me how good it was, the theatrical closed eyes as they taste it. Even the thought of it is exhausting.

Or I could enjoy it now and do my best to remember it later. Not everything has to be preserved, or even shared.

I stumble through asking the man behind the counter where I should buy bread and wine, hoping Michael's sanctioned places will prove irrelevant. But of course they're identical. For bread, go to the bakery on the corner, the one with the line out the door. For wine, there's a good shop on the way, but I'll have to wait until it opens at noon. I already have the names and addresses of both, scribbled on a folded list I decided to take, not leave. Zipped into the pocket of my suitcase, slipped between two bras and a last-minute paperback as the car waited to take me to JFK. A moment of weakness.

Any plans he and I made for Trastevere always included the Gianicolo Hill. We chose it for the view. At the height of the

Empire, Michael told me, it lay just outside the ancient city, at a time when the river formed a solid, natural barrier. This makes it one of the best places to see everything. Domes and bell towers and well-worn streets cutting through all of it like scars.

These bags are heavy in my hands.

Being this alone is something I need to get used to, like swimming in cold water. Wading in is better than jumping. Even now, walking this stretch of streets, empty enough that I pay close attention to everyone I see, makes me feel equal parts strong and exposed. I'm confident in one interaction and cower through the next. Smiling and asking the man at the salumeria about his family's goats, while ten minutes later getting flushed at what seem like judgmental looks from two Italian teenage girls smoking against the side of a church.

My dad understands this, how quickly our sensitivities can change, our awareness of who we are in a place or a moment. He sees the value, the delicacy. It's probably why he can make a song out of just about anything. A flock of pigeons settling, then taking off again. Where's the contemplation or loneliness in that? But he'd find it.

Growing up, I was never shy, always felt that I was more than enough for people. That confidence was born and fostered and held sacred by my parents, for as long as they had true jurisdiction over how I felt. This need to protect myself is a relatively recent development.

I was described as both precocious and prepossessing. Affirmed always, since I was old enough to voice an opinion or hold my head up without help. Even after Jack was born, my routine and sense of self were protected and preserved. I still felt pride and warmth radiating from my parents when I recited something from memory or was quick with a line or told a joke in just the right way. No hesitation, no embarrassment. Even when I was sixteen and loathed almost everything about myself, I could still be charming, still perform.

Sometimes I wonder what this has done to me. If there's blame to be distributed. There has to be some reason why the false modesty I playacted as a child has hardened into real, adult doubt. How everyone's once-unquestioned admiration became the praise I now search for hidden meanings, rooting out the actual contempt or sarcasm underneath. There may be advantages, ones I don't see, don't want to see. A born performer, Dad used to say. But then again, he had a vested interest in that.

Some of it came out with Michael, once I started to get comfortable and let more of myself show. The impulsive, demanding side. The parts of me that insisted on his time and attention. "You can't do everything," he'd tell me. "You can't have everything, princess." Always with a smile, though.

But mostly I didn't push things, didn't ask too many questions. I let him enfold me, then started to feel like it was something I'd earned. The sincerity of him asking me what I thought of a new story he'd written. His quiet, substantial approval of the way I looked and dressed and spoke. The softness that came over his face when I showed him one of my paintings. I believed all of that was unequivocally mine.

At some point, I'll need to stop consulting his list, make my own choices. His taste is still a series of mysteries: how this restaurant, this church, this shop crossed his path, what made him commit them all to memory. I keep trying to solve them with each stop, like they might reveal an answer. It's making it harder for me to forget him.

I drop his postcard into a yellow mailbox as I pass. I don't need to slow down or even skip a step; a slight push of my fingers against the slot, and it's done. It's not lost on me that, with no envelope as a barrier, anyone could read what I've written. I hope they do.

The heat here makes me forget all but the most essential, elemental things. The weight of the bag on my shoulder, the sweat underneath my hair, the last few steps in front of me, where I'll find the next patch of shade.

It's nearing the middle of the day, the hottest few hours. Anyone who knows anything about being here will start to find shelter now, has a long lunch planned, somewhere air-conditioned or hidden under an awning or tree.

I'm so grateful whenever I see a fountain. That relief doesn't fade with repetition. I rush toward them as I would a mirage, fill my water bottle, which is always empty. The label is peeling off from the cold of the water, the sweat of my hand. I splash more on my neck and arms and face, as if I'm at my bathroom sink and not a public fountain after climbing a set of worn stone steps. No shame, no self-consciousness.

My sweat, and the water that replaces it, would render makeup or anything I might do to my hair completely pointless. This might be the first time in years I've purposely spent a day without exerting any of that attention and not felt unsettled, like I'd forgotten something.

It's protection, more than anything else—a pattern I almost never allow myself to deviate from. Checking, evaluating, assessing myself always. And it's not that I have to look perfect either. It's little things, things no one else notices. Not just shadows under my eyes or zits on my chin or frizzy, messy hair. Something more ineffable. I know when I have it or when I don't.

Wherever I go, if there's a mirror or shop window or anything that shows me some version of my reflection, I have to look in it, just to be sure. It's not a choice. If I don't, or if what I see is at all wrong or embarrassing, any energy or ease I might have is gone. Maybe it's shame, that rigidity. It's powerful enough that it could be.

These moments, like the one I'm living right now, when I feel remarkably free, always make me consider the opposite: how malleable I can be, how susceptible to what surrounds me, whether that's a place or a mood or a person. How easy it is for me to move or dress or speak differently. Even erasing a word from my vocabulary, because of what someone else says or thinks about it.

Michael always found "enjoy" to be a dirty word, pale and weak. Two clunky syllables that merely fill silence. A placeholder for whoever's saying it, someone too afraid to have an actual opinion. So, I stopped merely enjoying things. I loved that play, was frustrated by that novel, looked forward to the risotto when I ordered it but was ultimately disappointed.

The change was subtle, but happened quickly. I barely had to think about it. Choosing my words was nothing new anyway. There was always distance between what I thought and what I said to him. Sometimes that gulf was wide.

His contempt for the word "amazing" (its overuse, in particular) inspired a series of drawings.

After overhearing a woman at brunch, he spent at least two blocks mocking her. "Your pancakes are *amazing*? Really? They astonish you? They inspire awe?"

I drew it a few different ways. My usual sorts of girls: eyes slightly wide, mouths agape, fingers pointing as they marvel at the shape of a friend's eyebrows, the fit of a new pair of jeans, a sunset, and, yes, a plate of pancakes.

I printed fifty of each. All of them sold out within hours.

"I feel used," he said later, but with a smile.

At this rate, I'll be climbing the Gianicolo at the hottest time of the day. Trastevere's obvious charm is starting to fade, the closer I get. Buildings grow shabbier. More Romans than tourists. No maître d's hunting for customers, no doors open anywhere unless someone is going in or out.

Heavy planters frame this doorway, painted just the right shade of dusty blue to accentuate the orange of the building they guard. A cat arranges himself diagonally underneath a step, half of his body in the sun, the rest shaded by stone. He allows a woman passing by to take his photo. She makes dry kissing sounds and coos to him in Italian.

Waiting this long was a mistake. The sun is already more ruthless than an hour ago and will only get worse. If I were with another person, someone who cared about timing or had more sense, this wouldn't have happened. Amateur hour, Michael might say.

A Vespa idles in the middle of the street. The driver's helmet rests in his lap. He scans the terrace of the café in front of him and, when he spots the woman he's looking for, calls her name, thrusts his arms and hands forward as if to hug or possibly shake her. He sits still on his scooter, showing no signs of moving. Her blond hair is messy and unwashed in an intentional sort of way. Even from where I'm standing, it's clear she's not wearing a bra. The day's newspaper, its sections pulled apart and opened, cover her table. A glass bottle of Coke keeps it all in place.

She tilts her head back in exasperation and barks a laugh. The decibel and pace of whatever he's saying to her are urgent, but it's unclear whether they're happy to see one another or on the cusp of a fight. The woman has kicked her shoes off under the table and walks out into the street with bare feet to meet him. His smile, her nonchalance, the abandon. They kiss in such a way that I have to turn my head.

My parents have been married for thirty-five years. This fact is a point of pride. They're held up as one of those couples that somehow survived the rise to fame, the attention and madness that accompany it, and came out the other side intact. They've succeeded where so many others have failed. My father is thought to be lucky, my mother superhuman.

She's always been described as some variation of a kind and generous person. Someone attentive, interested, empathetic, who truly listens. And it's true; she does give so much of herself to others. But there is a limit to all that patience.

It's early at home. She'll be drinking coffee, standing barefoot in the dewy grass, letting the dog out, surveying the hillside our house rests on, where it dips into a small stream. As a gift one Mother's Day, I took over an empty patch near the kitchen door and planted an herb garden for her. She stood watching, warning me to be careful where I planted the mint because it grows like a weed.

My parents met in Greece, another ancient civilization. They spent a year together on an island that was perfection for a time, then ultimately turned poisonous, ruining so many people's lives. Theirs, almost.

They haven't told me much, but it's all well documented elsewhere: in books and movies and folklore surrounding that time and place and those people. How this island became an oasis for artists and those who wanted to surround them. How Dad went there to try to write songs, met Mom at the bar where she worked. How everything was dirt cheap, from the beautiful houses near the beach to the acid dissolved into glasses of water and bottles of wine. Couples swapped husbands and wives while their children played on the wet sand and in the empty streets late into the night.

"I'm so glad we didn't have you there," Dad said once. Mom nodded along, but with a sideways look that ensured my growing up on Hydra was never even a kernel of a possibility. It was one of those decisions he thinks was his, but wasn't.

My mother had been living on the island for two years before Dad arrived. She'd fled what she always called a ghost town in rural southeastern France, worked at the local restaurants and tavernas at night, swam and sailed and sometimes painted during the day. "I wasn't much of an artist," she says, "but I was a pretty good muse."

She was twenty-two when they left together. Dad had the songs for his first album, and she had him.

It is, as Dad loves to say, a bit of mythology.

I don't know much about her childhood or her life before she met my dad, aside from a scatter of details I've picked up over the years. Occasionally, she'll open a window. The timing will be right and I can ask her whatever occurs to me and she'll answer honestly and openly. Like, her childhood in France? What was it like?

"There was very little there for me," she said.

"I left home quite early," is all she says when anyone else asks.

She has exact taste and specific opinions: the types that seem inherited, things a bohemian-turned-comfortable existence couldn't erase. Always use Dufour pastry and San Marzano tomatoes. Poking a needle through the throat of a tulip makes the flower last days longer. Wash your face with cold water, twice a day, without fail. A bed should be made in the morning, every morning, no matter what. Your home should always be clean, as if an important, uninvited guest could show himself at any moment. Certain things are facts, not suggestions.

She paints far more now than she ever did then. All in a studio built above the garage, her finished work in expensive, custom frames all over the walls, stretching up to the ceiling. They're still lifes, always small, sometimes claustrophobic. All classically done, like she's a Dutch master.

Her canvases are very dark, her subjects small and precious and dim. As if illuminated by winter light through a dirty window. On the surface, the compositions are simple, static. Things she can watch and adjust and obsess over. She spends days and weeks consumed by the details: peeled garlic; a pale-blue bird's egg; so many peonies or dahlias (depending on the time of year); a cracked teacup; a skinned, stuffed rabbit hanging from a hook, legs tied together. She agonized over its back feet. They took her over a week to get exactly right.

She's never tried to sell or give a single painting to anyone, even as gifts, even when people have asked. Instead they become part of a larger and larger collection, one that surrounds her as she buys more canvases and mixes more paint and labors to make it even bigger.

I have one, though. Three lemons in a shallow bowl, sitting next to a shallot that's starting to shed its skin. Morning light from somewhere. She gave it to me for no reason, as far as I could tell. I was home to visit her one weekend and she handed the small canvas to me, wrapped in brown paper, as I was putting clean, still-warm laundry in the trunk of my car.

The lemons hang in my kitchen, above the little table where I sit to drink coffee in the morning and pour a glass of wine, maybe bourbon, at night. Sometimes I toast them, with whatever I have, if the room feels especially quiet or empty.

In this moment, I think I'd be happy to turn this corner and find her sitting in a café, her eyes closed in the sun. With the same calm I've seen when she listens to Jack tell a story or sprinkles berries with sugar or dives into water with barely a splash. At times, I imagine I could spend the rest of my life trying to understand her.

The thought makes me dial her number, breaking my own rule. She doesn't answer, and I'm instantly relieved. Who knows if what passed through me in that moment would have translated, or if her mood would have met mine. Timing is everything, as ever.

When she inevitably tries me back later, I won't answer, will text instead, pretend to be surprised. I'll tell her I must have pressed a button inadvertently, that the call was a mistake.

I look at the menu for one of these restaurants, quietly open for lunch, and it turns out to be a place she would never go. Tripe, smelt, oxtail. Roman food rests on the foundations of what was left over: the offal and other discarded, rejected parts of the animal.

My mother's tastes may be exact, even expensive, but decidedly not adventurous.

It would be simple to say I'm braver than she is. I'll eat almost anything, stand in front of a crowd to speak, travel somewhere new all by myself. But she's dared in ways I never have or will. Staying and sacrificing is its own kind of risk.

It seems certain this hill will relent four or five times before it finally does. Every time the path winds out of sight, I have hope. This has to be the last turn, the last stretch with no shade, no relief. But it evades me, keeps its degree of difficulty a secret.

Graffiti is scattered along the wall that runs the length of the incline, separating this paved walkway from the houses and shops on the other side, the real Rome from the purely scenic version. I see *In bocca al lupo*, a phrase I've always loved, followed by three uneven exclamation points.

There are flowers and weeds and strands of grass peeking out of the cracks where the wall meets the cobblestones. Some of them have gotten creative and been able to grow, stretching up, looking for more sun or air.

My shoulder throbs with the weight of everything I'm carrying. I've stopped trying to wipe the sweat from my forehead. My feet are slick with it. They slip in my sandals.

With only a few steps left of the hill, the paper bag I've wedged under my arm, shading the once-chilled wine from the sun, splits open. The bottle falls straight down, somehow not breaking, then rolls on its side down the path. It rattles, glass against stone, but stays whole for as long as I can see it.

"Well, that's tragic."

I turn around, find a man standing, as if framed, beneath the open gate that marks the entrance to the park. He balances on his heels against the incline behind him, stretching his legs against the last of the climb.

"Kind of incredible though, right? I can't believe it didn't break." I look straight into his eyes—blue, I think—willing him to linger, for this not to be a passing comment. Is it possible to wordlessly force someone to stay?

He's walking over. How long has he been standing there? We didn't pass each other. I would have remembered.

Of the three bags I've dropped, he picks up the heaviest one, the one full of prosciutto and cheese and olives and a few of the little Baci chocolates I can never resist.

He lifts it as if it's a barbell, exaggerating its weight. "You expecting anyone?"

"No," I say. "I guess I overdid it a little."

"Easy enough. People have been overdoing it here for millennia."

I tell him he doesn't need to do that, that I'm fine on my own. "Not at all," he says, waving me off. The ricotta had fallen on the ground, still safely wrapped in its paper. But he's picked it up. It fits neatly in the palm of his hand. "Where to?"

"I hadn't really gotten that far yet. Anywhere?" A rolled-up sheet I found in the linen closet of the apartment is poking out of my bag. "I was told this was a nice place for a picnic."

"Ah, you were told."

His hair is dark, almost black, about to curl and would if it were an inch longer. No gray that I can see. He could pass for Italian, and probably does until he opens his mouth. A deep tan, long eyelashes, wide, relaxed shoulders, a mouth that looks sure of itself. Two days' worth of facial hair. His voice suggests a Brooklyn childhood, maybe North Jersey. I see creases deepen beside his eyes as he squints into the sun.

He's left the top few buttons of his white linen shirt undone, cuffs rolled unevenly halfway up his forearms. Chest hair, but not too much. I wonder if he tends to it or not. No gold chain, no saint, no talisman. No wedding ring. I've started checking automatically, without discretion. Any man I see, almost.

He wears shorts that American men would only wear in Europe, stopping at the middle of the thigh. Espadrilles that have molded to his feet, well loved.

"First time in Rome?" He looks straight ahead, toward the fountain, not the park, which stretches out to the right.

"No." Then, not wanting to seem reticent or dismissive, I continue. "But first time in a long time."

My legs feel light again, grateful even, on the level ground of the lookout.

I follow him to a semicircular pool, watch the chlorine-blue water lap against the limestone. A building supported by arches and columns emerges from it, all open to the air. Passageways cut out of marble show sunlight streaming through. We both stop to stare.

"I heard a choral concert here once," he says. "The acoustics inside are close to perfect."

He puts my bag down for a moment, dips his fingers into the water like a child would do, meeting the need to experience his environment fully. It's as if I'm not here for a few seconds, as if no one is. The water runs from his palm down his wrist, disappearing into the roll of his cuff.

"Almost too good," he says.

He shakes his hand dry, extends an open palm to me, still cool when I grasp it. His name is John.

"Do you live here?" I ask him, instantly envious, no matter what his answer is.

"Sort of. I'm at the American Academy." He waves his hand in the other direction. "It's not so much of a hike for me, coming up here, which is nice."

"What do you do there?"

"I'm an architect, or I was. That's what got me a fellowship years ago. I came back last summer for what was supposed to be a few months. They can't seem to get rid of me."

"I don't blame you. I'd keep coming back until they slammed the door in my face."

He smiles and laughs. Still here, still looking at me, still holding my food in his hand. I want to know more, but hold myself back.

"So, Emilia." He says my name carefully, letting the vowels at the end roll the way they're supposed to. He doesn't mispronounce it as Amelia, as most people do. "Are you a writer, a filmmaker...?"

"Artist. I'm a visual artist. Drawing, painting, that sort of thing." As if he needs to be told what a visual artist is. "What made you think I was creative? I could be an accountant."

"Just a feeling, I guess." And then, "Who says accountants can't be creative?" It's a pause I have to work hard not to fill.

"Well, your instincts are good," I say. I wonder what it actually was, something in the way I stand or the way I'm dressed or how obvious it is that I'm trying to figure him out.

"Sometimes." A pause. "You have that look about you, I guess."

"What look is that?"

"That you like to make things, or question how things are made."

What does that even look like? Always tearing things apart, overthinking, never satisfied. "So, does that mean you like to plan things? Or question how they're planned?"

"I prefer 'problem-solving.' Though I'm more of a spectator these days, instead of actually doing anything."

"How does that work? You look at something like this, the curves, the way the sound carries, and see logistics? All the ways it's still standing?" I sit down on the edge of the pool.

"I guess I do, yes. But it's more than that. More than technicality." He stands back, takes it all in as if seeing it for the first time. "I don't think I ever really lost my wonder at it, how an arch can support what it does or how a hole in a roof can be so ingenious. I never went cynical. Probably because I quit."

He moves back a bit, away from me and the fountain and the monument beyond us, to get a better look. With each step, I can almost see the bones in his feet through the espadrilles, their well-worn canvas. He moves with purpose, but lightly, barely making a sound, the muscles in his legs catching and letting go.

What does one of his days look and feel like? Aimless or liberated? Full of air and light and possibility, always an invitation to be answered or a conversation to be had? Or free and empty to the point of being oppressive, always too much time to fill with dwindling options?

Maybe he's the type of person who throws on something simple and makes it look tailored, chosen with care. Like his linen shirt: quickly buttoning it before meeting a friend for a drink outside, rolling the sleeves as he walks, feeling a precious bit of breeze find its way through to his skin. Choosing a life just because it seemed idyllic, finding a way in, making it look easy. He still has all my food in his hands.

We're moving away from the fountain and the small crowd that surrounds it, past the end of the path where I saw him, and into the park. His step slows, and I wonder what else he notices. Symmetry, maybe, a history that's hidden to almost everyone else. People who just see an old structure, a pleasing lookout point, a place to pause. He moves with ease. I'm a bit behind.

"So, your picnic. I'm guessing you'll want a nice view?"

"Please."

He extends his arm as if he's pulling back a curtain or showing me to the best table at a crowded restaurant, not a wild-looking park high above Rome, which makes me laugh.

The paved path we're following splits in two, each side circling a statue before becoming one again. Busts of famous Italian men dot this stretch of the park, perched on modest concrete pedestals of varying heights, the grass high and yellow around each base. They look in different directions, some just past one another. Michael would notice the missed connections, make up conversations between them on the spot, recite it all in made-up voices to make me smile.

"This is my goal for the next four days," I tell John, following him between shade and sun. "To be intentionally aimless."

"Intentionally aimless." He repeats my words, lingering on each syllable, delighted by the concept. Delighted by the turn his day has taken, maybe.

"You're only here until Tuesday?"

I nod.

"Not enough time."

"I know, wasn't my decision."

A few moments of silence strung together. I wonder if he'll ask whose decision it was. He doesn't.

"So, what's on your agenda?"

Since I'm not sure, but don't want him to know that, I say the first thing I think of. "I'd like to be inspired."

"That's why artists come to places like this, isn't it?"

And it could be true. I feel it, even now—the fluttering, open sensation of being a sponge. Everything I see has the potential to be useful, to fuel me forward in some way.

"I need all the help I can get," I tell him, part of a strong, uncomfortable need that's bubbling up. To tell him so much, and right away. That it would be safe, even welcome, to do so. It's the way he's looking at me, maybe. With eyes I know nothing about, whose routines and inferences are a mystery. This long, uninterrupted attention could mean mere interest or intense fascination or common boredom, hoping I've been sent here to help him pass the time.

The little road we've been following yields to green, left as wild as possible, cut through by a few paved paths. But he's stopped, moving my bags into one hand, offering them back to me.

"Is the tour over already? That's disappointing." My tone is light, but I'm surprised at how much I suddenly don't want to lose his focus, the possibility of his questions and answers.

"It's a little rude, isn't it?" The eye contact he gave me minutes ago is a struggle now. "Me barging in on you like this? I tend to collect people. It's a habit of mine, living here. I guess I've gotten too used to it. You came up here for peace, and I'm intruding."

I think, for the slightest moment, of Michael taking the seat next to mine on the train, barely waiting until I'd moved my things to claim his place.

"It's not rude," I say. "Really."

He's hanging back, still. It's a little painful, so plainly asking him to stay. But it's what I want. I swallow any desire I have to hesitate.

"Believe me, if I didn't want company, I'd say so."

"I guess I'll take your word on that," he says, still sounding unconvinced. But his posture softens. He leads me to a flat stretch of grass, between the roots of some trees and benefiting from their shade.

All of Rome seems to hug this hill, so panoramic it's not possible to take it all in without a turn of the head. He points out the Vatican, Hadrian's Villa, the dip of the Forum, the cool green lawn of the American Academy. "I used to live just beyond there," he says. "But I'm in Esquilino now. Real Rome, not the postcard."

The sheet I brought is white, printed with little flowers. Its folds are deep and don't disappear, even after we shake it open. The smell of the closet hangs in the air for a moment: years of dust, lingering detergent, a hint of a cigarette smoked long ago. He takes two corners. I take the others, watching him as he holds the fabric taut.

As soon as we lay it down, the sheet is covered in spiky bits of grass that attach and refuse to let go. "They look prehistoric," I say. "Something you'd use for torture," he offers. They multiply as we try to detach them. He starts to laugh at the futility; then so do I.

"A minefield," he says, watching me negotiate a place to sit. I kick my sandals off, heels resting on the border of the sheet, the part I've been taught to fold over when making a bed.

We both lean back and look out, deep breaths in appreciation.

"There's not a single thing I'd change," he says. "It's odd, how the mess makes it perfect. Beautiful."

"I would think it's a little perverse, the Academy being here. All those artists and writers and thinkers, surrounded by all this extravagance, all this beauty, done so long ago and still here. Must be discouraging, or frustrating."

"I think the hope is it will be motivating, that you'll want to add to it."

"Makes sense." I don't have much to say about inspiration, as it turns out.

"Where are you visiting from?" he asks.

It's a relief to be asked, as opposed to guessed at. I say New York. He nods and says him, too. Real New Yorkers, I'm convinced, aren't thrilled by the novelty of finding each other in a foreign country.

He asks me where, specifically, and my answer makes him perk up a little.

"Where in Gramercy?"

"Twenty-Second Street, between Park and Lex."

I moved in two and a half years ago, leaving the East Village and my sentient water stain behind. I found the place on the twenty-fifth of the month, packed my whole life in a fever. Once the rugs were picked up from the floor and all my shelves were emptied and plastic bins of shoes and sweaters pulled out from underneath the bed, I was surrounded by dust. The air was choked with it. I left that apartment far more spotless than I needed to.

I start unwrapping the ricotta. "Do you want some? I certainly bought enough."

"You don't mind? I swear I don't usually track down women for free food."

He takes the wax paper when I offer it, then settles back on the sheet. Propped up on his elbows, looking up, then out through the trees.

He tears a slice of prosciutto in half and drops a piece in his mouth. "You found good ricotta," he says, pronouncing the word with a hard *C*, wide *O*—the Italian way. I almost try my joke about the goats, then decide against it.

"One of the other things I was told," I say instead. "Where the good cheese is."

"That's important. You were given good advice."

"And I've got my priorities straight."

"Of course." He's not asking why I'm here alone or who told me where to go and for what.

"I know you must hear this a lot, but you're so lucky to live here. I'm envious." I sound a little ridiculous, but continue anyway. "It's always seemed like such a brave thing to me, something a true adult would do. Someone who has their life in order."

"I'm not so grown up," he says.

Only a few years older than me, actually.

"You just need some money to start and tolerance for a little uncertainty, for visas and all that bullshit. Not so hard." He exhales. "It's been a while since I just sat up here, looked at the city," he says. "I'm always passing by, on my way to something else."

I want to know what all that something else is.

It's strange to meet someone this way, without the circumstances that usually make a conversation easier. No shared commiseration over how crowded the bar is or stories about mutual friends that lead to more directed, personal questions. Aside from my asking his name and what he does, none of the usual ones have come up anyway. There's pressure to fill a silence or elicit a certain kind of response, but it's light pressure. Pleasant, even.

His feet are out of his shoes, too. One of his ankles cracks. Comfortable with whatever I might be making of him.

A pair of people walks by: a young woman in a tight dress and heels that clash with her surroundings, next to a much older man. The extra length of his belt hangs down, swinging with each step. His hand remains firmly, possessively on her ass.

"How miserable must that be for her. I wonder if he sent away for her through the mail." The words pour out of me, much more venomous than I intended, followed by a little shiver of regret.

John laughs at me. "People want all sorts of things from each other, I think." A little taken aback maybe, but not entirely put off.

I chalk it up to being out of practice. It's been a while since I was around someone whose opinion or reaction I couldn't reasonably predict. Even longer since whatever they were would interest me.

A breeze moves through the tops of the trees, making the slightest sound.

"My mother would call this riotous living," I say.

"Would she?"

It's a phrase she loves, to the point of overuse. "She had a favorite aunt. Well, they weren't actually related. But they may as well have been. They chose each other."

"Thicker than blood."

"Right, exactly. But whenever she'd give my mom some money for her birthday or Christmas, she told her not to put it away or save for anything, to spend it on riotous living instead."

"Everyone should have someone like that, I think. Especially when we're young."

"Riotous living changed her life, actually."

"How so?"

"She went to Greece and met my dad."

"Romantic."

I shrug. "I guess it is."

"Objectively, yes. Are they still together, your parents?"

"They are," I say. And then, "For better or for worse." With a smile. John nods as if he understands.

A father and his teenage daughter walk on the path in front of us, obscuring the view for a few moments. She's all legs, short steps that don't make proper use of them: not beautiful yet, but she probably will be. They speak softly to each other. The man's head is bowed, his hands linked behind his back. For some reason, the girl stops short, letting him walk three, four, five steps ahead before he senses her absence. When he turns back, she throws up her hands, starts to stomp away. There's a moment of conspiracy, both of us taking this in together.

"Makes me think I could see whole lives unfold if I laid here long enough." His voice is wistful. "It's fascinating, seeing that sort of missed connection in real time. Or shitty parenting, or teenage angst, or whatever it was."

"You think so? I hate it when people don't say what they mean. It's so clear that she's upset and he's oblivious as to why, or just doesn't care. What's the harm in actually telling the truth?" I'm surprised by how harsh my tone is, how dismissive. "Sorry, maybe I just had a flashback—being that age, feeling misunderstood. I swear I'm not actually this negative."

The look on his face betrays nothing. Maybe he can tell I like ambiguity, the excitement in it, how it can become a game.

"No, please, tell me," he says. "I want to know everything you hate."

"Everything? I don't think we have that kind of time."

He's reaching for his bag, standing up. It's startling. Even though he appeared out of nowhere, it doesn't seem possible or right that he could vanish just as easily.

"You want to get a drink later?"

"Why?" It sounds abrupt, but I'm genuinely curious.

Something cloudy rushes across his face, and is gone just as quickly. Fear, maybe? I can't imagine anyone who looks like him, who has his life, being afraid of rejection, or even being able to recognize it. But then again, I've made that mistake before, being so sure of what I saw in someone else.

"I like talking to you," he says. "You're not what I expected." Each word is weighted with the same degree of interest, even tenderness. "I'd like to talk some more."

I'd like to feel the linen of his shirt, cool from the shade, maybe damp from a bit of sweat, against my chest. I'd like to feel his hair between my fingers, touch the precise place where it meets his ears, threatens to curl over and cover them.

John doesn't wait for me to answer. "Seven work for you?" He names a bar in such a practiced, reflexive way that I can't make it out. But I smile and nod, wanting him to think I understand.

I waste so much time appearing confident. And for what? My conversations with friends are forever punctuated with different references and innuendos, all strategically placed just to make us feel comfortable. There's safety in knowing what someone means when they say their last relationship would have made a great Pinter play or that they can't believe the galleries are moving back to Tribeca, when no one can afford to live there anyway. Even when I'm not totally sure what people are talking about, it's a bit of deception I can usually pull off. But not here.

Or maybe this is how it's meant to happen, him coming into and out of my life just as quickly. He could be nothing more than temptation—something shiny, a distraction from the task at hand. My own stubbornness or vanity doing me a favor for once. Making sure I stay alone, stay focused. Even if it means standing him up.

But still, there's a pull, a curiosity that can't be explained or reasoned away. I can tell my unanswered questions for and about him aren't going to fade. It's not until his back is turning and he's three or four steps away that I finally give in.

"Actually—" I can feel the rush of heat in my face as I ask him to clarify. "Can you just tell me what's close by? I'm sure I'll be able to find it."

Michael would make use of this moment. He'd sense my self-consciousness and see it as an opportunity, try to prolong it somehow—a little laugh, a searching look. "Are you sure?" he might ask. One of his little power grabs that always masqueraded as charm.

But John just nods. Instead of asking for my phone number or typing the address into an app to show me, he rips a square of paper from the notebook in his back pocket. Using the palm of his hand as a flat surface, he writes the name of the bar and draws a little map, using the uneven square of the Piazza Sforza Cesarini as a landmark. His pen is thick. One word bleeds into the next. A flick of his wrist for the curve of the Lungotevere. A little asterisk for the bar itself.

Once the ink is dry, I fold the paper neatly in half, give a little wave, and lie back in the shade. The distance between us grows before I gather everything and start my walk down the hill. Both of us showing up at the appointed place and time is a test.

The street I'm following runs parallel to the Tiber, then curls away from the light, the sycamore branches and the canopy they make, heavy with leaves, cascading down toward the water. It finds shelter and shade and quiet.

In an unadorned alcove next to a church, two women are arguing. One of them is wearing a torn skirt and two sandals that don't match. Her feet look like they've been scrubbed clean.

"I've found your ring," she says, with a thick accent "Take it." Her hands are cupped together, holding a simple gold, more likely brass, ring. "Aren't you relieved? I could have kept it or sold it or worn it myself. Here, have it back."

"It's not mine," the other woman tells her, impatient while staying wary. "I'm not married. It must have been someone else." She sounds British, in a loose summer dress and canvas sneakers, sunglasses pushed hastily to the top of her head. Her confusion and uncertainty are bordering on anger, but it's uncomfortable to refuse a person trying to give you something. It's palpable; even I feel it.

"It's yours," the woman in the skirt insists. "I saw you drop it. The least you can do is give me something for the good deed." Her English is exact, like she taught herself from a book. But that doesn't matter when you've chosen the wrong mark.

The longer I stand here, the more starts to make sense. The clearer her choices become. The ring she dropped, then pretended to find. The price she'd ask of whoever happened to pass by.

She's alert and present in a way that's universally recognizable and undeniably true. Mostly it's her stare, devoid of anything but determination. This has to work.

Before I quit my last office job, I took the shuttle train every weekday morning for a year and a half, between Grand Central and Times Square.

I started hearing and seeing the same man, who would give the same speech, pacing the length of the car. He wasn't a drunk or an addict. He'd never been to prison. He had a daughter, who'd just reached the age when she started asking questions about everything. Why is the sun warm? Why is the sky blue? At that point, he'd always, without fail, burst into tears.

The details would occasionally shift and migrate, but there were only two or three minutes between stations, and he always timed himself accordingly. It seemed so real each morning, and made me furious at first. Seeing how that kind of emotion could be, if not manufactured, then so reliably duplicated, on cue.

Then I stopped commuting, and he was gone from my life just as easily.

"Just walk away," I half yell to the British woman. It's what I should have silently told myself, but instead say to her.

I struggle with the zipper on my wallet and pull out a five-euro bill left over from the bar last night and folded like an accordion. I put it in the other woman's still half-open hand, avoiding however she might be looking at me, and walk back the way I'd come.

A man is singing along to the radio. I can hear him above me through his open window, his voice shaky, but close to the melody.

I think of Jack's singing voice. Strong, though he hardly uses it. And low, like our dad's.

Last winter, a family friend was showing new work at a gallery downtown. Jack and I were expected to make an appearance at the opening, so we did. The portraits were seven feet tall, faces with features so large they were almost grotesque.

"Look at the size of those nostrils," Jack said. We laughed about how everything looked strange after a while, the way the spellings of words make no sense if you stare at them long enough. "I'm afraid to look at myself in the mirror now," he said. A few hors d'oeuvres, free champagne, smiles and congratulations, and we were gone.

"Want to stop and eat something?" he asked me, pulling up the collar of his coat. "I had all the mini grilled cheeses I could grab, but I'm still hungry." He rarely acts like he needs me for anything, but that night I could sense it, how he didn't seem ready to go home.

We ducked into a wine bar in Chelsea, a block from the gallery. It had started to snow, and we ordered excessively, for comfort. Grilled bread rubbed with garlic and tomato. Tortilla thick with potatoes and dotted with romesco. Octopus drenched in lemon and paprika. Croquetas so fresh from the fryer they burned our fingers. Two glasses became a bottle, and then another.

Dad's birthday was coming up in February, not a milestone year but he still wanted something festive, something big.

"What man in his sixties organizes his own birthday party?" Jack shook his head, stabbed a potato with his fork.

"I know, it's a little ridiculous." I laughed along with him, knowing I was inching into someplace perilous, unpredictable.

"The ego shouldn't surprise me, but it still does sometimes."

"It would be nice if you were there. I think it would mean a lot to him."

"To watch him pay yet another tribute to himself? Watch Mom continue to eat shit, the way she has for years? No thanks."

"I think you know that's not really how it is."

"Why do you always do this?" he asked.

"Do what?"

"You never let anything just be. Isn't it exhausting, always looking for problems to solve?" He wasn't quite angry with me, but it was close. "I'm fine with the way things are. You should be, too."

"Are you actually fine with it? I have a hard time believing that."

"I really am. And I don't see the point in continuing to talk about things that can't be fixed anyway. How is that better?"

"I think it must be hurting you, hurting you both to let something like this fester. I know he's not perfect, but he's our dad. And he's not the same person he was when we were younger." I wondered if that was actually true, but said it anyway. "You might regret not knowing him better, him not knowing you at all."

"Maybe he's someone I don't want to know."

There were times when I could lean on our age difference, talk to him in a kind, steady voice, spiked with authority, and he'd listen. I'd frame things a different way and he'd nod as if I'd actually changed his mind. Other times, like that night, he fought me even harder.

I leave Monti with plenty of time, maybe too much. As I pass the Forum, late light casts equal shadows on cavernous brick foundations and the columns that once held up temples, makes the weeds below look burnt.

I make my way slowly, not wanting to be early and waiting for him. Even though, at this point, it's probably unavoidable. Still, I linger wherever, whenever possible.

A couple leans over the railing separating the street above from the ruins below. They're both tall and blond, likely from one of the Scandinavian countries where people claim to be happiest, year after year. I watch for close to five minutes and she says almost nothing, looking out over all that history, maybe trying to imagine what it used to look and feel like. Deals being struck in the cool dark of the Curia. Arches welcoming triumphant soldiers or occupying enemies.

The man she's with speaks ceaselessly, barely stopping to breathe. He fills every silence so readily I'm sure he thinks he's doing her a favor. Eventually, she turns back toward the road, still without a word, and starts to walk, knowing he'll follow.

Being with someone else dulls the senses, like alcohol might, or sleep deprivation. I wonder about my friends who can't go anywhere without their significant other, or the ones who reliably jump from one person to another, so easily and predictably wrapping themselves in someone else. Do they give any thought to what they're giving up? I used to pity them, but now I worry that what ensnares them could be coming for me, too. This reliance on someone else, a breed of connection I tell myself I can want, but will never truly need.

Loneliness is painful, but what if it could be something else, too? Something worth the ache?

There's no doubt that Michael would be showing me a different sliver of this city. Many of the same streets and landmarks, I'm sure, but at another, faster pace and fueled by his own curiosity, at his whim. Dinner last night would have been longer, a celebration devoted to him, kept within the confines of a table for two. Some story or observation of his would have drowned out "Chain of Fools" on the radio this morning. When the wine bottle fell as I reached the top of the hill, he might have caught it.

What did I miss, in all that time I spent with him? What did he distract me away from feeling and thinking and noticing?

I picture John, leaning back on his elbows, inches away from me, looking up through the trees. He seemed more comfortable listening than speaking, though it's hard to know if that's true. One thing that's clear: He doesn't mind silence, doesn't shy away from a moment of discomfort if it holds the promise of something more. But is my curiosity about him worth the potential sacrifice?

When I was in college, Dad played a show at the Bowery Ballroom. I decided to take the train in for the night, bringing a few friends who would get a thrill out of going backstage.

The set list was familiar, about to reach a well-worn crescendo before the inevitable "Chaos" encore, when a ripple of unexpected energy filled the dead air between songs. A few gasps and scattered applause. People had turned away from the stage, toward a man and woman in the center of the crowd. He was down on one knee, wearing a nervous smile.

A few words muttered away from the microphone and the band launched into a rousing version of "Let's Stay Together." A song I'd never heard them cover before—one they all seemed to have memorized for a time like this. Dad did his best imitation of Al Green's magnetism, directed almost entirely at the newly engaged woman. She stared up at him, rapt. The crowd's focus snapped back where it belonged.

Later, I stayed for one drink at the after-party, which had expanded to fill the cocktail bar beneath the Woolworth Building. "This place is too cool for me," Dad said, stretching out on the leather banquette that lined a painted wall.

"Well, that was unexpected," I said, sitting next to him. "Have you ever had a proposal at a show before?"

"Not that I've noticed." He cracked his knuckles, opened his pack of cigarettes to one of the backup singers.

"I thought it was kind of sweet," she said, holding the Marlboro Red between her ring and middle fingers as she turned around to look for the door.

"I give it a year, tops." He leaned back, knowing his drink order had been placed, would arrive shortly.

I had to laugh. "Why? You don't know these people."

"It was obvious. The way he put her on the spot, in the middle of a show. You don't do something like that unless you're not sure of the answer." He rested his elbow on the table, dissecting my naïveté. "That 'yes' was coerced. She probably doesn't even realize it yet."

"If you say so," I replied. It was too dark for him to see me roll my eyes.

"One person always loves the other more," he said, turning to watch the waitress, the bourbon leaving the bottle and pooling in his glass. "Always."

The wine bar is dark and cool, like a cave carved out and held up with empty bottles. The sun won't set for three more hours.

And when it does, it will disappear slowly, luxuriating in color. The temperature dropping by one degree, then another.

Boxes of Peroni block half the staircase down to the basement bathroom. People repeatedly squeeze by, turning their bodies sideways, making a point of sucking in their stomachs. But no one says anything. The boxes never move.

A few people sit inside, but most are out in the street with their drinks. Two women sit on an old steamer trunk that serves as a bench, taking photos of each other. In the piazza, the one John drew as a lopsided square, two little girls run around a fountain, each giving a little scream when an errant drop of water hits her skin. There's just enough space between them that it's unclear who's chasing who.

I've made an effort tonight, but the right kind. Hair brushed smooth, enough makeup to look like I'm not wearing any, playing up the bit of sun on my nose and shoulders. So much work goes into looking as if I've barely tried, but it's worth it, I think. A shortcut to finding the subsequent confidence. I want him to know, instantly, that he's made the correct choice in meeting me here.

The Italian being spoken all around me is making its music. I consider all the twists and turns it would take to find me right now—in an unmarked bar on a hard-to-find street deep within an ancient city. It would be hard, if I didn't want you to. If you weren't the person I'm currently waiting for.

I'm a little early, trying not to watch the door.

Trying not to guess at anything, anticipate how this might go. Trying not to compare how I feel now with other nights when everything seemed aligned, when I looked exactly as I wished I always did. I would make up plans and recruit whoever was free, with no real motivation beyond wanting to be seen. There was momentum just beneath the surface. Buoyancy, pleasant surprises there for the taking. And even if nothing worthwhile came from it, I never regretted feeling happy to be out in the world, on display.

It sometimes happened without a plan, without me even knowing. Two or three winters ago, the night of the blizzard New York always seems to get in March, I convinced a friend who lived nearby to meet me at the dive on Third Avenue, equidistant between our apartments. It's the kind of place that keeps Christmas lights up year-round, just bright enough for me to be able to read a book on nights when I need a break from my own walls.

What was normally a two-minute walk took ten. Snow had been falling since the early afternoon and nothing was shoveled or plowed. Each step I took was cautious, the street completely quiet. Yellow light behind shut, locked windows.

The door swung open to reveal a man so tall he blocked any view of the snow outside. There were cross-country skis strapped to his back. He was a regular; we'd probably met and forgotten each other six or seven times. But I'd never seen him like I did that night. His eyes were a little wild, high on endorphins and whatever else.

He pulled off the hat he was wearing and threw it on the bar.

"You haven't lived until you've skied across the Williamsburg Bridge in the middle of a snowstorm," he announced to cheers.

My face must have looked familiar because he rushed over and wrapped himself around me. The back of my neck and side of my face were wet with his sweat when I pulled away. Had I ever noticed the sinew in his arms, the gentle roll in his voice from one word to another, how blue his eyes were? We saw each other entirely differently, transformed, even though it was brief.

The rarity of nights like that, the magic they carry, are apparitions I chase.

This bar is short, with only four spaces to sit. To one side is another woman traveling alone. She's asking me questions with an air of conspiracy, as if she and I are in on a secret no one else could possibly guess.

"Have you been to the theater here? It's not really that talked about for tourists, but I always find it so entertaining. Even though I can't understand nine-tenths of what they're saying."

I tell her I've passed some theaters but hadn't thought to go. She's a flight attendant, has one or two nights in Rome every few months. After all the bars and restaurants and monuments, she needed to start mixing things up.

But, she says, there's a sushi place on the roof of a hotel, not far from here, that's incredible. You wouldn't think so, but it's true. She starts to look it up on her phone, so she can give me the name and address. "And they have a great bar," she tells me. "Not a place you feel strange going by yourself."

I thank her, look at her pictures of sashimi and neon-pink cocktails.

"How'd you hear about this place?" she asks.

"Someone I met this afternoon. He's meeting me here actually, or should be." I resist the urge to look at the door again.

Her face loses a bit of its light. She raises an eyebrow. "Well, isn't that nice."

"It might be? I'm really not sure." I try to salvage her image of me, a fellow solo female traveler, braving the great unknown, but she's written me off.

I can't shake the feeling I've been intentionally cruel. Was that really even necessary? I don't need to feel better than her. I'm not. It's just as likely John won't show up anyway. And if he doesn't, that won't matter either.

I catch the bartender's eye. He seems like he might be a receptive audience.

"Prendo un calice di quello che mi consiglia lei?" I've practiced this one.

He pulls a bottle from the ice beneath the bar, lets it hang in the air dripping for a moment, then grabs it by the neck. It's cloudy and fizzes when poured, the color of a ripe lemon. It smells a little like feet, but tastes light, fresh, slightly sour, bubbling against the roof of my mouth.

He knows the family that makes this wine, is telling me about their vines, how they hug a certain hillside. I must look like I'm struggling because he switches to English.

"Have you ever seen a harvest?" he asks me.

I shake my head no.

"You can't leave Italy," he says, "until you see one. Until you step on grapes in bare feet."

On my other side, a man is eager to know what the bartender poured for me, what it tastes like, whether I like it. He's also alone, but not really. The screen of his phone keeps lighting up with texts from someone whose name he's saved as "Beautiful." She texts him over and over, and he smiles in a way he can't help each time the bar vibrates with her messages, whatever they are.

"This wine," the bartender elaborates, "the grapes for this are stepped on by women only." He turns the bottle clockwise so I can see the label: a pen drawing of a woman's legs, her disembodied hands holding up a long skirt, crushed grapes between her toes. "Makes the taste sweeter maybe? It's possible."

If Michael were here, would his arm be around me? Would he have asked for one of the small tables or been content standing at the bar? Would we be talking to these people or lost in our own conversation? What story would he be telling?

The bartender yanks open what looks like a cabinet door, painted the same deep blue as the rest, but actually pulls out to reveal the dishwasher. He's rough with it, taking clean glasses out, six at a time, clanging as they hang between his fingers, before refilling and slamming the door shut again.

As soon as he does, I can hear and feel the machine's low rumble. A sound that's always reassured me.

I turn my head and John is in the doorway. Another linen shirt, the palest pink this time. His hair wet from a shower or the rain that's just started outside, a smooth smile on his face when he sees me.

The guy with the buzzing phone gets up and moves to a single stool against the wall, so John can sit next to me without having to ask. The bartender who poured my glass calls him Gianni. They kiss on both cheeks.

"You made it," he says.

"Thanks to your map."

"No shame in needing a little direction."

The way he looks at me: direct, not lecherous. Then again, everything depends on the person who's doing it, whether that look is welcome to begin with. The warm water of this focused attention, heavy with suggestion, is something I'd like to float in a little longer.

"How is that?" He picks up my wine glass.

"It's good. I love anything that tastes like lemons."

He takes a small sip, shakes his head a little at the sourness, the fizz. "That it does."

I take the folded piece of paper out of my bag, lay it flat on the bar. It soaks up a drop of spilled wine or soda. "Your drawing was very helpful, honestly. Usually maps just turn me around."

"What is an architect, if not a really good, overqualified city planner?"

"So why'd you quit then?" I don't want to ask him something predictable or make small talk.

"Maybe I enjoy a life of leisure. Things moving so much slower. Shooting the shit with the old guys. Enjoying a drink in the middle of the afternoon. Not too bad."

"I don't think I buy that."

He looks straight at me, not distracted by my tone. "You want to know what I actually do all day."

"I guess I do. I don't know. I'm so used to people who never give details. Who emphasize certain things to make their lives look effortless. But people so rarely tell the whole truth."

"You've lived in New York too long."

"My whole life? Yes, I guess that is too long, isn't it?"

"Not like that bullshit doesn't exist everywhere else, but it's an art form in New York," he says. "It's been perfected."

He takes another sip of my wine, waiting for his own drink.

"I don't rent office space or anything like that, but I consult on different projects here and there. Offer my eye and advice, sometimes oversee renovations. There were a few referrals from friends and old colleagues when I got here, and it grew from there." The bartender brings him a tall, slim beer, foam perfectly in line with the rim of the glass. "And now I mostly take things on when I want to. It's enough to get by. Doesn't cost very much to live here, really."

I try to remember the last time I spoke with someone who wasn't trying to convince me of their ambition, show me how much what they did mattered. I'm not even sure how to respond. "It's funny, the hierarchy of what matters to people," I say, my tone the equivalent of a shrug.

"One of the benefits of moving so far away. Who gives a shit what people think? Right, Nico?" He raises his glass in the bartender's direction.

"*Certo, amico mio.*"

John answers him with a string of rapid syllables. It's obvious he loves to speak Italian: the joy in his pronunciation, the speed with which he finishes one sentence and launches into another. It's thrilling to watch, someone taking pride in his work.

"How long did it take you to learn?" I ask. "Not just enough to get by, but really learn. How long before words just came to you and sentences strung themselves together, without having to think about it?"

He considers it for a few seconds. "Enthusiasm is key, definitely. So is osmosis. But enthusiasm made it easy, an easy kind of love from the beginning. Any frustration that was there, not getting things right or saying the wrong thing, it didn't last for very long."

"I'd love to truly learn it, to be able to speak it the way I do French." He doesn't ask me to say something in French, the way most men do when I tell them I speak it. "But that's probably impossible. I'm too old now, to pick something up so seamlessly."

"What draws you to it, do you think?"

"How luxurious it is, maybe." I say whatever comes to mind. "And the fact that it lends itself to drama, like it's meant to be shouted. When people speak so quickly and it seems almost messy, as if they're making it up as they go."

He sips his beer. "It's true. Even the word 'moderation' is decadent. How can you not love a language that makes that possible?"

He says the word again for emphasis and Nico perks up, telling John he knows nothing about *moderazione*.

John introduces me.

"Emilia, *che bella*. Like Emilia-Romagna." Nico points to the label of a bottle he's just poured, made in that region. Just north of Lazio, where we are. "Is your family Italian?"

I laugh. "Not at all. My mother is French, and I'm not sure what my dad is, exactly. Some mix of English, Scottish, Dutch..."

"So, white?" The guy against the wall is eavesdropping, in between texts.

"Very. I was their first child, so I think they had some fun with naming me. A play at worldliness, maybe."

Nico speaks to John in English for my benefit. "It's been a few days since we've seen you," he says, tossing an empty bottle in the garbage. I hear it break, likely into deep green shards like the ones I've seen glittering under dumpsters and kicked across sidewalks. Nico picks up a new bottle, more of the same, without needing to check the label. "I was starting to worry. Maybe you'd found somewhere else to spend your evenings." A hopeful glance in my direction.

John doesn't bite. "No need to. You know I can't stay away too long."

Nico asks me how I'm enjoying my visit.

"It's beautiful," I say. "But it's very hot."

"Yes, this is absolutely the worst time to be here," he laughs. "August is worse, maybe." He says he's leaving for Puglia soon, to stay by the sea with his daughter and her family for the rest of the summer. "It's perfect there, the ideal pace, the sun, the water," he says. "The whole world wants to live the way we do."

"You could even call it riotous," John says, just short of a wink.

A man in the corner, cigarette behind his ear, is sipping what could be an Americano. The seltzer and vermouth are starting to separate. Apparently he has two drinks every night, sitting at the same table, speaks to no one, then leaves. His name is Agnello, John says, but he's only learned that secondhand. The most Nico has ever heard him say is good night.

"Why won't he talk?" I ask.

"No one's sure," Nico answers. "Probably because he listens."

"What is that?" I say. "An Italian haiku?"

They both laugh. I feel the swell of a small, but consequential, victory.

The rain that announced John's arrival has already stopped. The water rests in shallow pools on the street, between stones.

"When I was little," I say to John, once Nico has gone to take someone else's order, "I used to take showers in the rain."

I'm not sure why I'm telling him this. Maybe for no other reason than I can see it so clearly in my mind. A dark sky, my tiny feet kicking puddles. I explain it was all my mom's idea: her hand swirling shampoo in my hair, my face turned upward, her clothes soaked. The storm becoming something to embrace, even dance in, not run away from.

Every time I see a downpour like the one that faded a few minutes ago, whether I'm stuck in it without an umbrella or watching it through a window, I try to remember that feeling.

"That's adorable," he says. "It's a beautiful stretch of time, before we know to judge anything past how it feels, how free it makes us."

"A short stretch."

He exhales. "Unfortunately, yes."

The wine keeps changing, a different color with every pour. First, the deep yellow with bubbles that turn into foam. Then such a deep purple it's almost blue.

"Is it as easy for you as it looks?" John's eyes are calm, inquisitive, genuine.

"Is what?"

"Being so comfortable sitting here, talking to whoever, taking it all in. This effortless way you seem to have. I'm trying to figure out if it's real, if it comes naturally or takes a lot of work."

"I don't think I'd ever describe myself as effortless." I try my best to conceal the lift I'm feeling, having possibly fooled him. "You should see what it's like inside my head. Too much effort."

"Well, you do a good impression of it."

"Nice of you to say."

"The way you look doesn't hurt, I'm sure."

I think about that phrase "paying a compliment." It's apt, describing the exchange as something close to commerce. John's look is mostly generosity, but touched by expectation. He is giving me something, but I'm not quite sure what he wants in return.

Michael gave me rare, spectacular compliments. That I made him laugh like no one else. That I had an extraordinary eye for detail. That sex with me was perfect. Each one was unpredictable, startling, as if from nowhere, and therefore more true. Jewels I kept and polished until they lost their value from too much attention.

There's no offer of a menu. We never look at one. Instead, little plates of food appear every ten minutes or so. Placed in front of us with no explanation: caponata dripping through slices of quickly toasted bread, two forkfuls of pasta with garlic and oil, anchovies resting on potato chips, flecked with red pepper.

A woman announces herself at the threshold, waving her arm in the air to show off a new tattoo: a radish, just above her elbow. It looks fresh, an hour or two old. That singular shade of pinkish red, accentuated by drops of blood. She makes the rounds, twisting her arm, wrapped in the same kind of plastic that covers the cured meats behind the bar, for anyone who wants to see. Nico pours her a glass of deep amber wine.

"Why a radish?" John asks her, his voice light but not at her expense.

"I just love vegetables!" She says it over and over, punctuated with little yelps whenever she accidentally touches the radish with her other arm or the base of her glass. Every time she makes eye contact with her boyfriend, she dissolves into laughter.

"There's more to this story," I say, getting a little closer to John's ear.

The woman turns her head and there's a glimpse of another tattoo, a crooked star at the base of her skull. It's outlined in thick black, mostly hidden by hair. John touches the same spot on his head, maybe feeling a twinge of sympathetic pain.

"What do you think the deal is?" he asks me. "Is she turned on by all vegetables, or just ones with roots?"

"Or maybe she's deathly allergic to radishes. Maybe it's a constant reminder of her mortality."

"That's pretty fucked up. I didn't take you for such a downer." He looks back at her. "Maybe she does just like them. They're pink and pretty and taste like basically nothing."

"Unless you put good butter and salt on them."

"Yeah, but then they just taste like good butter and salt."

"Worse things." My left hand is resting flat on the bar, near his glass but not too close. He starts to play with the ring on my middle finger, moving the stone from side to side. As if it's the most natural thing for him to do, not the least bit daring.

A song Dad wrote for my mom is playing in the background. There's a sweetness in the recognition I feel, the sudden appearance of a melody and voice I know so well. Maybe I'm being reminded, or subtly told, that I am where I'm supposed to be.

John hears it and hums a bit of the chorus. Usually I might say something cryptic, invite his questions, but I watch him instead. After a few moments, seeing his appreciation, I want to claim it in a way I don't normally do.

"This is my dad's song."

"What do you mean?"

"It's his song. He wrote it, he's singing it. It's his."

Michael was a fan of my dad's. Lots of men his age are. He described these lyrics as verging on poetry, but the accessible kind.

John's gaze goes somewhere else. He's listening, nodding his head, not showing too much of a reaction. It seems me being this person's daughter is an interesting detail, but nothing more than that.

I have the privilege of deciding who gets to know. Dad performs under his mother's maiden name, so it's not immediately obvious who I am, who my parents are. It's hard to imagine he was thinking of his unborn children or their ability to navigate life unrecognized when he made that choice, but Jack and I have benefited from it.

Dad loved his mother fiercely, was always looking for ways to pay tribute to her. She died when I was four. One of the true things I know: she was so taken with my mother, always said that marrying her was the best decision Dad ever made.

She gave my mom an *Oxford English Dictionary* for her thirtieth birthday: several inches thick, covered in navy leather, title stamped in gold leaf. It sits centered on the desk in the library of my parents' house, like a totem.

Every party my parents have finds its center in that room. Maybe it's the fireplace or the thick, well-trod rug, or the blood-red walls—it draws people in, casts a glow. Our hearth, Mom calls it. She loves the way it looks from outside, through a window.

Last Thanksgiving, my parents hosted an open house, as they always do. We were opening bottle after bottle of Beaujolais Nouveau, another tradition. The flowered label, sweet, easy taste, light on our tongues. A fire was roaring. Jack watched closely, going outside for more wood to feed it.

Mom was talking to someone in the library, standing close and listening intently. Her wine at the same level in the glass for over an hour, her hand resting on the cover of the dictionary. As if to steady herself.

"To your parents, then," John says, a full beer in his hand. "To the love of a good woman." He's quoting the song now.

That song he wrote for my mother, it doesn't quite belong to her. The name in the title, repeated over and over in the chorus, is Christina, not Christine. And he's not saying thank you or I love you or I'm sorry. He's saying goodbye.

"You're not the easiest to know," she said to me once. "It might be tough, for someone new. Maybe. Something to think about."

She likes to do that—hide uncomfortable or even difficult truths, deploy them sparingly. Making her words all the more meaningful, occasionally devastating.

I sometimes wonder why my parents are still together. Then banish the thought, just as quickly. Their attraction or comfort or inertia for one another is forever ebbing and flowing. Though it's possible my mother's pull to him never actually wanes. She might just change how she shows it or doesn't, depending on what he did or didn't do.

I wonder if Michael's wife knows about me, or of me at least. How could I not?

Was there a conversation, Michael looking somber, chastened? Were the words "I met someone" ever spoken? Or did she figure it out on her own?

Does the name Emilia mean anything to her? Has she looked me up, scoured my website, parsed all the images of my work, told herself they were pedestrian, that I could never be a threat?

Or maybe, if she does know, the fact of me is irrelevant, because she's the one he's honoring, keeping. He could tell her I didn't matter to him, and probably mean it. Why wouldn't she believe him? He can be very convincing.

Even now, whenever one of Dad's songs comes on by chance,

my mom stops and settles and listens, almost always mouthing the words.

"So, if you hadn't swallowed your pride and asked me where this bar was," John asks, "what would you be doing right now? Crying into a plate of pasta somewhere?"

"I'd be eating pasta, I'm sure, but not crying into it. Don't flatter yourself." I give him a sly smile to soften any edge off what I've said. "But yes, I would be feeling pretty foolish."

"I'm just glad you decided to actually ask for directions."

"I prefer being self-reliant. What can I say?"

"You like knowing things. Being an authority. That much is clear."

I narrow my eyes, pretend to be incredulous.

"You don't like feeling out of control, at the mercy of someone else," he continues. "You want to lead, not be led."

"Says the man who's known me for a grand total of three hours."

"Oh, I think it's at least four by now."

"And that's enough to have me figured out?"

"Definitely."

So he thinks.

I give him silence and he fills it: "At least it's not passivity. That, I can't stand."

I lean back a bit and consider him: his calm and familiarity and embrace of everything around him. How seamlessly he's given up his former life for a new one here. And what did he leave behind? Beyond the usual: family, career, a relationship, friends, routine. Was there anything worth staying for, that he still thinks about? Or was it easy for him? And how is him being here, adopting this existence so easily, not an exercise in passivity?

But I keep that to myself, deciding to focus on how refreshing it is to find holes or flaws in a man's story without my interest dwindling. I think about it for a moment, formulating some version of what he might want to hear. "I think it's better to say yes or no, maybe even regret saying it, than to have no opinion at all."

"What if it's a no you can't take back?"

"Or a yes."

Whatever is between us has been pulled taut. Thankfully, the woman with the tattoo is back, asking John what beer he's drinking because her boyfriend doesn't like what he's chosen, is looking for a recommendation. She ignores me completely. Watching them talk doesn't make me feel weak the way a man's charisma usually does, a surefire sign I could lose him. Now, seeing his charm on display, I feel the swell that always comes with my instinct being right, followed by a familiar shiver of pride.

But I don't have any claim to John anyway, so what does it matter? All of this, the whole day and night, is extra, a gift I never sought out. Something I didn't earn, so don't have to pay for.

Michael was exacting always. He wrote all his drafts of everything on graph paper, each letter of each word perfectly confined.

I'd been seeing him for a few months when we first got stoned together. He rolled a slim joint very quickly, with quiet expertise. Instead of turning mellow or contemplative, he started bubbling over with energy: wanting to make something to eat, spy on his neighbors across the street, show me things.

At the time, he was starting a new novel, one he's either finished writing or abandoned by now. Normally, he'd mention a character, allude to a plot point, but push the topic away whenever I showed real interest or wanted more detail. Now, he couldn't stop himself, told me the whole story, what had been challenging him, moments that blessedly seemed to be working.

"Do you want to hear some of it?"

"Of course."

He flipped through those graph-lined pages, looking for the right scene. So excited and careless and desperate for approval. The next day, he was mortified, shuddering at even the memory of reading me something that wasn't polished or perfect. He'd given too much of himself away.

When I think of nights like that one, spent in his apartment, the light is amber and low. The conversation prickly, dotted with sparks that energized and sometimes stung. So many moments heavy with uncertainty and hope, never quite knowing where he'd go.

The little things I learned about him: his nickname as a child (and his impression of his mother calling him by it), his near-Olympic ability as an archer (before a car accident robbed him of his depth perception), the years he spent bartending downtown in the nineties (the famous people, the freedom, the evaporating invincibility he felt then). Our favorite French words: mine was *ivresse*—mostly because of the illicit, cryptic air it had when I learned it as a child, how it means much more than just drunkenness. His was *brindille,* for its delicacy, the fragility it evoked. I wove all of these discoveries together until I convinced myself they meant something.

I'm so sick of everything having weight. Every moment or

remark he's lodged in my mind stretches out, taking up too much space, insisting upon a response.

I look at John, study his face as he tries to catch Nico's eye, ask for the check. What could he say to me? What would hurt?

The streets and squares are still crowded, still loud with people drinking and laughing and walking to what's next. To our left, a man who's painted himself white stands on a pedestal, pretending to be a statue. This isn't a new routine: stay completely still until just the right moment, to scare and thrill tourists.

John is stopping to watch it play out.

And sure enough, the man jumps to life, just as a woman has leaned in to examine the folds of his toga, whether they're fabric or stone. She gives a little shriek that dissolves into laughter, then drops a few euro coins at his feet.

"A disguise." John says it absently, the way you might reflexively say "deer" when you see one through a car window.

We linger for a few more moments as the man composes himself, finds stillness again, waits for his next victims.

"What's yours?" I ask John.

We're standing side by side, our arms not quite touching, but almost. I can't deny the blind luck of it, of him being here, wanting to know me. But that gratitude is so close to uncertainty, even suspicion. What would I be seeing or doing without him? What else is possible?

He laughs to himself, puts his hand in my hair for a moment. Maybe encouraged by the beer, maybe suggesting there are no maps he can draw for that. I'll need to figure it out on my own.

I don't tell John this, but his apartment reminds me of Gregory Peck's in *Roman Holiday*. Small, utilitarian maybe, but suggestive of something more.

Even at twelve, watching the movie before my first trip to Rome, that sort of man, his sort of life interested me. Too consumed with his work to fuss with what his home looked like. His real life, the one that required consideration and effort and taste, happened outside.

The place is spare, but thoughtfully so: a well-used kitchen, notebooks everywhere, yesterday's newspapers in a neat pile. A bamboo canopy meant to shade his balcony from the sun. High ceilings and what I imagine, in daylight, is a view.

I think of my own apartment, sitting empty. Looking at John's bookshelf (paperbacks stacked horizontally and vertically, most of them in Italian, likely belonging to whoever owns this place), I try to see mine, all three of them. Two broad and accommodating, one thin and stretching all the way to the ceiling. I unpacked my books last, seeing it as a reward—the one part of the process I might actually enjoy. I arranged them alphabetically at first, but that was too constricting. Then by color, which made my living room feel too much like a clever museum gift shop. I finally settled on juxtaposing titles and colors and sizes that seemed right in the moment. I spent hours reacquainting myself with plot points and characters, looking at my notes and question marks and exclamations points in the margins, remembering the bookstores where I'd bought them, the time of year, the mood I was in. Opening any signed copies to reread dedications and pick apart handwriting.

I reserved a bottom shelf for the first editions my dad gets me for Christmas every year: books I hold on to and display and dust regularly, but never read, though I'm not sure why. Many are classics, depending on who you ask, and all suggest a degree of care. The fact that he's trying to know who I am, or at least show me that he's on the right track, *A Book of Common Prayer*, *Dubliners*, *The Mandarins*, Patricia Highsmith's Ripley trilogy. They get their own space.

I remember lying back, when it was finally done, my head resting on a couch cushion that had fallen to the floor. The end result is what I'm probably always going for in how I design my life, however you define it: a lot of time and focus spent to look casual and careless. The books bring some depth to what is otherwise a pleasant, airy, mostly empty living room. Though, on a Friday night like this one, under different circumstances, I would fill it with people.

It works for me, counteracting days spent alone this way. My apartment, wherever I've lived, has always been a gathering place because I put in the effort to make it one. And my current place lends itself to having people over, impromptu or not: an expansive (by New York standards) kitchen, floor-to-ceiling windows letting natural or reflected light into a living room large enough for a long dining table and separate seating area, my bed lofted and tucked away. Maintaining that sort of open-door policy can be tiring, feel calculating, but also offers moments of real, precious connection.

My favorite iteration is always an ambitious dinner party, surrounding myself with people who love to cook and eat and drink and never shy away from a challenge. Hand-crushing tomatoes to press onto grilled, oiled slices of bread. Frying oysters and folding them into omelets. Vegetables roasting in the oven while I dig through cabinets, hunting for an immersion blender. My bathtub filled with ice for bottles of beer and wine and a pint of ice cream that won't fit in the freezer.

Some friends do the dishes without being asked, others linger on the couch or lean into corners or take charge of the music. They'll bring expensive cheese, cheap Montepulciano, flowers from the bodega around the corner, baklava from Kalustyan's, filled with syrup that sticks to our fingers. I almost always fall asleep on the couch, a throw pillow pressing lines into the side of my face.

John has closed the door behind us, is getting me a glass of water. "I'd never lived alone, before living here," he says. "From my parents' house to college to roommates to being married." He's watching me feel the leather of his armchair, take a closer look at a print on the wall. "Can you tell?"

Is it possible he's still married? He's not wearing a ring and there's clearly no one else living here, but, as I'm painfully aware, that means nothing. Watching him walk toward me, I make a surprisingly easy decision not to care, either way.

"Well, now you've told me," I answer him. "But no, this place doesn't say 'scary bachelor' to me."

"What does it say?"

"I don't know. 'Man of taste finds shelter in the Eternal City'?"

He laughs at that. "Taste? How nice, you approve."

"I do."

"Well, you seem to have an eye, so I'll choose to be flattered."

"I don't know if you should. I once thought it was a good idea to paint a series chronicling a scab on my knee over the course of a week." I'd slipped on a patch of ice and sliced my leg open, but grown enchanted with the way it grew uglier while mending itself, then faded after only a few days. There were five canvases, the last one just a faint scar left behind.

He raises an eyebrow. "An interesting idea. Did you sell any?"

"A few of them actually did sell, incredibly. But the whole thing was kind of bittersweet. My parents didn't love them. Well, my dad didn't." I remember showing Dad the paintings when I'd finished, the neon oranges and greens I chose to use, the uncomfortable details, his outright disgust.

"How do you mean?" John's voice is taking a turn toward serious, so I try to change course.

"Oh, nothing, really." I play with the strap of my dress. "I told him if he couldn't see the beauty in healing, then there was something wrong with him." John is studying every breath I take. I can tell.

There's gravity keeping me here, urging me closer. A pull I haven't felt since the last time Michael pinned me against his wall with nothing more than a look, knowing I would stay and wait and give in. There's nothing wrong with wanting someone new. I know that.

The way John is looking at me now is no different than his palm flat on the inside of my thigh. Or so I imagine.

I sip the water from a cloudy plastic cup, the kind that comes with a short-term rental, the kind that no one will miss if it cracks or disappears and needs to be replaced. He takes it out of my hand, uses his thumb to erase a smudge of lipstick, leftover from the few moments I took to reapply it, assess myself in the mirror of the bar's bathroom, while he paid the check.

"I see you trying, you know," he says softly. "You don't have to." A lie, probably. Though how I move and look and sound has felt less important than usual, these past few hours.

He doesn't insinuate, like men before him, that he'll only end up hurting me or that he's worried I will, eventually, get hurt. I'm so used to being told that I'll ultimately be disappointed by those who know I'll see it as a challenge, not a warning.

I take the cup back, bring it to my lips again. This water tastes the same as it would from one of the fountains outside: mineral, elemental. I am trying my very best to be patient.

These moments thrill and terrify me. Heavy with precious attention and silence, pauses in which anything, or nothing, could happen.

The way he kisses me is a surprise. Soft, studying. Then, gaining courage, a little harder.

Everything is immediate; everything he does is new. I memorized Michael's breath, the pressure of his hands when he knew exactly what he wanted. I wonder how long it will take me to fully forget.

I can see a light go off through a tiny window, wrapped in ivy that looks black by night. John stands behind me, his hands on either side of my waist, moving slowly, tracing.

"You're so warm," he says, one hand under my dress now. "You radiate."

Do I turn and face him? Take his other hand, run his fingers across my collarbone, the outline of my neck, press the tip of his thumb to my lips, lean my full weight against his chest? I've forgotten how much I like making these sorts of choices. The power I feel is a living, breathing thing.

He sits back in the wide leather armchair, pulls me on top of

him with a pleasing amount of force. My legs fold in on either side
of his. I feel him hard beneath me.

"You need this," I tell him, a ragged whisper.

"I want it." So soft I can barely hear.

It's a profound relief, not having to think for a few moments. To
go where he directs me, to let my body respond. He feels me, slick,
pulsing, and breathes hard into my neck.

He's grateful. I can tell, while also knowing that all of me, all
I'm giving, still isn't enough.

The word I'm looking for is "insatiable."

SATURDAY

IN ITALY, EVERYTHING IS opera. So I've been told.

The last time I was here, on that family vacation, we stayed in a hotel on a short, sheltered street near the Piazza di Spagna. We had two of the eight rooms. Surrounded by luxury shops, black Mercedes forever idling.

Mom, Dad, and Jack were asleep after lunch, having taken to the local custom of a nap in the middle of the afternoon. I sat on the little balcony, watching two women argue for almost an hour over who was to blame for one's bike hitting the other's car.

I was up high enough that most of what they said, aside from the occasional high-pitched scream, was lost to me. Not that I would have understood it anyway.

They exchanged hand gestures, dramatic shakes of the head, series of what must have been expletives and threats. There were attempts to recruit witnesses from shops or parked cars on either side of the street. Both bluffed multiple times, made a show of walking away, only to turn around and storm back into the fray when inevitably provoked by the other.

I still remember their commitment to the performance. Each had her storyline, made sure she had an equal amount of time onstage.

This street, John's street, just as quiet and tucked away, is empty. It's early. The paving stones are still wet from the rain I thought I heard last night.

I feel his fingers twitch, his hand moving and feeling and noticing. The side of my hip, the uneven bones of my elbow. He's tentative, but working his way toward the courage and confidence of a few hours ago.

Michael always woke me up the same way—two fingers on the sharp point of my shoulder. He rolled over it, in a circular motion, as if trying to smooth it down. It started after the first night I spent at his apartment, and then became a habit. I barely thought of him last night and now he's everywhere.

I try to see myself from above—in a stranger's bed, his legs wrapped around mine like he knows me, like I'm solving a problem. His sheets are linen, same as his shirts. If I focus, I can see the strands, the stitches, looping over and under. How it all weaves together.

I slip out in a way that hopefully neither promises nor discourages anything. The soles of my feet feel tender and new on the tile floor.

There's a mirror on the other side of his bathroom door. It's startling, the length of my body so suddenly staring back at me. The two mirrors, this one and the other above the sink, create a tunnel, showing me the back of my head, my profile, all perspectives I rarely get.

A deep breath in, then out. I watch it happen, and make a deliberate decision with the exhale. To actually say what I need and feel and want, for a change. The doorknob is cool in my hand. It gives with the slightest touch.

He's watching the door when I open it.

"You came back," he says.

Between the sheets, I move to reclaim where I was before, curled up, facing away from him, but he grips my shoulder and shifts me onto my back. He treads the same line he did a few minutes before, but I let him this time. I welcome it.

I feel his hand skimming its way down my body, but I don't let my eyes leave him, tracing his eyebrows and lips and jawline, wanting to memorize them.

At first he seems to be wandering, his touch lingering in one place for a few moments and then moving on. But then his hand moves between my legs with purpose, such force and delicacy at once. It's hard to focus, so I stop trying.

"You're a revelation, you know that?"

He moves his fingers up with more pressure and then more, and everything in me gives way. Such release and relief it borders on pain.

"You must know."

His face is slack with desire, with watching what's happening to me. His other hand grips my leg. He keeps it there until I stop shaking, then replaces his fingers with the tip of his tongue.

He notices the bruise on the inside of my knee, rests a finger against the skin, presses it a little.

"Are you still married?" I ask.

He actually laughs. "No, I'm not. What makes you think I would be?"

"Nothing specific, just a question."

"That mind of yours never stops, does it?" he murmurs to himself.

I reach for the book on his bedside table. *Memoirs of Hadrian*. The imagined insights of an emperor, written by a French woman, translated into English, published in the 1950s, bought a week or a month ago from an English-language bookstore in Rome. Not what I expected.

"What made you choose this?"

"Hey, quit snooping." His fingers run the length of my spine.

I flip the pages. "I'm serious. Do you like it?"

"Are you bored?"

"No, I'm interested."

"I guess I'm pleasantly surprised by it. Though I shouldn't be. What's made men happy or miserable or reflective hasn't changed in two thousand years. Of course not. Why would it?"

I'm careful not to lose the dog-eared page, resist the urge to look at his notes, what he's underlined. "What makes us human can never really change."

"How profound," he says. And holds my arms above my head, both wrists in one hand.

The coffee bar is a rush of activity on the otherwise quiet street. It's John's usual place. He says he's come here almost every morning he's spent in Rome.

The walls are all lined with chalkboard, the café's name written in thick block letters, shaded to look three-dimensional. Two of the *L*'s are faded from brushes with passing shoulders. In between lists of menu items and the day's specials are cutely paired suns and crescent moons, playfully drawn espresso cups, their steam rising in loose waves. The artist has left their social media handle close to hidden in the bottom right corner, in lieu of a signature. A few pieces of chalk remain on a small ledge, encouraging people to draw and leave notes for each other. There are some flowers, hearts, messages I can't translate.

I catch my own eyes in the espresso machine, surprisingly bright. Even in the warped reflection: my skin undoubtedly flushed with signs of life.

We stand at the counter and wait while a British tourist makes the mistake of ordering while standing, then bringing his coffee and pastry to one of the empty tables. John shakes his head. He's watching a waiter try to explain that sitting at a table means ordering from someone, requiring an extra service charge. They seem endless, all the different ways of revealing yourself to be an outsider.

John greets the man behind the counter, who makes two espressos and places them in front of us. A touch of foam on top of his.

"Do you still notice them?" I ask him. "All the rules?"

"It's nice to be reminded." He smiles. "I used to care about all that stuff, but you make mistakes and get the hang of it." He licks the foam from his top lip. "And Italians tend to give the benefit of the doubt. It's not like we're in France."

I tell him to fuck off, in French, which makes him smile wider.

"Still, it must have been exhausting in the beginning, assimilating somewhere new like this. Making a new life."

He shrugs a little, smudges the surface of the bar with his thumb.

"I guess it was. Mostly I found that things worked themselves out, as long as I was open to learning and being wrong. One day sort of rolls into the next."

I try to see things as he does, as he must. Content with just existing, not trying to wring the last drop of experience or beauty out of a place. Letting it happen, or not.

But I can't help myself. "Don't you ever want more? Aren't there times when you get bored or restless or want to take on something new?"

"I thought you were enamored with a quiet life here." He looks past me, out the door. "Or does it not look the same in daylight?"

"It's not that," I say. "I think I'm just so used to having to fight for things, my life feeling like a challenge. I don't quite trust something when it looks easy."

"Believe me, I've had to fight for things."

As soon as it arrives, John drinks his coffee in a single motion, like the old men from yesterday. He searches for his wallet, for euro coins to leave on the bar.

"I should be going, actually," he says. "Have some things to do today."

Is this it? His abruptness throws me, considering this is the same person who'd been so committed to pulling me close an hour ago. Maybe he doesn't like being questioned, or even nudged, about how he spends his days. Perhaps I've crossed some sort of line. I press down the urge to tell him about all the things I've planned for myself today, lists I've made, maps I've consulted. Bullet points on an itinerary that I was ready to abandon.

"But would you like to have a real dinner tonight? I can pick you up later."

I tell him I would like that. He answers with a time and place to meet, close to where I'm staying.

"You're sure you don't need directions? Last chance to ask."

I laugh, tell him I think I can manage.

My body should feel this way all the time. Light, fluid, sure of itself. That it's doing what it's meant to.

But it makes me start to question how I've ever gone a week, even a few days without. Certain parts of me are highlighted, reliving the attention he paid. The different ways he was able to make me fall open, relieving me of some excess, an unnecessary weight.

This is dangerous, such reliance on touch and attention from another person. Someone likely just as changeable as I am. And I can't tell if this clarity, this focus that John has given me, is real or some apparition I'll scold myself for later.

But I also know that, at least historically, this feeling doesn't last. Intimacy, for me, has the shelf life of something expensive and temperamental, like peonies in April or heirloom tomatoes in August, so ripe they're almost rotten. Maybe it's not destined, for me to have it. I let the thought rest for a moment, consider it clinically, then push it away.

John buys me another espresso, settles the bill. He puts his lips to my cheek, waves to the barista, and is gone. I breathe in the smell of his soap before that fades, too.

I know what intimacy looks like, though—that true understanding, maybe even acceptance, between two people. Even if I can't seem to hold on to it myself. Aside from reading novels and watching movies and stealing glances at couples holding hands on the street, my friends share glimpses of it with me, sometimes on purpose.

There might be hesitation, as there always is before telling a secret or testing a boundary. Then they realize there's little to no risk in telling me anything. I'm a reliable confidant, or I make them feel that way. Maybe it's the reverence I have for their situations. Or they just don't see me as a threat.

Adam, a childhood friend and son of one of my dad's band members, works as an art dealer. Well, he's managing a well-known gallery and looking to eventually forge his own path. So he tells me whenever I ask if he'd like to see any of my new work.

Last summer, he was in New York to introduce himself to artists and do some studio visits on his boss's behalf. I met him at the Campbell Apartment for a drink just as the commuters started to clear out and catch their trains. Before long, we had the bar almost to ourselves.

After two whiskeys, he started to tell me about the girl he'd been seeing, that the two of them had started watching one another have sex with other people, both men and women, bringing strangers home, speaking openly about what they wanted and making it happen for each other.

"I had no idea how different it could be." He paused, not sure if he should continue. "These things—urges, desires, whatever you want to call them—that were always a part of me, I just kind of assumed I'd never act on them, that I'd never be able to."

"But now you can," I said. "I would think that might be kind of scary, actually being able to do something you never thought you could."

"Oh, it's terrifying." He laughed. "But in the best way. And the fact that this is something she's given me. I think I'll be grateful for the rest of my life."

Not long ago, I visited Taylor, a friend of mine who'd defended her PhD, gotten married, and had her first baby all within a year. As I crossed her childproofed threshold, a gift-wrapped swaddling blanket in my arms, she apologized in advance for how much she was going to talk. Her brain wasn't used to all this idleness. She worried it would lead to atrophy.

"Giving birth is insane," she said to me. "But I was ready for it, especially being two weeks past my due date. It felt like it was never going to happen."

The night their baby was born, she and her husband had cleaned the house and were lying on the couch, watching *Seinfeld*. "And of course that's when Luke decided he wanted to fuck me for the first time in three months," she said. "Two hours later, I was in labor, my legs in the air. Mean nurses screaming at me to push. One of them told me I was going to tear like a sheet of paper."

She told me this while we sat under the lemon tree in their LA backyard, sharing a joint while her infant son slept in his nursery, painted perfect robin's-egg blue.

Michael was the first man I ever really wanted more from, something close to that kind of connection or reliance or symbiosis. I thought that was healthy. Maybe it would have been, if the object of that wanting had been different.

A month or two after I met him, we woke up to a storm in the middle of the night, the violent, summer kind. With each strike of lightning, the walls of his bedroom turned bright white, our faces and bodies visible for just a second or two. In the darkness, he pulled me close, his breath against my neck, touching me in just the right ways. When he moved inside me, I felt such gratitude, such safety. Powerful, here and gone just as quickly.

A late afternoon in September, lying in the park as the sun was starting to slant sideways, he held some of my hair up to the light, watching its color change.

Months ago, crossing the street toward his building, I didn't check for traffic and a messenger slammed into me with his bike, leaving a tread mark on my toenail to prove it. When I limped off the elevator, Michael called me roadkill, but in a loving sort of way, and rubbed my foot for almost an hour.

The street outside is dirty and getting louder. I turn left and the Colosseum is all I see.

In a city that's constantly reminding you of its age, the Roman Ghetto looks and feels even older.

There are statistics carved into the sides of buildings, memorializing the Jews deported to almost certain death in 1943. Or even further back—when the popes decided this tiny neighborhood was the only place they were permitted to live, in squalor, walled away from the rest of the city. There's no shortage of pain that's been inflicted in this four-block radius, under watch of these statues and ruined temples. But when I try to envision it, to sympathetically picture or feel that struggle and fear and loss, all I see are well-kept piazzas, restaurants playing American pop music at full volume, and quaint streets, tightly wound and unraveling.

A couple browses near me in a shop selling leather goods. A tannery that, the owner's son tells me, has been open and family-run for two hundred years. The bones in his wrist are half-hidden by a worn bracelet, deep brown, likely warmed by his skin, marbled by water and soap and sweat.

The woman consults with her husband over the price of a wallet, her earlobe straining under the weight of a heavy hoop.

I turn a pebbled coin purse over in my hands, resist the urge to smell it, and almost walk out. Until I'm stopped by a pad of good paper, covered in leather the color of cut grass. It's displayed next to a painted cup filled with pens. Not the width or weight I usually like, but one of these will do.

I wander toward Octavia's Portico, trying to see it as the gateway it once was. An entry that enclosed a gathering place and protected temples and libraries, or so some signage tells me: its brief explanation spelled out in five different languages, side by side. Chunks of what used to be its roof are missing, looking like they've been bitten out.

Augustus built it for his sister, in a type of familial gesture that doesn't really exist anymore. Though I like to imagine that maybe the roles brothers and sisters played for one another haven't changed that much. Him being a defender, a sounding board, or lightening the mood when needed. As a sister, if you were a good strategist or ally, you got a portico or a theater or a war fought in your name. In place of any real, demonstrable power.

Jack doesn't speak up for me often, but when he does, it's for good reason, and with conviction.

I notice a man taking a picture of one of the walls. He gets as close as he can, legs straining the chains of the barricade. He's not focused on the whole structure or a still-standing column or even the carving at the top, but on two blocks of stone, next to each other but different colors. He thrusts his arms forward, focusing his camera on the mismatch, this one piece of the foundation different from all the others. There's a smile on his face as he examines the screen. What does that mean to him, one part separate from the rest?

I'm standing under the open window of an adjacent building, designed and built to blend in with the ruins. A voice is trickling out, and it takes a few moments of too-seamless understanding before I realize it's speaking English. At first, I think he might be the designer of whatever space he's describing, but the forced friendliness and hint of desperation suggest a real estate agent instead. I linger and listen, trying to match the enthusiasm in his voice to what he might be showing them. Vaulted ceilings, intricately tiled floors, maybe a faded fresco running the length of a wall.

A deep voice says something about the width of a doorway. A woman, probably at his side, murmurs agreement. Not to worry, the man assures them. Everything can be customized. Is that the right expression, "blank canvas"? He must know it is.

"This place is an opportunity," he tells them, reiterates that this or that can be fixed or adjusted to give them what they want without sacrificing any historical detail. "No one else," he insists, "has the outlines of an ancient column bursting through their living room ceiling."

"What is that," he asks, "if not a conversation starter?"

What I'm hearing and seeing belongs to no one else. And would another person even notice or appreciate it all, pay this degree of attention to these particular details? These scraps of life I likely wouldn't even notice if someone were here with me.

I take a deep breath, and with it, a rare calm is starting to find its way in. A feeling I always wish for and rarely get. When it does bubble up, it leaves me far too easily. This lightness, or whatever it is, feels comfortable, or safe to flourish, only when I'm alone. The moment I slow down or stop somewhere or open my mouth to speak, I risk losing it. I know this from experience. So, I keep moving.

I take so many wrong turns on the way to the Piazza del Popolo. Two hours of walking and barely any closer than when I started. This little square is relief, more like a cove: quiet, secluded, protected. Unassuming, with only two small cafés, a few compact cars parked at angles, out of the way. Its only distinguishing feature is the fountain at its center, surrounded by topiaries spaced unevenly along the perimeter. Four male figures, all riding dolphins, hold a shallow pool above their heads. Bronze turtles rest just past their fingers, sunning themselves.

A sliver of an image comes back to me, part of a dream I had last night and am now only halfway remembering. I was late for something, a flight or meeting or show, a date with a fixed deadline. One I was about to miss. But there was still a chance I could make it, whatever it was. I know I felt that. It helped me move quickly, with confidence. Until my legs suddenly went dead, leaving me crawling toward whatever was so important. Their useless weight, trailing behind me, felt so real. My helplessness, too.

I wonder if John heard me say anything in my sleep, if I fought my made-up paralysis and braced my body against his.

I sit outside, order prosciutto and melon, but don't realize how ravenous I am until the plate is in front of me. The side of my fork slices through the curve of the melon with barely any pressure. I tear a piece of meat apart with my fingers, like John did yesterday, and wrap it around a chunk of the fruit. Bright orange, so ripe it almost drips. I give myself real time to focus on the taste. Sugar and salt will never not be perfect together.

The cap leaves the pen with a satisfying click. The paper cushions its felt tip with the right amount of give. I look through the marbled glass of the table and start to sketch my toes, which look exactly like my dad's. Long, thin, starting to curl. Still ugly despite their polish, fresh from a pedicure the day before I flew here. I add shade where my feet hover above my sandals, draw lines that seem to swim.

There's cruelty in connection, I think. In the fact that yesterday and last night weren't simply gratifying or a pleasant surprise. Or meeting him—the coincidence—wasn't just that. Maybe he's stealing my solitude and showing me how alone I really was, all without trying. And while I'm working so hard to keep some-one else at bay. Is this loneliness, what I'm feeling now, or is this peace?

At the other café, to my left across the piazza, I see a woman sitting alone. She could possibly be, but isn't, Michael's wife. The same hair, long waves cascading to the middle of her back. The same angles in the face, the same air of effortless knowledge, of infallibility.

Yes, I've looked her up in all the usual places, studied photos, even started to listen to an interview she gave, aired on Berkeley's radio station, just to hear the pitch and timbre of her voice. I don't know what I hoped to gain, searching her face and tone for some kind of answer to all the questions I was asking myself.

Warm, shimmering hatred starts coursing through me, coming from everywhere: the base of my neck, the spaces between my ribs, the tender skin underneath my fingernails. The only reason being resemblance, a passing one. I watch her sneeze, check the screen of her phone before putting it facedown on the table and writing a sentence in her notebook. I study the joint of her shoulder, the ski jump of her nose. She has the same fluid movements I've assigned to his wife, the same delicate way of picking up a glass, looping her wrist through the strap of a bag, a loose grip on the pen while signing a check. Attributes I always assumed I had, and actually valued in myself, before I knew she even existed. But she must have them in greater quantities, more artfully deployed.

Surely she's always measured, in control. Never disappointing or embarrassing him in any way. Pushing him to be better, even. Making him wait.

The woman smiles my way as she leaves, mistaking my focus for friendly attention, maybe even kinship. We're both women traveling alone, after all.

The first time Michael and I went out to actually eat something, we searched his neighborhood for close to an hour, but nothing sounded right. I wasn't in the mood for Thai. He'd had a burger the night before. Eventually, we figured out what we both really wanted was oysters and French fries. I remember exactly where we sat to eat them, full of the thrill that comes from knowing precisely what will satisfy you—and actually getting it.

There always seemed to be a table for two at that place whenever we had a collective craving. It became a shtick, a sometimes ritual.

What are theirs? They must have hundreds, jokes and flirtations and memories of tenderness I couldn't imagine or even guess at. I'm hungry for details, and repulsed by the thought of them.

My mother's favorite place in this city is inside Santa Maria del Popolo, the alcove in front of one particular Caravaggio. *The Conversion of Saint Paul.* His prone body, lying helpless beneath his horse. He's fallen as one type of man, legs and arms spread, ready to receive, even embrace, a vision and rise as someone else.

On her first trip to Rome, which would continue south and east, eventually taking her to Greece and my dad, she wandered into the church, past a nun who was trying to close the doors. All part of a story she loves to tell.

It was raining, the day she found the church. A downpour that had started to taper off. When she walked in, despite the nun's protestations, the sanctuary was empty, thin streams of light struggling through the front door. The paintings on every wall were moody and dark. The air was still, as if it were all there just for her.

There was a leak in the roof, drip after drip of dirty water into a neon yellow janitor's bucket, "so close to all that precious art, the marble and the relics. I couldn't figure out whether it meant people were being careless with such spectacular, beautiful things, or they were so used to being surrounded by them that they took it all for granted. It had been there so long. What was a little rain going to do?" Whenever she talks about that afternoon, those paintings, her focus drifts. Her tone becomes exasperatingly dreamy.

I've pushed her a few times, asked her what exactly it was she loved so much. Then, she turns evasive.

"Oh, I don't know if I could explain it," she'll say. "You're so much better than I am at putting those reactions into words anyway." For whatever reason, she always keeps it to herself.

Today it's bright and hot and sunny, no cloud that could even suggest rain. The church's vaulted ceiling is, as far as I can tell in the dark, intact. No scaffolding or signs of disrepair to be found.

Even after giving my eyes time to adjust, I need to squint to see details in the canvases, on walls and ceilings. Moments of light, when so much of it has been shut out, are startling: the bright white of skin, pale blue folds of a veil, a beam of brightness meant to serve as some divine message.

Tourists move through the outer sanctuary in packs, whispering. A woman follows a priest into confession, which, a sign tells me, is available in Italian and English. Spanish, too, but only on Fridays.

The Caravaggio is hard to miss, imposing even by Roman standards, in a little side chapel of its own. Paul's face is relaxed, receptive. The folds in his clothes, I can only describe them as voluptuous. Same as the muscles in his forearms and the lifted leg of his horse: coiled and perfectly tense. It's the kind of thing an artist could study only so much. At a certain point, he had to just know—how desperation could masquerade as openness, how outstretched palms might welcome a moment of ecstasy.

I look for similarities between this painting and my mother's. The darkness, that's obvious, but also these pressure points of warmth. Brightness that has no identifiable source, but still somehow illuminates. Whether it's Caravaggio's religious transformation or my mother's single blooming flower in a vase, the glow from within, to me, is the same.

But I'm just examining. Evaluating technique, observing the results. Whatever transcendent experience she had years ago is escaping me. I keep waiting to feel something more, sitting in a pew until a nun tells me the church is closing and watches until I leave.

A boy, maybe eight or nine years old, is crying on the church steps in a way I can tell is fake. He pauses, looks up at his parents' faces. Then, finding them insufficiently concerned, he takes a theatrical inhale to fuel the next high-pitched scream. I wonder if he'll end up getting what he wants, whatever that is.

In school, the human body haunted me. My whole first year, it seemed drawing people, in all their various flexibilities, was the only thing I could do reasonably well.

So, instead of branching out or trying to take on a new challenge, I settled into what was safe. Even during my winter and spring breaks, I spent afternoons at the Art Students League in life drawing classes, questioning every choice I made. The men with chewed-down fingernails. The woman with a long silver braid that hung down to the backs of her knees. How one model held a handstand for close to ten minutes, her curvature being pulled the wrong way by gravity—how to capture that? Was her neck really that long, or did I just want it to be? What if I exaggerated the curl of his toes or the valley of his spine?

I caught my own poses in mirrors. Forever trying to understand what people meant when they spoke about composition and space, how one gesture could be meaningful, another mundane.

I can't escape here either. Halfway up the steps to the Borghese gardens, I find myself at eye level with the sculpted woman who guards the piazza below. Her hand up, her fingers folded just so. I don't know who she's supposed to be, but there's no doubt she represents someone specific, a particular goddess or symbol, chosen with care. I'm sure the exact placement of her fingers is deliberate, meant to identify her, or translate whatever benediction she's offering.

In Rome, almost every piece of art I see has an assigned story behind it: a piece of mythology or religion or history or some combination. They're marked by agreed-upon details, meaningful to those who know. The Virgin Mary always wears blue. Saint Peter is seen with a book or holding a pair of keys. The angel Gabriel plays a trumpet. Those signals are everywhere, the looks and postures they accompany. Captured by artists who held tight to tradition and those eager to see what diversions they could get away with.

The figures I draw now, the ones I duplicate over and over to make money, are caricatures, nameless women. Types, not individuals. And I can't lie, I like that I'm able to hide behind them. I'm comforted by the lack of originality that surrounds me here, at least surrounding the female body. Everything is shown, or nothing is.

I can either spend weeks on a painting that actually means something to me, or sketch something in an afternoon that will pay my rent and barely register in my memory as anything other than popular. Maybe it's no different from the decision Caravaggio made between showing the full, traditional scene of Paul's conversion, as told in the Bible, or focusing on a moment instead. The former sinner, on his back, ready to be redeemed.

Maybe I was destined to feel and think this way, being the child of two artists. One of whom the world has embraced and enabled, the other a secret, even to herself. Once people learn who my father is, they tend to assume that the life I lead, any talent I have, is all preordained. And it never really occurred to me, when I was growing up, that I wouldn't be able to create and feel and act the way he did.

But that assurance didn't just arrive in my mind. It was placed there. Dad's always taken great pleasure in knowing and noticing the things I was better at, where he believed I'd surpassed him in the ways that mattered. Whenever people come to the house, he shows off my painting above their mantel like it's a stop on a museum tour. There are times, at a dinner table or sitting on their terrace, when I'll make a point in such a way that he sits back and nods and smiles, close to possessive. Though it's far from unconditional; he claims me when it suits him, when he likes what he hears or sees.

Still, he's always made me feel as if I'm full of promise, capable of anything. After all, he found and married the most beautiful, intelligent, indulgent woman he could. How could their daughter, their firstborn, not embody what was best in both of them?

My brother, and where all of this leaves him, has always been complicated. I wonder if he knows how much he's discussed and dissected when he's not around, which has become the rule instead of the exception.

"Jack's a leading man," Dad always says. Mom and I roll our eyes, as we do when he gets in one of his moods, starts speaking in riddles and stanzas. But we know it's true. And we know how Jack chooses to fight that, blending in, smiling neutrally, fading into the background.

I wait to meet John on Via Baccina, squinting into the light. It's just before sunset.

I'm standing near the fountain, as discussed, wearing a long silk dress that flows and clings exactly where it should. A green so dark it's almost black. It seemed ridiculous to bring it with me. Five nights of solo dinners, aperitivi at a table for one, maybe an introspective nightcap or two. And no one to dress up for except myself. What use would it have? But I rolled it carefully, tucked it in my suitcase the way I usually do, hung it in the bathroom when I arrived so any wrinkles would evaporate with the steam while I showered. The hem brushes the tops of my feet, a little burned from the sun.

I let my fingers rest on the insides of my wrists, where he held them tight this morning. Even now, with my feet firmly on the ground, I'm aware of the muscles that stretch the length of my legs, the way they shook just hours ago. An enveloping warmth, the sort I feel after a long run or a deep stretch. My body, as usual, serving as a reminder I can't ignore.

I'm slightly wary, standing here with nothing to distract me, looking so in need of his arrival. But waiting for him is what I'm doing, so I embrace it, even work to embody it further. I make a show of looking down each street that empties into the piazza. We'd said Via Baccina, by the fountain. He could be coming from anywhere.

But I didn't realize he'd arrive on a Vespa. We walked the twenty minutes back to his apartment last night, so I assumed there'd been no other option. He's easy to spot, even with the helmet on. His posture is that distinctive: the width of his shoulders, the way he holds himself.

He pulls up right in front of me, shakes his hair free from the helmet. It's obvious he loves the Vespa but isn't quite comfortable on it. His feet are flexed and gripping the ground on either side, one hand still on the brake, to steady himself.

"You look beautiful," he says, forcing me to fight back a smile. His eyes taking in the length of my dress, he asks, "But how's that going to work?"

I last wore this dress to a friend's wedding on the North Fork of Long Island. Michael was my date. We'd gone strawberry picking, then wine tasting in the afternoon. He turned quiet at the vineyard, either contemplative or bored.

The wedding was extravagant. A monstrosity of a tent, its poles camouflaged with flowering ivy, and a floor built to resemble hardwood. Flickering candles on every flat surface. A top-shelf bar, open all night. All of it benevolently ruled by a very thin wedding planner wearing a floral dress, sensible shoes, and an earpiece so small and shaded so close to her skin tone that it was almost impossible to see.

After the cocktail hour and before speeches from the bride's parents, a group of horses in a nearby field ran up the hill, hooves pounding in unison to everyone's buzzed wonder. Michael wondered out loud if the moment was choreographed.

I rested my head on his shoulder as we swayed to "Midnight Train to Georgia," singing along silently. *I'd rather live in his world than be without him in mine.* I felt safe in how true that line was for me, in that moment. Is it still?

People were talking about how expensive the band was. The groom had heard them at a friend's wedding in Virginia and wouldn't think of hiring anyone else. There were lighting cues and a tightly curated set list and a horn section like I'd never heard before. The lead singer's makeup stayed perfect all night, even as the stage lights revealed the sweat pooled at her hairline, running down her temples.

I gather the length of the dress and tie it into a knot above my knees, wrapping it around and through itself, the way I might a scarf. Pulling it tight. It almost looks like a considered, if dramatic, detail, there on purpose.

John leans back against the scooter to get a good look and nods his approval. "That'll do it." He hands me my own helmet and I climb on, as gracefully as I can. The jolt of the engine is a surprise, even though I'm expecting it. John's careful steering and gradual acceleration aren't.

We cross the Tiber and speed up the winding roads that lead to the crest of the Aventine. I'm clinging to him in the way that feels most natural, considering we've barely known each other for a full day. What crosses a line? What's just close enough? My hands on his waist or hips or shoulders? My breath on the back of his neck?

The houses here are built into the slope. Shades of yellow and orange and burnished brown. All of them behind high walls, locked doors. I can only see their tile roofs, second-story windows, flowering bougainvillea as it climbs. More expensive quiet.

John is comfortable here. The tension leaves his neck and shoulders. His grip loosens a bit. He leans into the turns and so do I.

We slow to a stop where the pavement levels off, in front of an unadorned church that looks more like a fortress.

He turns his head as the engine fades, his voice so clear after all the noise and speed. "Thought we could take a walk first," he says. "Have you been up here before?"

There's a line of people to my left, waiting to look at Saint Peter's through the keyhole of a locked garden door. I remember doing that, waiting and watching, but none of what surrounds me now feels familiar. Did I really see the basilica, perfectly centered, through the door, or have I just heard about it secondhand, seen photos, and kept the image for myself? Did my parents bring Jack and me up here, stand in line with us, convince us it was worth the walk and the time? Or did I make up a memory? I can't say for sure.

"I don't think so," I tell him. "Definitely not in here."

The gate to the church's courtyard is closed but not locked. He pushes it open just enough, then shuts it behind me. The church blocks the low sun, throwing the whole entryway into relative darkness. We're alone—everyone else is chasing the last bit of light, avoiding the shade. Under cover of this entrance, standing next to John as he studies the church's carved wooden doors, is the coldest I've been since I arrived in Rome.

Inside, the candles are arranged in tiers that remind me of seats in an amphitheater. Different lengths for different prices. A few of them are lit, close to the ends of their wicks. I consider lighting one or two of my own for someone I've forgotten, but I'm out of ideas. John leans over them for a moment, as if testing to see how much heat they're giving off.

There's wax on the floor. He scuffs it with his shoe, wanting to kick it free.

"Santa Sabina," he says in a low voice, even though we're the only people here, as far as I can tell. "There's a symmetry to it that I like."

I know what he means, in both the alliteration of the church's name and its long, simple nave, columns and arches mirroring each other on either side, leading to a simple altar. It's restrained and expansive, all at once.

I follow him to a hole carved out of the stone floor, nominally protected by a chain-link barrier. We look down. Whatever light typically illuminates the space is turned off, but John says it's left-over from what used to be a temple devoted to Juno, during the days of the Empire. My mother lingered on descriptions of Juno when she read to me from *Mythology*. The golden throne she sat on, how she protected women in childbirth, her fondness for pea-cocks, how devoted she was to revenge. Starting wars to punish a man who said another goddess was lovelier; brutalizing all the women her husband pursued. She never forgot a slight.

I search the dark, but can't see anything.

Santa Sabina was built in the fifth century, he tells me. Long enough ago for the priest who commissioned it to see the ruins of what he was replacing and, in this way, honor them.

The fountain guarding the entrance to the orange garden out-side looks like a mask. It's an old man's face: untamed beard, concerned brow, gaping mouth emptying into what looks like an always-overflowing bathtub. The stone that surrounds his forehead curls in, like the pages of a book left outside.

Once we're through, gravel crunching under our feet, a beagle trots in front of us, gnawing on an orange he's found under a tree. His owner sits on a bench nearby, leash in hand.

Tall stone pines line the path that cuts through the middle of the garden, like an aisle leading to the altar that is the lookout point. They're spaced symmetrically and curve toward each other, natu-rally or not, to offer shade. The garden culminates at a stone terrace, built into the crest of the hill: one of the best places to see the city.

The tops of buildings look dipped and dripping in gold. Clouds, turned peach by the sunset, cut streaks across the sky.

A teenage couple basks in the light, against the stone railing that's been chipped away and carved with initials and dates. She can't be more than sixteen; he looks a little older. A sad attempt at facial hair, a tight black T-shirt. But it's her I watch, the way she leans back, eyes closed, letting the last of the sun hit her, turning her head away from his attempts to touch her cheek. Knowing he'll still keep trying. The sparse knit of her shirt, the precise stack of her bracelets, the music they make.

This thought passes through me sometimes. Maybe it's more of a lament, a pointless one. The fact that I'll never have a different childhood, different parents, a different perspective. I'll never truly see the world any differently than I do now, the way I've learned and taught myself to see it. My gaze, my instincts, what I value and pay attention to will never truly change.

It confronts me through details, like the exact cursive handwriting all French people seem to have—the same on bistro menus and the handwritten sign explaining why the park is closed. Children must learn to write that way in every French school, and even if I tried to change my own script to match it now, I'd probably never learn. Or the jewelry this girl is wearing, the effort she's made in balancing its proportions. Her necklace is delicate and unassuming to allow for flashier, dangling earrings. Maybe her mother still buys her clothes for her, at one of the markets, cheaper than she'd like. Maybe she longs for more.

What matters to this girl—her mother's nagging, her father's indifference, the way she likes her boyfriend because he lets her get away with anything, the flutter she gets in the back of her throat when she sees the last of the light dance on the surface of the water— will never matter to me, not in anywhere near the same way.

We move to the side to avoid the worst of the crowds, and I need to crane my neck to get the full view. There's a stillness here, the kind I associate with being at the beach at the end of the day. That same lull, a collective pause, touched with exhaustion. A sigh to acknowledge all the energy the sun and sea have taken from us before we pack our things and leave. Sandy feet, tired steps, salty hair and skin.

As an experiment, I take this, one of the moments I usually keep for myself, and share it.

"It's kind of sad, isn't it?" I ask. "That we'll never see the world the way a Roman does. Or an Italian. Or a Brit or a Swede. Or even someone from LA or Arizona. We're stuck in the way we were brought up, what we've been reinforced to notice."

John nods slowly, looking out at the city. "It's bittersweet, to me. The fact that we can only be one thing." He's quieter than before. Or is this who he really is? Was yesterday the departure from character?

"Maybe that's why I tried to teach myself Italian in a month and a half, because I knew I'd feel this way, being here. It seems, sometimes, like it could maybe be that simple, adapting identity, with enough time and motivation. Especially when I see other non-native speakers do it. You do it so seamlessly." I pause. He's listening, but looking past me, into the quickly fading light. "But what else is it, even beyond language? There's so much, all those little things you don't even notice about belonging somewhere. That are locked and irreversible and impossible to change. You can change your life, but only to a point."

He's quiet.

"But I'll come back," I continue, hoping to pull a response out of him. "I'll see this city again."

"It won't be the same, though," he tells me. "Neither will you."

"That's true."

"It's funny you say that, that 'you can change your life, but only to a point.'" Turning my words over in his hands. "There are things, you know, things you can't escape or leave behind, no matter where you move or what language you speak."

"Of course not. I didn't mean to suggest..."

"To a point," he repeats it, as an invitation.

"What's that point, for you?"

He puts his weight in his elbows, leans forward to look down toward the river. "My son dying." His words are level, even.

My throat constricts immediately. My first feeling is one of surprise, but that makes no sense. What right do I have to be surprised by him? I didn't sense weight, no deep sadness, but why would I? There was nothing to compare him to, nothing to warn me.

So many questions flood their way through me: How could something like that happen? Was it an illness or an accident? How long did he live? What has this done to you? They all push against my tongue, wanting to be asked, but I stay silent. Maybe it's only a few seconds that pass, empty and heavy, but the pause seems endless.

"I'm so sorry. I have no idea of what to say."

"You've never lost someone?"

I shake my head no. "Not someone close. Or young."

"You're lucky."

"Yes."

I've wanted to read minds before, but not like this. I want to infiltrate him, understand exactly what he wants from me, and give it to him.

I'm about to ask, as carefully as I can, what happened, when he starts to tell me. How his son Henry died at six months from a very rare, very cruel brain disease that he'd had since birth. How the marriage couldn't survive it. How something like that, something unimaginable, either binds you to one another or makes life together impossible. How they had nothing left to give.

"So that's what brought me here. I couldn't stay in New York. None of it made sense anymore." He sounds exhausted by his own history. "Not that what I'm doing now makes sense to anyone at home."

We walk the perimeter of the garden, slowly. It feels like turning a light off, putting the view behind me. John looks down at the pebbles he's displacing with every step. He's only a few years older than I am, but life has been so much kinder and uglier to him. Finding a person who thinks you're good and kind and safe enough to align their life with yours, maybe forever. Feeling secure in that bond, fully accepted and understood, and later realizing how fragile it actually was. Becoming a parent, with all its joy and terror. Being filled with that indescribable, all-consuming love, having it ripped away.

"I'm sorry. This is a lot to tell you, I know." He pauses where the path curves toward the exit, out past the church. The dog is lying under a tree now, still chewing on his orange. "Something about what you said. Or the way you said it, maybe."

"I'm glad you feel you can. Tell me."

We turn the corner. I can see the Vespa, leaning where we left it. "You can think you've accepted something," he says. "You can feel safe and be sure of that feeling. Permanence." He speaks so softly, like whatever he's saying is illicit or dangerous. "Then everything under your feet just shifts. And suddenly you're sideways, unmoored. I'm not sure how else to explain it."

I try to place John in New York. Living near Union Square, walking to his immaculate, airy office in the morning, a scarf wrapped around his neck three times in the winter. Probably a well-curated social life, dinners with certain couple friends on certain nights. Summer weekends spent out east at the house they either own or rent religiously every May through Labor Day. A careful equilibrium, a happy life. Until it wasn't. "What made you feel leaving, coming here, was better than staying?"

He thinks about this for a moment, knowing what to say but determining how to say it. "Something senseless and tragic can make people mean," he says. "I think it has something to do with the randomness of it, like your suffering could be contagious." He shakes his wrist so his watch slides closer to his palm. "People are afraid of their own powerlessness, of course. How little we comprehend."

He tells me how connecting with other bereaved (he hates that word, but uses it anyway) parents helped at first (they're the only ones who really understand), and then didn't.

"Rome has always been open and kind to me. That's how I remembered it, so it made a certain sort of sense at the time. It's also not a bad place to disappear."

"Absolution maybe? A fresh start?"

"There is no fresh start." His response is immediate and I'm worried I've said something offensive, but then he softens a little. "But I appreciate the optimism."

I laugh, relieved. "Sure, anytime."

"I like that about you," he says.

"What?"

"How you see the world, or how you talk about seeing it." He's gauging my reaction. "You're always thinking, considering, trying to make sense of things. It's obvious, even when you think you're hiding it so well. Makes me feel calm for some reason."

"Really? That calms you?" I would never think someone could find peace in how I do just about anything.

"It does, oddly enough." He sounds just as surprised as I am. "And I think you might be an optimist, in spite of yourself. You want to be."

"An optimist?" I smile at him, give one of the Vespa's tires a little kick for emphasis. "I wouldn't be so sure."

A few years ago, my parents spent another summer on Hydra. I joined for two weeks. Jack could only spare four days.

Our schedule revolved around the sun: when it grew bright enough to wake us up, how strong it was on which side of the island, which terraces it shone on during lunch, where we could get the most light into the evening. One afternoon, for old times' sake, we hired a boat and sailed to the cove where my parents met. Jack perfected his flip off the side. My mother still had command of her swan dive.

Most nights, we went out for dinner, spending long stretches of time at tables in different tavernas, ordering food and wine in spurts, as the mood struck. Eggplant and potatoes and oiled cucumber and blocks of feta served with still-hot pita. Shredded chicken and beef and so much lamb. Everything doused in oregano and lemon juice. Wine in a never-ending parade of copper pitchers.

The nerves I always feel whenever Jack and Dad are at the same table at the same time started to fade. Both of them brought their guitars and played together in the lull between sunset and whenever we left for dinner. Locals recognized or pretended to remember my parents, toasted to their health and their love and the family they'd made.

Even though we were on the water, the nights in that house were hot. I slept fitfully with the thin sheets twisted around my legs, a pillow over my head to block out the morning noise. We kept all the windows open, all the time, encouraging the air to move. Late at night, Jack and I talked through the open door between our rooms, maybe the longest conversations we've had since we were children.

"He's so mellow all of a sudden," Jack said.

"I know, it's a little surprising."

"Makes him almost fun to be around."

I had to laugh at that.

"But seriously. When did he get so old?" Jack asked me, as if I actually had the answer. "It's been happening, obviously. But it seems sudden to me."

"Of course it does. You're hardly ever around." I wanted to tell him that he wasn't just selfish, but wrong, too. I lay there silent instead.

On Jack's last night, he said he was tired of going out, wanted to stay in. So we did our best to recreate the kind of meal Mom would make at home, in her own kitchen. We bought whole fish, stuffed them with lemon and garlic and olives, roasted them in the rented oven. I chopped cucumbers and crushed feta with my fingers. Mom barely had to touch the tomatoes with a knife, they were so ripe. A salad of local lettuce and herbs, dressing of olive oil and mustard and pepper, tossed with bare, clean hands. It always surprises me, how adaptable she can be when the situation calls.

Dad and Jack toasted us, even clapped a little when we brought the roast fish to the table. They did look beautiful, charred in just the right way.

Jack caught a drop of condensation with his finger before it dropped from his wine glass to the table. He was in charge of the dinner music. I looked out at the calm water, listening to some obscure cover of "You Can't Always Get What You Want." None of the swagger, all of the resignation.

Mom tipped her head the way she does when she needs a moment to consider something, fully concentrate. "This is a little morose, though. Don't you think, honey?"

"It's true," Dad said. "I'll never understand your obsession with covers, Jack. A copy is so rarely better than the original."

Jack said nothing, had no reaction at all, which I found admirable. Especially when it would have been so easy to remind Dad of the fact that covers of his songs had been paying his bills, and then some, for decades.

"Whenever I hear this song, the original version," I said, "I always remember listening to it while looking out the bus window, passing Madison Square Park. It's strange—I know I've heard it hundreds of times, but somehow that's the image that sticks."

"I can't believe you take the bus," Jack said, grinning.

"Me and all the other little old ladies, just trying to get from A to B," I replied, before genially flipping him off.

Mom exhaled loudly through closed lips, in that French way she has. "Emilia, you're not old, my God. Bite your tongue."

After dinner, wine turned to ouzo. Dad and I climbed up to the roof, which wasn't much more than swept-clean stone, two wooden chairs, and a pot containing a long-dead plant, fried by the sun. We were, obviously, without the expensive, comprehensive stereo system he was used to at home. So I taught him how to angle his phone in an empty water glass to amplify the sound: a bit of ingenuity he found delightful.

He played "Out on the Weekend," loud, and the two of us sang to match it, fighting the breeze that tried to mute our voices. *The woman I'm thinking of, she loved me all up.*

The sky was impossibly big and black and pricked with stars. Water lapping at the sand in the little cove below. He danced around, in his always-controlled sway, a glass of cloudy booze in his hand.

I remember thinking, as I watched, *Is he being natural onstage, rehearsed when he's with just us?*

That night, I nodded my head to the guitar, laughed at Neil Young's harmonica, knowing Dad wanted me to. Mom and Jack were washing the dinner dishes downstairs, their muffled conversation drifting up through the windows we wouldn't close. Jack speaking to her in French, in a tone I recognized: light, at ease, almost conspiratorial. The way you talk with someone you trust.

"Do you remember the first time you were stung by a bee?" Dad asked me. It might seem like a non sequitur, but that's not too unusual in conversations with him. You can't be misled by it, though. He always knows where he's going.

"No, I don't think so."

"You were four, maybe five years old. Running around the yard the way you did, telling yourself a story, making up some kind of world we couldn't see." Even in the dark, I could tell his eyes were going soft. "Anyway, you were running, with your arms spread out like airplane wings, and a bee stung you, right in your armpit." He winced a little at the memory.

"Ouch. How do I not remember this?"

He waved that off, not unkindly. "Who knows what we remember from childhood and why?" What was important was his memory, not my lack of one. "You cried a little, of course, but you were more shocked than anything else. It was that that upset you, much more than any pain. After maybe a minute or two, you were out there playing again, as if nothing had happened."

A wisp of the afternoon came back to me then. And he wasn't wrong: it was a surprise, to be found out and hurt in such a vulnerable place, with no warning. Other moments, too: Mom pulling the stinger out in one smooth second, telling me that bees die once they sting you, and that meant I was safe.

"I remember watching you and thinking, *She'll be fine, whatever life throws her way.*" He leaned back to get a fuller look at the sky. "I found it so exceptionally *comforting.* That, even at five, you could see past temporary bullshit. You know what matters."

"You think so?"

"Without a doubt."

People wonder what it's like to be his daughter: to be constantly in his orbit, to understand the intricacies of his moods, to know the meanings behind lyrics and titles and clothing choices, to know he loved me all the time.

And they're not wrong to be curious, or even assume that being so bound to him might be magic. Sometimes it is.

Yes, I grew up in a house that was filled with music almost

always. There were fresh flowers and good artwork and expensive instruments in almost every room. People with the kinds of bold-faced names you'd expect visited often, joined us on our vacations and we on theirs, sent cards and presents all year long, served as godparents. I feel comfortable, if not at home in foreign places. I speak a second language fluently. My parents did and still do know how to throw an excellent party. But much of the glamour and ease that used to be there has shifted; the energy that fueled it may have dimmed, if not gone out.

Dad is at his best when he feels "awake, creative, and alive." His words. For some musicians, that means time spent alone to write and play songs, away from the real world and other people and outside influence. Dad always wanted the opposite; he craved and craves connection. Especially with age—the way hours of sunlight become much more precious in winter.

When I was growing up, there were journalists from *Rolling Stone* or the *Village Voice* or the Arts section of the *New York Times* at our dinner table, hanging on Dad's every word. Their questions were predictable: asking for details about the set at the festival in Montreal that launched his career and what it was like to play the Isle of Wight that summer and always the same fascination with that rare musician who'd managed to grow older creatively and productively.

They sometimes paid attention to my mother, rarely to Jack and me. If they did, it was transparent—a ploy to show Dad they cared about him beyond the songwriting and the legendary shows. As a full person, a family man.

With time, he's grown more sentimental. Which means he's let more people in.

The pilgrimages, as we came to call them, started maybe ten years ago. As soon as the weather turned warm, groups of people (mostly men, mostly in their early twenties, but not always) would start to gather in town, eventually making their way down the back roads, into the woods, and to our front door. They were always jumpy, somewhat apologetic for the trespassing, and full of expectation, as if they were going to see some kind of mystic or preacher. But unlike Salinger in his New Hampshire bunker, Dad welcomed them.

He spoke to them about the difference between poetry and song, how something can lie gracefully on the page or in the throat. They took notes and asked him for advice: Should they marry their lover, take back the person who wronged them, pursue their dreams of writing or singing or both? How to stave off the depression and regret and fear they feel? I think he liked sending each group down different paths, wielding the power they gave him.

I've wondered if he's ever wanted to be a better man: a truer, more content one. Maybe that was him trying.

Jack has never been under our father's spell, but even he's had moments caught in that current of charisma or love or whatever it is. Whenever that happens, he retreats, confused and feeling betrayed by himself. Which, I have to imagine, is an especially horrible breed of loneliness.

My parents didn't really go to Hydra that summer to show their children where it all started or commemorate their time together, though that's what they told people, and maybe each other.

The truth is, my mother wanted to put a stop to it. No more offering iced tea and shade and polite smiles to his acolytes. No more watching them sit at his feet, asking questions and waiting with rapt attention for his answers. The pilgrimages were that rare, tangible thing—a presence she could see and grasp and banish, without question or doubt. Dad, as he does so often now, just went along, followed where she led.

John's Vespa is deep navy, a hint of shimmer in the paint. It's the color I focus on, looking down instead of ahead at the traffic he's weaving through. The farther we go from the city center, on to what I assume is a highway, the less my surroundings look like a preserved European capital, and more like the wide stretch of asphalt that connects Midtown Manhattan with northern New Jersey. The only real differences are the font on the signage and the size of the cars that speed past us, as I try to hold tight to John without making it clear that I'm terrified. When I do look up, I see the trees that line the road are full—all that shade deepening into vivid shadows, blues and greens becoming purple, then black.

We stop at what I can only describe as the Italian version of a strip mall. A series of storefronts barely off the main road, separated from traffic by a row of stout hedges. A neon sign announcing the restaurant I assume is our destination. There's no way this place was ever on Michael's list.

I only notice the embossed flag above the Vespa's taillight, a she-wolf with two figures kneeling beneath her, when I climb off, legs still shaking.

"You're a Roma fan?" I ask him. "I guess that's a given, right? Living here?"

He smiles and shrugs. "Not really. I wish I could take credit for that."

"You're not? I thought being obsessed with soccer was a requirement for living in Europe." I act shocked to cover my amazement
that I've arrived in one piece. "If you want to have a social life,
anyway."

"It helped in the beginning, definitely. Watching the matches,
learning the chants and the songs, getting a little invested. But any
enthusiasm, I was mostly faking." He brushes dirt off the side of
his shoe. "To be honest, I bought the scooter off a neighbor. It still
feels like something I'm trying on."

I could lie and tell him he's a natural, but I smile at the thought
of his nervous driving, and don't. "Well, it definitely gives the air
of legitimacy."

"I thought about covering it with something else, some other flag
or symbol I cared enough about. And then, when I couldn't think
of anything better, just painting over it seemed too boring."

"I like it," I tell him.

"Me too. I'm doing as the Romans do."

I roll my eyes at that, and in this moment, my mock annoyance
at his pun and his satisfaction in making me laugh, the speed and
intensity of whatever this is, feels close to miraculous.

We turn toward the restaurant's terrace, crowded with families
finishing early dinners. His hand placed gently on the center of
my back, guiding me, a sign of the type of chivalry my mother
taught Jack to practice and me to look for. Like standing up when
a woman joins or leaves the table. Or always walking on the part
of the sidewalk that is closer to the street.

As first impressions go, the place isn't much to look at. White
walls and tablecloths, a low ceiling, black metal chairs you could
find in any office park, generic light from wall sconces that are

supposed to suggest warmth, but don't. Any full view I'd get of the room is blocked by thick white columns, spaced haphazardly. The only detail that suggests any real personality is the variety of water glasses. Each one a deep shade of a different color, dotting tables with pops of eggplant purple, emerald green, the yellow of a dandelion.

I've been noticing this, how a Roman restaurant's focus is on food and comfort and connection, rarely on ambience, the way it is at home. That need to create a particular kind of environment, obsessing over the spacing of candles or the height of a chair or the art on the walls. In hopes that all of it will wordlessly communicate something inviting or universal.

A man who looks my dad's age bursts through the swinging kitchen doors and shouts John's name. He's wearing a full navy suit, an expensive watch. His hair is long enough to curl at the nape of his neck. It shines silver.

They grasp hands, hold one another by the shoulder.

"Emilia, this is my friend Tommaso. He owns the place." John's hand on my back again, in the same neutral place. "Tommaso, Emilia."

Tommaso takes both my palms in his and kisses me on the cheek. His tan is that Italian shade of terra-cotta, and he smells of a just-smoked cigarette. "A joy to meet you." The lines around his eyes remind me of an orange peel forgotten in the sun, hardened but vibrant still.

How often does John come here? The closeness between them seems cumulative, hard-won. Though it's not easy to make assumptions based on how people greet and react to one another in this city. It seems you could meet an Italian twice and be greeted like an old, trusted friend the third time. That degree of kindness and hospitality could be deceptive, I imagine. How do you determine when you actually know someone, when you've crossed the divide between casual acquaintance and actual friend?

I wonder if John has been misled like that since moving here, starting a new life while healing, thinking he was making progress and finding a safe haven when he wasn't.

"Here," John tells me in a low voice, while Tommaso scans the room for the appropriate table, "if a restaurant looks like it belongs in New York, that's usually a sign of trouble."

We sit near the door, close enough to have a view of the patio, the ivy drifting down from the arbor above it, while also benefiting from the air-conditioning.

"How are you, my friend?" John asks, settling in, feeling at home. "How's tricks?"

"Well, I could complain, but you know what they say." I can hear the rough skin of Tommaso's hand as it runs over his hair, the beginnings of a bald spot. He stands behind a chair, leaning against it for a few moments, then sits down. "If everyone on earth threw their troubles in a pile, I'd want mine back."

While they talk, I flip through the wine list, which is more of an encyclopedia, organized by region. Some bottles have been crossed out with a felt-tip marker. Others are annotated by different sets of handwriting, words I don't understand.

But there's no need to look at the list at all. I've barely turned the page from white to red before three short, fat wine glasses appear, placed with force against the tablecloth, which muffles the sound. A waiter stands between John and Tommaso, opening a bottle still dripping from the ice bucket. It's white wine made in Abruzzo, a hand-drawn, smiling sheep on the label. Sharp, salty, a little rotten in the back of my throat.

Just like the wine, food starts to appear. Fritti misti, spread out over four plates. Crisp cod fillets, cut to bite-size pieces. Anchovies fried to barely more than a crunch. Baby squid with curled legs and squash blossoms wrapped in basil, overflowing with ricotta. Lamb brains, creamy underneath the crust. All served in overflowing paper cones the color of saffron. John rains lemon juice down from the wedge in his hand. Burrata so fresh it spills open and floods the plate, dotted with roasted tomatoes, their oil bleeding fiery orange. Basil snipped thin with scissors.

At the table next to ours, a boy contemplates a chessboard. The portable kind, pawns and bishops and knights with magnets on the bottom, brought along to occupy him through dinner. He's the only child at the table, playing a match against his dad, who pauses the conversation between what seems to be himself, his wife, his sister, and her husband, takes a sip of water or wine, and then makes his move.

Tommaso is charmed by the fact that John and I are both New Yorkers, or, in John's case, used to be.

John nods. "I think we were actually neighbors at one point."

"That's true." I bite into a squash blossom, which promptly falls apart in my fingers. "Mere blocks away."

Tommaso asks me how I'm finding the city, as if it's a car I've decided to test drive. A question so ridiculous I have to laugh a little.

"It's very calming, to be here," I answer. "I'm feeling peaceful, happy."

"Only someone from New York could find it calming to be here.

John is the same," Tommaso laughs. "For real peace, you have to leave the city. That's what we do."

I reach for more wine, wonder who's deserted all those grand, empty palazzos I've been seeing, where they've fled. "So, where do you escape to, Tommaso? Where do you find peace?"

He takes the bottle from me, fills my glass. "My country house, of course. My family has been there for a month already. My wife, our two daughters, their husbands, their kids." It must be the same in every culture, this desire to convey our life's abundance and good fortune as a pleasant sort of burden. And always with a self-deprecating lilt. "I'm making it sound much grander than it is. John knows all about it. Much more than he probably ever wanted to."

I watch John's face while Tommaso talks about the dynamics between his children and their spouses, the nonstop energy of grandchildren: how they run through the garden, build forts in their bedroom, splash so much water out of the pool. John seems to have no reaction beyond a neutral smile as he reaches for a squid and navigates burrata and tomato onto a ripped-off piece of bread.

But should he have one? Why should he fall to pieces every time he sees or hears about a child? Why assume he's that fragile?

"But yes, John has been there many times, knows the house very well by now," Tommaso says, finding his way back to his original thought. "All the insides and outsides. It's very temperamental, my house. Very old but very beautiful."

"Just like you," John teases.

"You're helping him with his house?" I ask.

"It's a beautiful place, just outside Todi, in Umbria." John describes the stone farmhouse, in Tommaso's family for generations:

its sloping, Spanish-style roof; windows carved by hand; cool, clean-swept floors paved with locally handmade tiles; thick wood beams supporting the ceilings; mulberry trees that mark the entrance; olive groves that surround it on all sides. His voice grows a little louder, his eyes focused, hands waving, describing arches and staircases and fireplaces and a veranda that he and Tommaso know to be real and I can only imagine.

"There was an addition, then repairs, which turned into more changes," Tommaso says. "But it's worth it, to make it perfect. It is my favorite place." He puts his hand over his heart, swirls the wine with the other. "And John knows everything. He's helping me keep it that way."

"A little pro bono work," John leans over and tells me.

"Pro bono? I wish," Tommaso says with a laugh. "No money, maybe, but plenty of food and wine. Emilia, don't let him fool you. This man's no saint."

"Don't worry about me," I say. "I have an instinct for those sorts of things." If they only knew what a joke that was.

"Emilia's an artist," John tells Tommaso.

I feel it in my throat, the urge to qualify that statement somehow. Some favorite ways: "Well, kind of," or "Depends how you define artist," or "Only in small corners of the internet." But I let it stand alone this time, along with the hint of pride in John's voice. It feels undeniably good, but also makes me wonder, what kind of person lets someone else in this easily?

"Then you must give us some pro bono work as well." Tommaso waves a waiter over. He gives me a sheet of paper and a few of the crayons they reserve for children. "Try to make me look respectable, if you can."

I almost make some comment about having to sing for my supper, but study Tommaso's nose and chin and earlobes instead, assigning different colors to different parts of his face. "Like your water glasses," I tell him. He can feel me watching, raises one eyebrow before telling John he should look for a house of his own.

"Home is a funny idea," John says. "Changeable. We end up having so many different kinds, the older we get—with parents, with wives, with children."

"And once you move on to a new sort of home, the one before is gone," I add.

"If you're lucky enough to have all these homes in one life," says Tommaso.

I sneak a look at John. Does this upset him?

I try to change the subject, or at least divert it, maybe more for my own comfort than his. "I love my parents' house, but maybe I only love my version of it, as I like to remember it: the sky flushed pink in the mornings and evenings, woodsmoke thick enough to smell." The hillside leading to the front door would be especially beautiful now, washed in the bright chartreuse of summer. "I don't know if the house and the way I've felt when I'm there have ever actually lived up to how I think of it when I'm away."

"Maybe we all imagine what we think we deserve. We see the best in our parents and what they've done for us, convince ourselves that a home like that is possible." John's voice has gone a little dreamy. "It's inspiration, for when you set out on your own."

"And to make a new life, like John has done. This takes courage." Tommaso leans forward, turning serious. "To go away from the darkness, toward the light. Don't you think so?"

"Admirable," I say, putting my hand on John's arm under the

table. Hoping this will be enough to satisfy Tommaso, or at least put him off for a little while.

Tommaso pretends he wants to know me, but he doesn't really. I've learned what it looks like when a man is actually interested in what I'm saying. He's showing me this translucent courtesy out of respect for John, some condition of their friendship that dictates whoever he finds captivating enough to bring around must be worthy of conversation.

The table is suddenly crowded with three trough-like bowls, narrow and deep and full of bucatini all'amatriciana and tonnarelli cacio e pepe and rigatoni carbonara. Men are standing behind us, grating pecorino and Parmesan; cheese rains down in a thick, uniform stream.

"*Ecco a lei come richiesto,*" the waiter says, before he walks away.

"Yes, this is something very important I learned from Tommaso," John explains, his voice close in my ear. "That pasta should always be cooked *al chiodo.*" He lifts a tangle of the cacio e pepe onto my plate, steam rising. "It means hard as an iron nail, a little less done than al dente. Cooked the rest of the way with pasta water and the residual heat. So there's a little bite."

Tommaso mimes a hammer hitting a nail as we start to negotiate the bowls of pasta in front of us. "It seemed only fair you should be eating well," he says with a wink in my direction, "after you kept my house from falling down." I wrap some of the bucatini around my fork, glistening with tomato and oil and fat and cheese. I taste spice and salt and hear a little crunch.

The wine turned from white to red without me noticing. *Dolcetto di Dogliani*, the label reads. "It's table wine, *vino della casa*, if you like," Tommaso says, "but very good still." Sunny and ripe and a little heavy on my tongue. After a swirl, I can still see a shadow of color on the side of the glass.

All the tables outside are full now. Tommaso leaves us to greet and tend to some more regulars who've just arrived, then gets pulled into the kitchen by one of his staff. It's a bit of a relief, to feel back in this new sort of equilibrium, sitting opposite John, trying to know him.

Tommaso keeps seating any new arrivals as close to us as he can, so we're surrounded by activity and attention. Energy seeming to radiate out from our little table.

Looking up, I can suddenly see all the ways the room has changed from day to night. The white walls and generic tables are made distinct now by different orders and outfits and voices. The garish wall sconces burn low like oil lamps.

We clean the bowls with bread, passing them back and forth so both of us can taste it all one more time. Each refusing to leave anything behind.

As soon as those plates disappear, there's oxtail braised with tomatoes and celery; fish with garlic, raisins, and pine nuts; spinach wilted with olive oil and lemon juice; fried lamb chops we eat with our hands, nibbling on them like rats.

The boy with the chess set, looking for a distraction while the adults finish their wine, smiles at our messiness. John gives him a little wave.

"Did it bother or upset you, when Tommaso brought up family?" I ask. "Or when you see parents with small children?" This is more direct than I'd ever think of being, but his openness seems to invite my questions. He might even be eager for them.

"Sometimes. But I don't want to stop living. Or be afraid of other people's happiness. That seems like barely any kind of life at all."

"How long ago did it happen?"

"Three years, which feels so long ago and also like no time at all. But it also feels like he's always with me, in some way. So I try to move forward, knowing that."

He pushes a piece of fish around the plate, leaving a trail of oil. "It burned away a lot of stuff that, ultimately, I never really cared about. For the rest of my life, I told myself, I'm not going to talk about or do anything that doesn't genuinely inspire me or anger me or make me afraid."

"So Tommaso's country house was a source of inspiration?"

"When I first saw the state it was in, that did scare me a little." He laughs. "But I loved it, too. Loved that it was a challenge. I'd never done anything like that before, reconstructing something. It was well built, but basically falling apart after years of neglect. So I helped him, negotiated with builders and stonemasons and glass purveyors in a foreign language, saw the whole thing come together. Knowing that if I fucked up, it would be such a huge loss for him and his whole family. It's a truly beautiful thing, a house like that. That contains so much, and continues to."

"Can you tell me what he was like, your son?" It's the simplest thing I can think to ask, while still hoping it's not a painful question.

He thinks for a few moments. "He was so little, so young, but he knew himself. Even then. Very sure about what he liked and what he didn't, from his favorite food to which book he wanted us to read to him at night. He made up his mind, quickly and absolutely." He tilts a knife so he can see his face in the silver, then mine. "The thing about him was, he caught your heart and held it."

It feels perverse, maybe even wrong, but I examine his face, sated and seemingly happy, and try to picture it grief-stricken, broken, without the bit of hope he seems to wear now. Three years is hardly any time at all, I imagine, when faced with the task of bringing yourself back to life. Rebuilding something fragile that could fall apart at any moment. And likely does, over and over.

He blessedly pushes the thought from my mind by spooning some tripe with tomato and mint onto my plate.

"I want to be adventurous enough to try it," I tell him, "but I'm just not."

"Oh, come on. It's *trippa alla romana*, food of kings! At least take a bite." I focus on the acid and pepper I'm tasting, not the mysterious sponge of the tripe, and swallow as quickly as possible.

When John leaves for the bathroom, Tommaso sits in his chair, so I'm not alone for even a moment. I pass the finished portrait, folded over once, to him across the table, as if we're negotiating a price.

He opens it, holding the paper away from his face and then up close. "This is very nice," he says. "I can see you're a good judge of character."

"I don't know about that, but I'm glad you like it."

"No, I can tell. You see people for what they are." He's insistent, so I let him have his way. "And you're kind, drawing my nose much straighter than it is. Not quite so big."

"Every artist should know how to be a flatterer," I tell him.

"John is a good man," he says abruptly. "It's easy to love him."

Maybe I've read Tommaso wrong, thinking this was indifference. It's possible I'm being assessed instead.

"From what I know, I have to agree," I say.

And then John's back, just as quickly. Our wine glasses and plates are swept away and replaced with short, sturdy highballs. A waiter shows us a bottle of amaro, the label blank except for a carefully drawn artichoke. He leaves it on the table.

We drink shallow pour after shallow pour, as if giving ourselves only a little at a time is some show of restraint. Again, I've lost any concept of how early or late it is. I refuse to look at my phone or John's watch to tell me.

He's a little drunk. His laughs at Tommaso's jokes have turned closer to giggles, like he can't control them or doesn't want to.

We should probably take the taxi Tommaso has offered to call for us, but we don't. Driving back, as we cross the Tiber and speed through Testaccio, I can tell, from the tilt of his head or the release in his shoulders or some other detail I can't quite name, that John is smiling.

"Your place makes me think of my mother's studio, a little," I tell John as I sit on the floor, leaning back against his mattress.

And it's true. The exposed beams, the slope of the ceiling, how John's drawings and prints are hung to look nonchalant, though it's clear how much thought they've been given. My mom made sure her studio inspired the same feeling, transforming an old barn on the property into a space that happened to perfectly fit her intentions. The way that money can honor what used to be there and make it unrecognizable at the same time.

There are obvious differences, though. Her space was gutted and remade in her precise image, not pieced together from a top-floor rental studio in a quiet, residential part of Rome. Her walls are full, using every inch of space all the way up to the ceiling.

His are spare, frames separated just so. He's considered size and color, the proportions of a painting as they relate to the angle of a chair. Two wildly different rooms; attention is the only thing that unites them.

"What's she like, your mom?" He lowers himself down beside me, ignoring the couch and nearby chair. Aside from a weak lightbulb in the kitchen, we're sitting in darkness. Our eyes adjust. I can see the outlines of rooftops, the night as other people are spending it.

"She's quiet, but not in a passive way. Maybe she's leaned on that, to balance out my dad. But it's clear she's always thinking, definitely has opinions about basically everything. She's talented, kind, still beautiful, a good friend, good listener. I guess you could say long-suffering." I laugh like it's a joke.

"Do the two of you get along?"

I shrug. "Mostly we do. She can be very hard to live up to, sometimes. It's hard for me to know if she thinks I'm making the right choices, living the right kind of life." I listen to my own words. The right kind of life. What is that, for her? It's not what she's chosen, what she's accepted. That's a safe life, a known life, a life that's an argument she ultimately wins, every time.

"She's an artist, too," I tell him.

"Like you?"

I shake my head. "No, much more exact, technical, secretive. She never sells or shares what she paints with anyone."

"Do you think she wants to, or wishes she could?"

"I don't know." And I actually don't. I've never really asked, just wondered at why.

He doesn't ask me to clarify, just nods. I endure a few moments of the discomfort I always feel when I've talked about myself too long, when too much time has passed since I've deflected the momentum of a conversation.

We look out the open French doors, past the balcony, to the dip of the river and the Vatican in the distance. He's drinking gulps of water from a glass bottle, picking a song on his phone that starts to play from a speaker, the type designed to hide in plain sight. Any thought I try to isolate or put words to is vague and fleeting, my head just short of aching from the wine. I am waiting for him to touch me.

"It's amazing to me, how so much is still standing." Michael would give me shit for saying something like that. Too sentimental, too naïve. Not to mention, does it *really* amaze me? But John murmurs in agreement.

"I find it kind of heartening. People adapt, sure, but history here will be preserved, built around, allowed for, always," he says. "If something is considered old and valuable and beautiful enough."

"Right, but who's doing the considering? How does one villa become a public museum and another is locked away, so you can only see it if you know the right person? Is one more valuable? How are people even supposed to know, if so much of it is hidden?"

Why am I trying to poke holes in what he thinks? Kicking at the surface of still water, just because it's calm?

"Like the locked door to that garden on the Aventine," I continue, "with all those people lining up to look through the keyhole. Why not just let them in?"

He gives me a smile that's just short of dismissive. "For the same reason that's always been true. Some people have those keys, others don't even know they exist. It's not right or fair." He wipes away water that's pooled in the corner of his mouth. "Having the father you have, you must know that better than most. There are privileges, deserved or not."

Yes, I want to tell him, but more often than not, you have to pay for that privilege.

I ask another question instead. "What do you think has made you stay?"

"It's okay for me to just exist here. Not like at home." He tips his head back, cradled by the cushion of the mattress. "There isn't that insistence on getting better, on continuous growth and improvement. I don't miss it."

"I can see how that would help. There's so much beauty and ugliness here, so much history. Maybe it's nice, how straightforward that is." It's a challenge, ignoring his weakness or pain or whatever it is that makes him say things like that, navigating this part of him I'll never fully understand—but it's invigorating, too.

He shrugs. "I'm not trying to be whole. There's no one I'd care to convince of that anyway. It's a reality. Why should I lie?"

"You shouldn't."

"But it's probably more hopeful than I'm making it seem," he says. "There's ruin, a lot of it, but there's life, too."

John has lit a candle near the window. I see the flame's reflection in the glass.

Its scent, a masculine take on orange blossom and jasmine, is already in the air. Maybe it was burning while he was getting ready to meet me, hastily blown out as he reached for his keys, checked the mirror one last time.

The bed has been made since I left it this morning, the pillows punched back to life.

It's hard to tell if my being here, my ease and comfort around him, is real, or just a reflection of his openness or kindness or pain. Is it possible for a choice to be deliberate and also involuntary?

"There is one song of your dad's that I love."

"Let me guess." I take the phone from his hand, turn the screen so he can't see what I'm doing, find "Chaos" on a short list of "Most Popular" titles under Dad's name, and press Play.

"Am I that predictable?"

"It is a crowd pleaser," I admit. Then, taking a risk, "And it's a little sentimental, so I can understand why it resonates."

"What's that supposed to mean?" he asks, in such a way that I know he doesn't need an answer, putting his hand over his heart to signify he's not insulted. It's funny, how some men like to be teased and others don't. Or how one man can want both, how it changes with his mood or circumstances.

I try for a few moments to listen to the song for what it simply is, just music and lyrics, as if I haven't heard it a thousand times before. Dad's voice is deep and a little scratchy. He navigates the familiar melody with the caution that comes with age. "I haven't heard this version in a while." My voice sounds far off. "Usually it's the original recording that people play."

"How old was he when he recorded this?" John asks. "The original, I mean."

"Thirty-four, I think. Maybe thirty-five."

John leans back, maybe remembering himself at that age, just a few years ago. What mattered to him then, what still lay ahead. Was his son still alive? Were they expecting him then?

He rests two of his fingers against the curve of my knee, plays with the knot I've tied in my dress, and I breathe out, grateful, wondering how to shift or otherwise wordlessly tell him not to stop.

"I wrote this chorus, you know." Another risk. A bigger one.

He looks up toward the ceiling, interrogating the air as if it actually holds the song itself, my father's voice. "What do you mean? This song is from the nineties, maybe earlier."

"Nineteen ninety-two, to be exact."

"So you were, what, seven years old?"

"About that, yes."

"How did that even happen?" John asks, but not in the light, curious way people usually do. The few people I've actually told about this. The ones who act like it's kindness, a paternal gesture, maybe even sweet.

I give him the short version, while making little allowances for my dad, though I'm not sure why. How he saw and sees my words as inspiration, the tenderness in his voice when he dedicates the song to me onstage.

"I know it's not a question of whether or not it bothers you, but how much."

"What makes you so sure? How could you be?" My tone turns immediately, instinctually shrill. I try to smother it back to normal, a deep breath. "Maybe I think it's an honor, the fact that I could contribute to his legacy like that." Am I just testing John, or does a small, mostly hidden part of me actually believe that? Either way, the words feel like vomit, painful and involuntary.

"Because you're not a doormat. This is a story you're telling me. I don't think it's true." I give him silence in response, but he continues. "He's still in your life, so it must not be too much for you to handle. Or you've found a way to deal with it."

"With what, exactly?"

"That kind of disregard, or callousness, or ego. I don't even know what to call it, to be honest." I can almost taste the disgust in his voice.

And how does that work? I want to ask. How does he think I do that kind of mental arithmetic? What I'm willing to tolerate, how much I can reasonably swallow. At what point do you decide, even though you've dealt with, even accepted something for most of your life, that it's no longer possible?

"To have your own creativity, something pure, taken from you like that, when you're just beginning to understand it. Has he ever apologized?"

I shake my head, trying to be as calm as he is incensed. "I don't think he's ever really seen a reason to."

"And for all these years, he just keeps on singing your song." I can't tell if his sympathetic anger has turned to tenderness or pity or both. And why, exactly? Given the loss he's had to live with, is he looking for someone, anyone, to save?

"Well, it's not really my song." I say the words not because I think they're true, but because hearing John call it my song is enough to make me wince with guilt or bury my face in his chest or cry with rage. None of which I'll let myself do, though I'm tempted every time he speaks. "Just those few lines are from me. The rest is all him." I let my eyes lock with John's, watch him evaluate this new information, add it to his vision of a person he's so convinced he sees. What is it that he wants to hear? Is this enough, this lie?

"Of course you'd say that. I bet he's quite invested in you actually believing it, putting yourself down."

"God, you make it sound like he's been walking all over me, my whole life."

"Hasn't he?"

"How on earth would you know?" I picture my dad, just briefly. The rare shadow that crosses his face when he knows he's fucked up. I've seen it only a few times—waiting outside the front door when Mom wouldn't let him in the house, that dinner we had in Providence, the few moments of weakness he's shown me and just me. "That's quite an assumption to make. You don't know anything about him."

"No, I guess I don't. Though it says a lot about him, I think. To do that in the first place, take you for granted, and let it fester all these years. Maybe I feel like I know him."

He's so sure of himself. Is this the stance he always takes in a fight? Find the high ground, hold it at all costs? Did his wife have an opposing, equally effective tactic? I wonder if she was the loud one, the one who pushed him to do things that scared him, knowing he'd be grateful later. Or maybe she was quiet, patient, complicated, posing problems he could reliably solve. If this is a pattern, do I fit into it?

"None of this even matters," I tell him. "I don't know why I said anything."

"Why did you?"

"I'm not sure." Though that's hardly true. "Please don't analyze me. It was clearly a mistake."

"Why do you care what I think anyway?"

Not an unreasonable question. But I don't want to tell him his opinion matters. That I do, in fact, care. I know what happens when I give someone unfettered access to me—the destruction that follows. Michael and the damage he did would be the obvious example, but now, hearing John's surprise and anger and pity, I wonder if my life hasn't been a wasteland for much, much longer. Any peace or happiness I've felt just thin grass and the bravest flowers covering what's actually been barren all along.

"I know I just met you and you're only here for a few days," John says, suddenly sounding far away. "But am I not supposed to care? Am I not supposed to want you to be happy, not supposed to be pissed off by something fucked up that happened to you?"

Of course he's not supposed to care. He doesn't know who I am, what matters to me, what hurts and why. But the fact that he wants to is keeping me rooted in this spot. Something else, something ugly and protective, keeps me looking out the window, out at the dormant city, and away from him.

"Can't you be a little more open, honest with me? Would that be so hard?"

A shirt he's left hanging on the desk chair sways the slightest bit in the breeze. I hate to even think it, but Dad would understand this feeling. The push and pull of it.

What would he say if he were here, observing this, as he might put it, sorry state of affairs? He'd find John laughable, probably, for his lack of ambition, or pitiful, for his loss. The way he ran away from it.

And me? I need to wait for someone who deserves me, stop selling myself so short. What happened to the little girl who could see through the bullshit of life?

More likely he'd just give me a look I'd be expected to flawlessly translate. To read that face, capable of so much, telling me in equal measure, "You're the best thing I've ever done" and "You're nothing even close to what you could be."

The song, his song, my song, keeps playing in the background, taunting me. It's long, indulgent. In this later version, as the chorus grows in intensity with each repetition, Dad brought in a gospel choir, to underline the point. They're singing my words now, in beautiful harmonies. I've gotten very quiet, I'm realizing.

"If you want to leave, leave." There's finality in John's voice now, maybe even anger at my silence. I turn around and see him sitting on the edge of the bed, his hands clasped together, waiting for my decision. Him becoming certain that if I leave, this, whatever this is, is gone.

I wonder if anything I ever make, for the rest of my life, will come close to this four minutes and thirty-seven seconds, and what it's grown to mean to people. If I'll ever have a hint of the affirmation Dad must feel when he strums the first few chords and is met with shrieks of love and acceptance and gratitude, no matter where he is. He's received that recognition so many times he probably thinks he deserves it.

I'm not sure what gives me away first: my shoulders shaking uncontrollably or the surprising strength and volume of the cries leaving my throat.

John approaches me slowly, the way you might a skittish, unpredictable animal. *Now look what you've done*, Dad might say. *Making this poor guy feel like he has to take care of you. Good luck with that. He can barely take care of himself.*

I'm not remembering him as he's almost always been with me: generous, vibrant, loving, even indulgent. All I can conjure now is any pause that may have entered his mind when he recorded this song, sang my words. Not just once, but four separate times. As recently as two years ago. Or maybe he didn't give it, or me, any thought at all.

"I've never been good enough for him," I sob. "It doesn't matter what I do." I can't stop saying it, over and over. My mind and tongue are suddenly blank, except for those words.

John doesn't tell me it's not true or insist, "He's crazy if he thinks that," or even whisper for me to calm down. Instead he lets me lean against him while his hand runs up and down my back, over and over.

It takes a while to breathe normally, to realize he's brought me over to the bed, to see the room around me again, the lights outside. But mostly darkness now. It's late.

John lies back and guides me, his hand gentle against the side of my face, so I follow. My head is on his chest, feeling his heart beat fast and loud at first, then slower and softer.

SUNDAY

THROUGH THE OPEN WINDOW, Rome is peaks and valleys. The weathered dome of a church, faraway but big enough for me to see its details, the precise curves of its roof dipping down to the street. The top of a bell tower slopes to a terrace. Squat palm trees, one scorched brown, sit in glazed pots. From where I lie now, wrapped in a cool linen sheet, washed soft, John's arm draped over my hip, I can just see into the dining room of an apartment across the street. Plates left on the table. One lone wine glass, the last sip still in it. A crooked satellite dish clings to the incline of the tile roof. Birds gliding and landing. John's thin curtains fill with air and empty, just as slowly.

His body emulates mine. His legs fit neatly in the angles mine have made. Even the ledge where the bridge of his nose meets his forehead finds a place to rest in the nape of my neck. How can he breathe like that? But he is, softly.

The street outside is almost completely quiet. I envision it close to empty, since I can only hear, not see. Every sound is magnified:

a cart carrying groceries or laundry rattles as it's pushed over the stones. A man's voice calls out to someone, to say good morning or comment on the weather. It's equal parts encouraging and maddening, this almost-understanding.

He's definitely not awake, not even stirring. His breath is steady and calm in a way that can only be genuine. His face betrays absolutely nothing, not the infuriating things he said and assumed a few hours ago, not the care beneath all of it, no shock at how I reacted. How I fell apart.

Just a bit of pressure against his shoulder or a too-loud noise would change all that, bring him back to life, make my tears and denial and anger real all over again. If he were to open his eyes to look at me, that's likely all he'd see. I'm careful, move as quietly as I can.

I take a few minutes to stare at his bookshelves, his pots hanging from hooks, wishing I didn't have to keep so still, that I could investigate the way I used to when Michael was in the shower or ran downstairs to get the dry cleaning or meet the food delivery. Opening books and cabinets, reading the labels of wine and liquor bottles, skimming my fingers on top of picture frames to check for dust.

I slip out of his bed, hunt for my clothes, avoid the mirror and with it the opportunity to see how swollen my eyes are, the redness in my face, to possibly change my mind. I shut the door without a sound.

It's very early. I know this instinctually, seeing how fresh the light is, without needing to look at the time. When I was little, I was always up before everyone else, sometimes before sunrise. My mother tried to wake up with me for a while, or find ways to get me back to sleep, but eventually she gave up and let me do as I pleased. By the time she woke up to make coffee or, when he was home, fry an egg for Dad, I'd have been roaming the house and yard for hours. That time was precious. If I sat to read a book behind the crumbling stone wall in the backyard, no one would find me until I wanted them to. I walked through empty rooms that took on new meaning—our dining room table looked abandoned and ridiculous with nine vacant chairs pulled up to it. It was easy to tell if it had rained the night before by looking at the river, either glassy smooth or rough and clouded with mud. Back when that stillness could be an adventure, not the lonely way it occurs to me now.

Ever since, I've had an awareness of that deeper kind of quiet, knowing when I'm more or less alone in the world, even for just an hour or two before other people start to emerge.

When John wakes up, he might think this is me wanting to be chased, pretending to be lost just so I can be found. I can tell myself that's not true, but it's hard not to wonder how he'll react, if he'll see this as an invitation to look for me or start doing whatever people do to forget someone as quickly as possible.

There's undeniable release in descending his circular staircase, no quieting myself anymore, letting my feet fall at full volume from one step to the next. The walls are made of still-cool stone, curved around the stairs like a well or shelter built into the earth.

With every move I make, the knot that's still tied in my dress knocks against my knee. A reminder of what seemed like such an ingenious idea last night. His smile as I tightened it making me feel so game for whatever might continue to happen. When I loosen it now, the fabric spills down to the ground; the wrinkles that have set fan outward.

I should probably find my way back to Via Clementina and the apartment I've barely used. But the quiet here is close to hypnotic. The breeze is still crisp, despite the sweat already beading on the back of my neck. Monti might be louder, busier. I might not find this calm again, so I linger in it, staying away from any hint of noise or activity. There's hardly anyone to ask for directions anyway. Every café or shop I see is locked or dark or covered by a metal gate. My phone is dead.

I remember it's Sunday and laugh into the empty street. Another one of Michael's proclamations—in Italy, nothing's open on Sundays. A fact that we were going to prepare for and work around. If it were the two of us, we'd still be in bed, high above the street in Monti, listening for church bells. My messy suitcase on the floor next to his neat one. He'd have bought coffee. It would be brewing. I'd be smelling it now.

I look up to see jasmine crawling from a rooftop arbor down to one window and then another, as if it's water running over stones. The building façades on either side of me are so close the street feels more like a hallway. The scent is everywhere. A few petals catch in my hair, and I leave them there.

Even the churches I pass are closed. It's late enough for the faithful to be awake, but too early for them to start gathering for the first mass of the day.

There's a little coffee bar on the corner, marked by a curved Madonna etched in stone above the awning, empty but definitely open. So not everything is closed on Sundays, apparently. The man behind the counter is reading a newspaper. He makes me a caffè doppio quickly, silently. I put a two-euro coin on the bar, smell and sip the espresso while he reads his paper, swats a fly away from the cornetti he's arranged in a straw basket for a euro each. No one walks by the propped-open door.

I follow a series of streets that lead me out of Esquilino, notice them growing wider, losing more and more of their charm. Then a turn onto Via Barberini, lined by bank branches and luxury hotels, before it disappears into a Y-shaped piazza dotted with palm trees. Three new streets fan out, but I'm suddenly too tired to care what their names are or where they might take me. On a weekend morning, during the city's busiest season, in a wide-open square, I am completely alone. A long line of parked motorbikes sits baking in the already hot sun. I can't see shade anywhere.

But I can hear running water from a fountain on the other side of the piazza. An empty double-decker bus, the kind designed for tourists to hop on and off, narrowly misses me as I cross the street toward that bit of shelter. The closer I get, the larger and lusher and more bizarre it becomes. The man at its center, a king or a god judging by his size and crown, points resolutely down at the water. A row of lions, all reclining with front paws crossed, water flowing steadily from their mouths. Some of them look fierce, others confused, with raised eyebrows and conflicted stares.

The fountain faces a church, made of the kind of bleached white stone that never gets hot, no matter how direct and prolonged the sunlight. It could probably pass for a government building, were it not for the wiry iron cross marking the highest point of the roof, the Latin wrapping around its angles like a stock ticker. The façade is imposing, substantial enough to allow for curved alcoves—probably built to house statues of saints, though these sit empty.

But from the side I can see it's actually thin, fragile-looking in a way that makes no sense. I wonder if that's the point, building something that looks so strong, but isn't—an optical illusion almost. John would be able to explain that, how such a narrow, detailed piece of stone could support that much, last all this time.

I climb stone steps that start wide and narrow at the top, the kind of approach designed to communicate importance, inspire devotion. The doors are worn, weathered, and look painted shut. But the past few days have taught me that there's almost always a side entrance, unassuming and tucked away. This church is no exception.

Before passing through the little gate to try the door, I reach for the shawl I folded into my bag last night and never used. It's just large enough to cover my shoulders. I'm not sure if that's still a requirement for entering churches, but it was years ago, when we came here as a family. The sign of respect was lost on me then, groaning at being forced to smother my arms and knees in the heat. My mother went a step further and covered her head. Old habits die hard.

The door is open. I'm able to slip in silently. From the entryway, I can see only one other person, a woman, maybe my age or younger, up on some scaffolding, tending to a fresco. She's wearing white coveralls and holding a very thin brush. Her focus and precision and outfit give her an official, maybe surgical, air. It's unclear whether she's stripping away age or amplifying detail—the pearlescent white of a beard, the pale pink of a shroud. I watch her work until my neck starts to ache.

Dad was never sold on the idea of restoration. A year or so ago, I met him and Mom for a late dinner near Film Forum. They'd just returned from Amsterdam, where she'd gone to meet him at the tail end of a tour. I remember being encouraged by their moods that night—light and easy with each other. How I like to imagine they interact when they're alone.

"We went to one of those coffeehouses and your mother ate a brownie," Dad said. "Can you believe it? I wouldn't if I hadn't seen it with my own eyes."

"Well, part of one," she corrected him. "And you know, there was a time in my life when that wouldn't have been such big news." She winked at me and I felt a lift, enjoying the stem of the glass in my hand.

Mom had been struck by the Rijksmuseum and Rembrandt's *Night Watch* in particular, how they were keeping the painting partially on view while they restored it. She went twice during the three days they were there, fixated on the details. How to address the abuse the painting has endured over the years: two different knife attacks seventy years apart, a spray of acid in the mid-nineties, the canvas rolled up and hidden from the Nazis in an underground bunker. The different methods the team used to perfect Rembrandt's specific whites and yellows and reds. The enormous, temperature-controlled glass enclosure they built around the painting, complete with a mechanical perch where the technicians could cover the height and width of the canvas with the touch of a button. She compared it to the moving platforms used for window washers on the outsides of skyscrapers. Tickets were, of course, discounted.

"It was fascinating." She spread her arms wide to show me the massive dimensions of the glass box, illustrating her points as she always did. "They even call it Operation Night Watch, like it's part of a military campaign." She gave an amused laugh.

"I guess I understand the impulse," Dad said, bursting the yolk on top of his steak tartare, "but I still felt a little cheated. Having to squint and stare, just to see a fraction of it. Sometimes, something isn't better than nothing."

I smiled, to give him that, and also to cut out any tension I could, before it settled and became real. My parents, the way they are with each other, can be difficult to predict. Sometimes, everything he does irritates her. Others, she's in his thrall.

He went on. "I don't trust it. How do you restore something"— he punctuated "restore" with air quotes—"without changing it? Lessening it even?"

"So you think the painting should just be left to decay?" Mom typically let these strangely specific, strongly held opinions of his go unchallenged, but this one incensed her.

"It's been hundreds of years." His tone got professorial, pretentious. "These men probably never dreamed their work would last a century, let alone forever. Wouldn't you rather something fade away naturally? Instead of being propped up and added to like some Frankenstein monster?" Whatever calm I'd initially walked into was decidedly gone.

"So, deep down, you don't believe your work will live forever? That's not important to you?"

Smug silence from him. She poured water into his half-empty glass.

"Show me an artist who doesn't," he said.

All the churches I've been wandering in and out of have numbed me to a certain amount of opulence and drama, but this one still sets itself apart. The interior isn't just made entirely of marble but different shades and striations, all bound together somehow. Gold leaf and frescoes on every possible panel. Incense hangs in the air, a smoky reminder of the excess, the heavy quiet.

I haven't been to Mass in over a decade, haven't sat and stood and knelt in unison or taken Communion or smiled at strangers as a sign of peace. Though I'm confident I'd still remember how. Certain responses and refrains stay memorized, probably forever.

Dad was raised Catholic, and it's something he's tried to preserve in himself, or at least not forget entirely. God is all over his music, explicitly and not. A little laughable, all things considered, though religion and hypocrisy certainly can go hand in hand.

When I was a child, every Sunday morning he was home, we were sitting in a pew at nine a.m., earlier if possible, to get good seats. The Gothic-style church in Hudson, with its vaulted ceilings painted deep blue and flecked with gold to resemble stars. It wasn't even something I bothered complaining about. I didn't think up excuses not to go or say anything about the dresses I was forced to wear. That's how inevitable it was. Until his presence was no longer a given and our routines no longer fixed. Around the time I started mouthing the words instead of actually singing them.

It's hard to remember exactly when it started. Mom decided to skip one Sunday, which made it easier for me to ask to skip the next. Sunday mornings became a time of illicit freedom. I grew out of those dresses. When he'd call from the road or a hotel or wherever he was and ask me if we'd been to Mass, I'd lie. By the time he was let back into our lives, it was too late to start again.

Is that why I linger at the *madonnelle* I pass on the street or dip my fingers into every pool of holy water I see or cross myself on the way out of every church? It feels good and obedient, but also like some kind of statement, something I'm determined to acknowledge despite all I know about science and history and human nature. I guess that might be faith.

I take a few more steps down the aisle, turn to the left, and suddenly realize why the name of this church was familiar to me, why it was starred on Michael's map and recommended by the guidebooks.

An angel holds a golden arrow delicately between two fingers, face at an agonizingly indirect angle and smiling gently, as if about to give a gift. Saint Teresa, her head thrown back in the ecstasy that gives the statue its name. Both their bodies dissolving into folds of fabric that become clouds, all carved out of marble so white and flawless it seems impossible. Natural light from a hidden window in the dome above illuminates them both, emphasized by rays of gold in the background. It's a little maddening when something is supposed to leave you breathless, and then does.

The woman is still up on her scaffolding, still protecting or heightening whatever marks that bit of plaster. I make sure no one else has seen me, and then sit beneath the statue, my ankles crossed and pulled in. I lean forward, chin tilted up toward Teresa, and feel my hips open. That pleasant ache is still there, evidence of the different ways I've just been discovered, opened, interrogated.

Sex is the obvious conclusion people draw when they look at her face. I see that, but so many other things, too. Pain, sweetness, vindication, release, loss of control, and freedom from shame. Possibly fear, possibly rage. I start to shake with both.

The last time I saw my parents, or spoke to my father, we were all having dinner at their house at the end of April. A twist in the weather, suddenly warm enough to eat outside. I didn't know yet that Michael was married, that he'd decided to finally discard me. I'd find out soon.

Dad had been given a generous offer earlier that day, for a new record compiling his most popular songs. Something he'd always said he would never do.

"I wonder why you're so resistant to it," I said to him. "It doesn't really mean anything, certainly not that you're done making music. People release greatest hits albums all the time. Maybe just think of it as a reflection of all you've done so far."

Dad was plainly drunk, which didn't happen much anymore. His eyes settled on me with an ugliness and conviction I hadn't seen maybe ever. "You're like me," he said. "Such an eye. You see the world your own way."

Dessert was on the table—berries folded in thin dough and baked until they bubbled. Jack's topped with vanilla ice cream. Azaleas wilting in a shallow vase, candles burning low. More wine if we wanted it.

Mom had gone into the kitchen to refill her water glass and, I imagine, after hearing his tone, decided to stay there.

After a few moments of silence, he went on. "And you're capable of so much more, too. You're just afraid." Which, to him, is the most staggering sort of insult. There is nothing worse than fear.

"No, I'm not like you." After a few long moments, I finally spoke, but with certainty, knowing what would cause him pain. "I'm not selfish."

"Selfish? Well, maybe I am. But at least I followed my talent, did something with it."

"You're right, Dad. You did, no matter what. You didn't even let it stop you when Mom made you live in the Airstream at the end of the driveway because she couldn't stand to look at you. But then again, you do everything with style, even banishment." I wasn't sure where my anger was coming from, but I knew he wanted it. So, as usual, I provided.

I also knew I was nearing truly dangerous territory, like an animal accustomed to navigating cliffs and mountain roads. If I fell off, it was my own fault. I had been bred and trained to maneuver situations like this, to step lightly, disturbing as little as possible.

"You think you could do better?" His voice started to rise.

Did I say anything or just stare back, trying to show him that whatever frustrations he held, however I'd disappointed him, he'd done so much worse? I can feel it, even now: my nails digging into the thin cushion of that chair. Mom had chosen the fabric carefully; it covered all the outdoor furniture. A cream-colored linen: both attractively rustic and smooth enough to lean against, woven to hold up against direct sun and sudden storms and still look refined. Even though it masked nothing more than a cheap layer of foam. How unsatisfying it was, to grip something that gave so little back. Whatever I said or, more likely, didn't say, it could have changed everything or nothing at all.

He pointed through the front window, toward my painting above the fireplace, the way a lawyer might, mid–cross examination, at a damning piece of evidence. "You have power. Do you know how rare that is?" He's suddenly screaming. "Why the *fuck* don't you use it?"

"Well, you were certainly able to make something of it, Dad." Jack's voice is clear and strong. I'd almost forgotten he was there, sitting next to me. Did I tell him, as I always did, to stop? Not to bother? I think so, something like "Don't, he's drunk." Or "Please, this isn't worth it." Or "Come on, we know where this ends. It doesn't matter." Forever looking for the familiar path, the one of least resistance.

"What's that, Jack? What was I able to make out of her little cartoons?"

Dad's lips curled around his words. He bit the hard *T* in little, taking pleasure in making me feel small. I leaned back against the cold wrought iron of my chair, and said nothing more.

"No, not the drawings." Jack's tone started to match his in cruelty, and I knew what was coming. "You weren't afraid to steal from your own child, if it meant giving you the greatest song you ever supposedly 'wrote.' All while you made a fool of our mother for years. If I had power like yours, I wouldn't use it either."

I shut my eyes then. They may have pushed, even punched each other. Or not. I remember it both ways, depending on how angry or sorry I am. I can't be sure if that's what made me leave, or how weak my defense of our dad had become. Or just the confirmation that he actually thought what I never quite let myself believe. Letting myself remember it now, it's hard not to shudder at his spite, my silence.

I drove back to the city that night, sobbing so hard I could barely see the reflection of my headlights against the median. But the painful void in my stomach that usually comes when I'm doing something wrong or hiding from the difficult choice was nowhere to be felt.

There are tears on my face now, too. They're silent, but I still want to scream. At my dad or Michael or maybe both of them at once. *You never took me seriously, I never even had a chance.*

It's not a new concept, something hurting so much it feels good. Or the opposite, actually.

I walk out, into the light, into a city that's started to stir.

There's a steady stream of traffic on the main road now. People are starting to gather on the side streets, but the pace is slower. No one looks my way. A monk notices the gate I left open and closes it roughly, with a clang.

The steps are warm, not hot yet. I sit and rest my lower back against them, let the sun start to burn my wrists and ankles. It's the kind of heat I always try to memorize, so I can recite it to myself in winter.

Church bells start ringing, not from where I'm sitting, but very close. Close enough that their rhythm and vibration travel through the air. I can feel it in the sheet of bone that covers my chest, protects my heart. I rest my fingers on its ridges, taking a moment to feel what makes me up.

The last time I was alone with my mother, a few hours before that dinner, we went on a hike near the house. A web of trails, with views of the river and the Catskills on a clear day, which this was.

Most dogs can and do run free on the trail, but ours is ruled by her nose, not any kind of command, so we kept her close and on a leash, the two of us taking turns holding her back. The dog looking up from her sniffing every few minutes to make sure we were still there.

Sometimes there was a lot to talk about on these walks, gossip to catch up on, advice to be asked for and given. But more often we were mostly silent. When the dog decided to run, we'd speed up to match her, laughing at her howls, letting her take us in whatever direction she chose. Mom knew where all the paths led anyway, what turns we ultimately needed to take to get home. "It's nice," she said, "to give her the illusion of control. She wants to be top dog, so we'll let her."

"I think she appreciates it," I said, scratching the dog's back while she took a drink from the stream.

We walked out of the trees into one of the open fields that always makes us pause. Depending on the time of year, that stretch of land could be mowed flat, left fallow and covered with hay and dying grass, dotted with purple chive blossoms, or transformed into a slowly waving sea of yellow flowers. "It's why I love coming here," Mom always says. "Every day it's different."

That day, she stood silent longer than usual. "When I die," she said, "I want to be left someplace like this."

My mother is not a sentimental woman, usually. Which makes moments like these seem like a choice of hers. I'm not sure why her deciding to be vulnerable, even for a few moments, has the power to make me so unsettled, but it does. I didn't want to meet her eyes to encourage this train of thought or ask any questions that might prolong it. I was also worried she might see me cry.

It's a battle my mind is always fighting—trying to reconcile all the time and energy I've watched her inexplicably waste and all the light of hers I've only ever seen glimpses of.

"This is important to me. I need you to listen." There was a slight shift in her tone, one I always pay attention to. A warning.

"I *am* listening," I said with that impatience she can still inspire in me, that I show when I'm not careful. I took a breath and made an effort. "Go ahead."

She described the specific stretch of California coast where she wants to be scattered. How she wants Jack and me to be together, somewhere beautiful, when we say goodbye to her. "That's the kind of remembrance I wish for," she said, her breath a bit short as we made our way down the hill, stepping over raised tree roots and running our fingers over the waist-high weeds and flowers.

"It's what I've always wanted and will want, to be free like that. At peace," she said, in that wistful way she has that always makes me want to pull away from her.

Still, there was a small part of me that felt glad I was the one getting this information, not Jack. Though it may have only been because I'm the oldest, the one expected to make these sorts of decisions or respect specific wishes. Or maybe she'd already told him. I chose to believe otherwise.

"And what about Dad?" I asked her.

"Your father probably wants a mausoleum. A monument." She snorted. The dog pulled on her arm, her tail doing figure eights. "She must smell a rabbit."

I opened my mouth to defend him but stopped short. Because, then again, he might.

Campo de Fiori is certainly not closed on Sundays. The market vendors are out already. Their dirty canvas umbrellas are open, creating aisles of shade over their pallets of fruit and flowers and laundry detergent and off-brand children's toys.

My hair is still wet from the shower, but won't be for long. I left the dress on the bed, changed into one of my mother's shirts, perfectly worn at the elbows, the collar relaxed in just the right way.

One of the lower buttons is missing from all the times she tied it up to show off her stomach. I pulled on a pair of her old torn Levi's that I cut up and turned into shorts when I was in college. The hem stays just frayed enough, no matter how often I wash them.

It would make her happy, knowing I was dressed in her clothes, walking around a city she loves. I think about calling her again, but don't.

I keep close to the edge of the piazza, hugging the side of a building painted the color of saffron. The restaurants aren't open for lunch yet. In a half hour, the maître d's will try to entice people into sitting down for a meal, but for now they smoke and adjust menus and yell greetings to each other. One is bent down on one knee, plucking weeds from between stones.

They've already turned on the outdoor fans, the standing ones that blow not only industrial-sized bursts of air but also shocks of cold mist at the same time. I adjust my path to make sure I'm always in the line of fire, my face damp and cool for a few blissful seconds before the sweat takes over. Then I do it all over again.

I turn the corner of the piazza, avoiding an early line starting to form outside Mamma Mia Gelateria, a dirty, narrow doorway marked by a laminated poster of a woman licking a small plastic spoon clean.

The path I'm taking starts and ends at Forno. Even if I didn't recognize it from Michael's list, the lettering of its sign and the purpose on the faces of people filing in and out would be a signal that the place is a classic for a reason, that whatever they do is done well. By the time I've done a full turn, they've shifted from selling cornetti and biscotti to sandwiches and slices of pizza and loaves of bread for lunch.

A small tour group waits outside, speaking what sounds like German, while their guide orders for them. Why actually stumble through the language barrier or make a decision about what looks good, when all of that effort and discomfort can be sorted for you?

She's carrying on a lengthy conversation with the men behind the counter, her tone light and familiar. She might be catching up on gossip, maybe complaining to them about the day's group. I bet she brings people here every week, the same routine each time.

After a few minutes, she emerges, offering the Germans a bit of everything, translating it all as she goes. Pizza rossa, shiny with tomato and olive oil. Pizza bianca, crispy with potatoes and rosemary. Another baked with zucchini flowers, anchovy, and mozzarella. All cut from long sheets into equal squares.

When I walk in, the small storefront is full of people, all of them crowding the counter. It's not difficult to pick out the Romans from the rest. Their confidence is palpable, parting the sea of hungry tourists with little to no resistance. Two college students pause midorder, speaking English to each other, and an older man, wearing his hat at an angle, turns and steals their place in line with a smile.

One of the men behind the counter unfolds his palm and points at me, indicating I should do the same. He drops a few fried olives in my bare hand. They're almost stale, but not quite. Still a bit of crunch, just enough to preserve the brine and bite inside.

I chew one and smile at him in gratitude, but he's impatient now, waiting for me to order. His eyes darting, telling me to hurry up or lose his attention. I know what I'd like, but I'm not sure if they'll make it for me or not.

"I should never underestimate it," Michael said once. "Your ability to order off-menu."

I think I responded with something along the lines of "So what? I know what I want." The lies I told.

But at this moment, in this hot, crowded, deliciously confusing corner bakery, I actually do know what I want. And I stumble through asking for it.

"Per favore, un pezzo di pizza bianca con prosciutto e fichi?"

He thinks about it for a few seconds, then nods and turns his back to me. I watch him adjust his grip on the communal serrated knife and cut the already thin bread in half, steam spilling out. He spreads fig jam on both pieces, messily but still even. Three large slices of prosciutto draped on top and pushed together.

This spell of my competency, if it ever existed, is quickly broken once he's handed me the sandwich and a scrap of paper I'm guessing is a receipt. He's telling me to go somewhere and do something, but I just stand there until the tour guide, back for seconds apparently, points to the woman at the register and tells me how much to pay her, in English.

It's a bit of a shock, to be dropped back so quickly to where I was two days ago. Stringing words together, pointing and miming and hoping to be understood. It was so easy to just rely on John's fluid Italian and fast friendships and knowledge of which street led where. I felt relaxed and capable, just by being near him, but it almost felt like my mastery, too. Because he literally crossed my path, a foreign place became a little bit familiar. I gave up the peace and challenge of being alone so readily, without even needing to think.

The pizza bianca is dotted with salt and oil, wrapped in wax paper and warm still. It crunches a bit with each bite I take. The meat is sliced so thin it melts. The fig seeds stick in my teeth.

All of this is happening, or none of it is. Depending on what I decide to tell people, or not. John is himself, in all his accurate and complicated detail, or he's ten years younger and a Formula One driver I met at a club, or he's that bartender who pressed ice against my knee. Or he's no one and I sat alone with my own thoughts for six days in Rome, in cloistered contemplation. There was no fling, no diversion, no whatever this has been. No glimpse beneath the veneer of him, no surprise at the depth of his pain, no feeling unworthy or afraid of it. Certainly no breakdown, no pent-up rage or sadness fighting its way out. I kept all my plans and dinner reservations and slept in the room I rented every night, alone.

I could return home and convince everyone I've been invigorated, changed. Never in danger of making the same mistake over again, falling for someone just because he's there, losing myself in another person, or whatever the lesson here is. No one would know the truth but me.

The exhaust from a passing truck smells sweet, almost medicinal.

Last night swims through my mind. How presumptuous he was, how unfair I might have been before my complete, mortifying collapse. Why his uninformed opinion seemed to matter so much, or matter at all. Why it was so successful in making me feel I was betraying and banishing my dad, all at the same time. It's hard not to picture John's face, imagine his first thought when he woke up this morning and I wasn't there. To wonder if I'm all right, to shake his head at my need to run away.

The weight of the wine and the amaro and everything he told me in the orange garden clouds my memory a bit, but the important details still persist. Though I always wonder, in those moments when I lose even a bit of control, what did I miss? And I lost so much, last night. Gave so much away. There's no way of knowing what he thinks about any of it—I don't have John's number; he doesn't have mine.

But there's always distance between who we really are and what we allow other people to see. John sees me, or he did, as someone who floats gracefully through the world, who feels and appears to be at ease. He said it himself. A little bit of learned sophistication and well-deployed flirtation go a long way, as it turns out. But clearly he could smell the truth on me last night, the fact that so much of what I'm built on is crumbling, maybe always has been.

Twenty years ago, someone thought it would be a good idea to follow Dad around on what would be his biggest tour ever, filming everything. Not just the shows themselves, but long rides on the bus or plane, frenzied rehearsals, crowds that trailed him everywhere, whatever happened backstage. They even filmed his then routine of starting each day by swimming naked in the pool of whatever hotel he was staying in. He gave them full, unfettered access.

They made what was called at the time a "hyperrealistic documentary." No strategic cuts or reframing anything in service of a narrative. There's no cohesive story to it: just 165 minutes of everything that they could capture before they ran out of film, in chronological order and uncensored. It's thought to be ground-breaking, maybe even art, by some people. In my family, it's never discussed. On the few occasions it has come up, any details are either laughed off or coldly ignored.

The full film is hard to find, other than some pixelated illegal downloads and VHS tapes floating around on eBay. But clips are all over the internet, available for free to watch over and over again.

When I was nineteen or twenty, I got curious and did some research, since an internet connection could maybe give me the answers that asking my parents questions wouldn't.

I scrolled quickly through live performances and interviews with reporters, surprised by how many people spent so much time dissecting my dad's set lists and side-glances, wondering what it all meant and how it influenced the music that would follow.

I was looking for something different when I clicked on a video titled "Sing-along." And I got it. The version of him in those three minutes and forty-three seconds was completely new to me: wide-eyed, hungry, unmistakably high.

He's in a shabby room backstage in London, at the Royal Albert Hall, where he'd just played the second of two sold-out shows. After looking up dates and doing the math, I realized that my mom would fly to meet him in Madrid a week later, leaving Jack and me with a family friend, and decide to stay married.

People are sitting on the floor and the arms of couches and leaning against walls. I recognized longtime members of his band (a few of them unofficial uncles to me) and the man who's been his manager from the beginning, also Jack's godfather. I didn't recognize at least fifteen women, all of them younger than I am now at thirty-three.

Dad stands in the middle of the room, commanding all the attention like the conductor of an orchestra. He holds a big platter above his head, once piled with deli meat and cheese but now picked over. They all sing a song I've never heard, a capella, while he plays at being a good host, passing the tray around.

The camera moves behind him, surveying the room and mirroring his eyeline before ultimately settling on a redhead in the corner. She appears to have been waiting for him to notice her, allows herself a small, smug smile when he does.

As he approaches, her eyes stay locked on him, not bothering to look down at the plate or what's on it, what her choices are. Her fingers move blindly for whatever's closest: a few slices of raw red onion. She slips them into her barely open mouth, never giving up his gaze. Regardless of the drugs they've taken, or maybe because of them, this dark, brief moment of connection between them is palpable, serious, undeniable.

Dad has always loved attention. So, it's not a shock that he drinks hers up, meeting her smile, reaching out and giving her hair a tug before dropping the tray to the ground and doing a little spin for the camera, his eyes shiny with speed or whatever he's on.

She responds with a look that's aggressive, almost mean. She knows she's going to fuck him later. In an hour, maybe two. But it's certain. In her mind, it's as if she already has. An expression I've only ever seen on men. Except for her.

The red-haired woman never makes another appearance in the film. It's not her he puts his arm around when the airplane descends in Berlin. She's not one of the girls lying by the pool on the roof of the hotel in Spain either. Believe me, I've looked.

Not long after I found the videos, I made the mistake of showing them to Jack, convincing myself, in my young wisdom, that all of this added up to something he should see, that he had a right to know, too. He was fifteen at the time.

I watched him watch it, then rewatch it. His face was blank and also fierce, somehow. He never raised his voice and only asked me one question, at the very beginning: "Where's Mom?" But then it quickly became clear she wasn't there, and that was very much the point.

I wanted a reaction, of course. For him to be as visibly outraged and hurt and confused as I was. I didn't know then that Jack was capable of doing more with silence than I ever could with sound. He closed my laptop, went to his room, and shut the door.

For someone like Jack, someone who thinks and lives in absolutes, this was a condemnation, simple and swift. It colored everything, and it has ever since. He quickly, effectively became a ghost.

His relationship with our dad has been cordial, shallow, and consistent. When we were younger, it was accepted, even laughed about. How he always ran to and talked with and seemed to prefer our mom. But I had been the opposite when I was his age. And Dad was on the road so much anyway. It's probably to be expected.

But the fault lines started to show as he got older. The way he'd avoid any time alone with Dad, even shying away from topics of conversation that interested only the two of them. Or the fact that, as soon as he could, Jack went to college an ocean away, found a girlfriend who conveniently takes up all his free time and is all too ready to add him to her family. Even though he lives in New York, so close to my parents, he's devoted that life to money and numbers and the kind of quick, magic-like intelligence it takes to be good with both. A focus our Dad will never understand or truly value, which is its own kind of self-perpetuating barrier.

Neither of them ever acknowledges it. Our dad is a narcissist, yes, but it's hard for me to believe he's that blind.

Jack's approach may seem extreme, but it's never changed. I keep giving up, going back, pretending to forget.

In his defense, Dad never really tried to hide any of this. The clues, if you can call them that, are woven through the songs. The girl with the stone-cold stare, his ode to her underlined by two faintly operatic backup singers. Being poured Dalmatian wine by a steady hand, long fingers, a thin wrist. Resting on the shores of Bohemia. An apartment in Mayfair, empty except for a mattress on the floor. How different bodies have healed his soul.

I remember it as an abrupt realization, watching those videos again and again—understanding that, in all those songs about love and sex and longing and heartbreak, he was writing and singing about more than just my mother. That it's just not possible to feel that much for one person. For one single relationship, no matter how long or complex, to provide that volume of material. How the anger she kept simmering below the surface suddenly made much more sense.

Still, considering all those women over all those years—no one ever replaced her. Or, she never allowed herself to be replaced. Through some mix of finesse and brute strength, she kept him. That ruthlessness, that's a gene I didn't get.

I imagine how John would react to all of this, if I decided to tell him. The details likely wouldn't be a surprise. My dad's reputation as a womanizer is a given for anyone even slightly familiar with his music.

"Have you and your dad ever talked about it?" he might ask, careful not to take as strong a stance as he did last night. "That time in his life?"

The answer is yes and no.

I've asked him directly about the documentary, hoping his response might at least provide an effective lie I could tell myself.

"I don't know what I was thinking, letting those guys film everything. They made themselves out to be these genius directors, auteurs even. I was an idiot then, as you well know." Always insinuation, standing in for the more difficult conversation we could be having, but never do.

He was sitting by their fireplace, drinking coffee from the moka pot he uses every morning without fail. He loves that it brews perfectly each time and came without instructions.

Never pack the espresso, he would tell me. That's the mistake everyone makes.

"Honestly, who were those people, capturing this shit for what kind of posterity?"

As for the rest of it, he explains himself in his own way, in his trademark mixture of charm, deflection, humor, the occasional moment of genuine remorse.

When Jack and I were young, Dad coming back to us was an event. He appeared, suddenly penitent and present. And then, just as quickly, he'd be gone again. It's a tired cliché, but, to me, he was like the sun then—powerful, central, life-giving, and changeable.

Around the time I finished college, Dad came back from meetings with his label in LA, and stayed. She hasn't kicked him out since. He hasn't left on his own. At the precise moment I didn't need him anymore, and Jack wanted nothing from him anyway.

A year or so ago, I noticed a painting or a piece of music, some work of art I'd loved when I was younger, but now found flat, uninspiring, maybe even ugly. I called him to tell him about it, worried that all that love and enthusiasm I once had could be lost so easily.

"That doesn't surprise me at all," he might have said. "Your sense of what's beautiful, what moves you, has become more complex and formidable, as you have."

His ability to say something perfect, out of nowhere and off the cuff, has undoubtedly saved his life many times over. The deep voice, the well-cut suit, the sideways smile: all could be weaponized, if that was his choice.

There are times I've seen those moments as acts of love—him helping my mind protect itself, making it possible for me to love him still.

A few cars are parked in the corner of this square, in accordance with lines or rules that either have worn away with time or never existed at all. I still can't figure it out—why it's okay to park at this angle and on this side, not that one? And for how long? Yet another thing Romans must intrinsically know.

"Isn't that part of the pleasure in going to a different place, though? To realize how much we don't understand? The world is so much bigger than what we know."

I can hear, even see Michael as clearly as if he'd just turned the corner in front of me, intersecting my path. But would he ever admit to that kind of humility? That's something I'd expect from John. Everything is growing hazier.

The longer I'm away from Michael, in a place where we've never been together, the harder it's becoming to predict his reactions, know what he'd love or hate, or even care.

I don't know, will never know, how much of his effect on me was true connection or just chance. Did he happen to know precisely how to talk to me? Or is what interests me, what I prefer, what turns me on, just a blueprint he drafted, left for other men to be measured against?

I step into a little bookshop. The table in front is piled high with American novels that have been translated into Italian. None of Michael's among them.

One wall of the store is devoted to magazines, the expensive kind that people keep and leave on their coffee tables as signs of their good taste. They're thick, made with high-quality paper, words printed in bold, self-conscious fonts. Names like CULTURED, L'APPARTMENT, FANTASTIC MAN, WOMANKIND, COURIER, FOAM, LUNCHEON.

Most of them are familiar to me, thanks to a newsstand on Eighth Avenue, a place I've come to memorize. It occupies a popular corner, and has for more than thirty years. They stock fashion and design and culture magazines from every country that prints one, all fitted into plastic slots that scale the walls from floor to ceiling. Back issues of the *New Yorker* and the *Economist* and *Lapham's Quarterly* are stacked into leaning columns, near copies of French and Italian *Vogue*, all creating narrow walkways in and out. Piles of that day's *Times* and *Post* and *Daily News* always crowd the doorway.

The owners order scrambled eggs from the diner next door, drink coffee until they close at midnight, and answer the phone in Arabic. After a while, they started to recognize me and eventually learned my name, what I looked for and why. When I asked for a specific back issue of something or if the new *Artforum* had come in yet, whoever was behind the counter would use a laser pointer to show me exactly what I was looking for, immediately and without fail.

Before long, it became a place where I hunted for new ideas for commissions, looked up the names of artists and photographers I wanted to pitch and work for, flipped through other people's ideas, the risks and liberties they took.

This shop carries a magazine that's devoted itself to conspicuous consumption. When I met with the editor in chief for the first time, she described it to me as an exploration of the relationship people have with their interiors. From grand architectural statements to the intimate details that make a home feel lived in. It sounds a little ridiculous, I know, but they've published my work a few times.

I check that it's the new issue, from July of this year, and flip to the table of contents to make sure my name is actually there. The shop on Eighth Avenue is probably the only place in New York I'd be able to find this, and not for weeks anyway.

I was hired to produce a portfolio of summer accessories, what to buy for the Hamptons host who has absolutely everything, or for yourself, if you have too much money and are out of ideas on how to spend it. Instead of photographing everything, the editor commissioned me to draw each item. I used pastels for all of them, on thick brown paper, the sort that looks recycled, that people use to wrap presents, finishing with twine for a bow. Flipping the pages to see my name in print, my brush or pen strokes glossy and final, is still something that makes me smile, no matter how pretentious or commercial the source.

The spread starts with a Gucci tea set, hand painted in an exaggerated floral print. The flowers were large—I made them more asymmetrical than they actually were—and decadent in their proportions. Hard outlines in black to balance the white curves of the china.

The accessories editor let me keep it, as a gift, I guess. But I insisted on drawing it at home, in my own light, so they probably didn't want to ask for it back anyway. It does make me wonder how valuable these things actually are, if so many of them are given away—for publicity or goodwill or, in my case, convenience. It's still sitting above my kitchen cabinets, dust gathering inside the cups, the divots in the saucers, the spout of the pot.

I flip through to the other drawings. A pair of equestrian-style boots, half-zipped and hanging open. The laces dangling. I made them thin like spider webs. A heavy ceramic mirror, its border the perfect shade of peach, flecked with an almost-white blue. I sketched a poodle in its reflection, just because.

The last one they printed was by far the most difficult to capture. A French fashion house, one that typically embraced simple, iconic design, had given one of their signature handbags to a talked-about artist to interpret as he wished. He kept the silhouette the same and amplified everything else, almost beyond recognition. The leather was dyed bright pink, stiff handles. I spent an hour posing it like a difficult model.

I hold the copy up to the woman in the shop, busy rearranging the bookmarks and pens for sale next to the register.

"*Quanto costa?*" I ask her.

She answers quickly, but I think I understand the number.

I give her what I hope is exact change, and it actually is.

Miraculous. I walk out with the issue under my arm, satisfyingly heavy and impractical.

There are parrots in the palm trees. They sound just a little different than the other birds I've heard. Then I lean back against the base of the fountain where I've been sitting, look up between the leaves, and see their colors.

A friend of mine tells a story about her childhood cat. How, when she was growing up in New Hampshire, he spent most of his time grooming his long, white fur and sleeping in the sun. How, one day, he sauntered into the house, his mouth full of red and blue feathers—remains of a neighbor's pet parrot. How he was a hunter all along. The postcard I chose for her is fairly generic: a photograph of some ruins intersecting with a modern-day Roman traffic jam. It's similar to the three or four others I picked for certain people, friends who have become something close to family.

One for a classmate from RISD who unofficially adopted me in our second year, took me to parties, lent me Elizabeth Hardwick's essays, taught me about existentialism, that oysters were better with hot sauce, and how much coke would keep me up for days, instead of hours. I returned the favor later, driving two and a half hours out to the Hamptons one night to rescue her from a boyfriend who liked to smack her around when he'd had too much to drink.

Another for a girl I met when she was a model in my life drawing class—a dancer who liked the way I shaded her outstretched arms and insisted on watching me paint. She'd come to my studio in Queens, when I still had it, sit next to the electric heater in the dead of winter, and read poems out loud while I worked. We'd share a thermos of milky tea and go find hot toddies at the nearest bar as soon as the sun went down.

I told them all I'd write. Their postcards are sitting blank, probably folded or stained, in the bottom of my bag.

The Spanish Steps look exactly as I remember them, unfurling from the church and its obelisk above down to the shallow Fontana della Barcaccia below. Two small children on the inside of its low barricade are contemplating stepping into the pool itself, egging each other on. The piazza that surrounds us is paved with stone walked smooth by centuries of people. Bougainvillea wanting to overflow the neatly spaced planters that contain it. The lamps have just flickered on.

I turn down a side street, ugly with too-bright signs advertising drink-shot specials and free tiramisu with dinner, in search of pasta. "Don't let the location or the look of the place put you off," a friend told me before I left New York. "It's so worth it."

The chef makes three different types every day, she said, based on what's fresh at the market or whatever's inspiring him in the moment. You can order one or two or a bit of all three. All options laid out behind glass in heated metal trays, like an assembly line or a school cafeteria. Everything is takeaway, only ten euros, and, she claimed, the best pasta she's had in Rome.

Not only is the storefront completely dark, but the metal gate is pulled down. A padlock connects a thick, rusting chain through the Push/Pull handles of the door. Just in case all the lights being off wasn't clear enough. "I told you," Michael might say. "Remember?

About Sundays?" But there's no one else's disappointment to manage tonight, just my own.

By now, I'm so hungry it doesn't matter that I'm wasting a precious dinner in Rome on a slice of pizza. All that counts is finding some, and soon.

It takes effort not to turn into the first pizzeria I see, one whose windows are plastered with laminated pictures of tomatoes and chefs wearing white hats, lovingly holding bottles of olive oil. But I hold out until I find one that doesn't look objectively like a tourist trap, even though it sits between two souvenir shops playing techno music. And there's a line, which I choose to believe is a good sign. Once it's my turn, the man behind the counter spins his spatula around two fingers and waits for me to say something.

I start with *"Io vorrei...,"* but the word for mushroom is suddenly a total mystery. Instead of fumbling and trying to explain myself, I start pointing, with an apologetic smile, at three different slices. He warms them in the oven for me, packs them in a box.

I should probably look for a place to sit and eat, but I can't wait, pull out one of the thick, square slices, balance its weight between my fingers, and take a massive bite as I walk. The oil from an artichoke, baked into a layer of mozzarella and shaved fennel and chili flakes, slides down my chin.

The rumble of Campo de Fiori at night is palpable, so I sidestep down Via dei Farnesi. My eyes adjust a bit to the darkness—the only lights here are barely strong enough to clarify the numbers of buildings or give drama to window-boxed flowers. I know I'm walking toward the apartment and away from the crowds, but it still feels strange that everyone I pass is going in the opposite direction. No one seems to notice the mess I'm making or the satisfaction it's giving me.

Monti is still loud, even though it's late. I can hear the laughter and tipsy conversation in the piazza from a few streets away.

I walk down Via Urbana, almost tripping twice, thanks to the downward slope and the weight of my legs, heavy from the heat and miles of hills and stone steps. I'm close enough to the apartment to find my way without consulting anything but my memory. To my right, there's live jazz coming from a tiny bar, its glass doors thrown open. A slow, patient take on "All of Me," or some other standard that sounds just like it: the trumpet clean and clear, drums so steady and measured they're almost imperceptible. Subtle scaffolding holding the rest of the song up and together. But the room is too full, the lights too bright. It's not a place to hide, which is what I want, what I'm looking for.

I find it, oddly enough, in the busy piazza, sitting on the lip of the fountain, set apart but not so much as to be conspicuous. I'm even careful of how long I stare in which direction, watching the conversation at one table, then moving my gaze to another. Then to a woman walking her dog once more around the corner before they both go to sleep. Her sandals quickly kicked on, the buckles that slap her heel with every step, left unfastened. It's strange, learning how to be alone again. The sudden, but not unwelcome quiet of it.

Though quiet like this can be easy to puncture. It's more likely I'll remember the shift in John's face when I started to cry, how he seemed to be practiced in comforting and calming not just me, but anyone, maybe himself most of all. How, two weeks before I flew here, the doorman handed me an envelope enclosing a smooth, cream-colored card that read, in my dad's unmistakable scrawl, *The older you get, the more forgiveness you need.*

I almost jump when a man sitting a few feet away offers me a Peroni, cold and dripping, from the cooler between his feet. He smiles and nods at my *grazie,* then turns back to his conversation, never looking my way again. A simple gesture, asking nothing in return.

A slight breeze lifts the hair off my neck as I take a first sip. The coolest air I've felt all day.

MONDAY

I'D EXPECT TO FIND a cottage like this—quaint, low-lying, built with warm, pink stone—in the countryside of Italy, or even the South of France. But it's just off the piazza in Monti, covered in unruly ivy. Trimmed back around the windows and doors, but barely. I can see new green shoots, starting to creep in.

I've been here an hour, possibly two. My flimsy chair pushed back, flush with the corner of the room so I have a better view of the street. I give myself thirty seconds to sketch each person who passes by. My notebook is already half full of them, these wisps of people. Swinging arms and handbags, careful steps, tucked-in shirts, too-big sunglasses, and pursed lips.

Morning has become afternoon; my espresso has become a spritz. I prop my phone up against the side of the drink and film the strokes of my pen, the flips of pages.

Via del Pozzuolo is empty for a few minutes, so I start to draw the waitress. Her black shirt, black jeans, black apron tied tight to accentuate a waist. Every stray strand of hair noticed and pulled back with a pin. I rotate the paper one way, then another to get the shading on her nose ring just right. I want it to be a little unclear whether or not she has one, depending on which way her head is turned, whether that bit of silver is catching the light. Ambiguous, the way it looks to me now.

"Excuse me," she asks, suddenly over my shoulder. "This is me?"

I hope she isn't irritated, me drawing her without her permission, but she seems interested, maybe even flattered. I tell her yes, and then, in the most fluid Italian I can muster, "*Vorresti tenerlo?*"

She nods, excited, but wants to practice her English. "You can sign it?" She mimes the scribble of a pen.

I fill the bottom right corner with the little curl of my name and, after considering it for a moment, my social media handle, giving each equal billing. In case she wants to find me again.

I see SPQR everywhere, so often I've almost stopped noticing: on coins and manhole covers and tattooed on the arm of someone walking by. The she-wolf, too. Carved into fountains and statues and monuments, standing guard over the two future founders of this city. They're always reaching up, grasping for her, for more attention and food and life.

I know, without fully admitting it, that I've been making my way back to Esquilino. Obeying a subtle but strong gravitational pull.

Decadent façades and dripping ivy are interspersed among buildings in varying states of collapse. Some of their roofs are visibly crumbling, outlines in sharp contrast against the sky.

A café has set up a few tables on an otherwise empty street. I see John sitting outside, reading *Memoirs of Hadrian* and drinking what looks like a vermouth and soda. It's hard to tell whether he's lonely or just alone. I wonder how long I can stand here before he notices. My feet throb with gratitude at the chance to rest, the soles of my leather sandals worn and starting to curl from sweat. The hem of my tomato-red skirt, long and thin, rests against my ankle.

But he sees me first.

"Haven't had enough of Esquilino yet?" he yells across the street to me. It echoes.

I walk close enough to answer without raising my voice. "I guess not."

He gestures for me to sit. "If you want."

I do. He puts the book down and looks at me.

"I never asked. Why did you choose here to live, this neighborhood?"

"All the history seems incidental around here. Things don't have so much weight," he says, leaning back in his chair, looking up at the sunbaked peach of the building behind us. "I like that. The Porta Maggiore, the aqueduct that runs through the market in the Piazza Vittorio. Some things stay, others are gone stunningly fast." He takes a sip of his drink. "They dug up more ruins just recently. What used to be an ancient fountain, less than a mile from here, by chance, while expanding a metro station. There's not much reason to any of it."

If he's not going to acknowledge it, then I will. "I'm sorry you had to see me like that, the other night. And me leaving in the morning, without saying anything. Especially after you were so kind. I'm sorry."

"You don't need to apologize. I overstepped. And I shouldn't make assumptions, like you said. We don't really know each other, after all." He smiles.

"I don't know if that's completely true." He's giving me an out, but I don't want to take it. "My relationship with my dad... well, it's complex. Even I don't fully understand it. I know it's far from perfect. That's pretty clear. But there are certain things I can't change. Or haven't been able to."

"I understand."

"But I should have handled it better. Something in me just, I don't know. Broke."

He shakes his head. "You feel deeply. That's a good thing."

True relief floods me, the release of a muscle I didn't even know I was taxing, pushing too hard. I want to give him something in return.

"Meeting you, spending this time, all of it, it means something to me," I say. "Truly. Even though it's only been a few days. It matters."

"Nice to hear you say that." He's trying not to smile, I think. Looking down at his hands.

"I'm sorry I couldn't tell you that the other night. You've been so honest with me."

"Don't feel like you have to reciprocate, that's not what I meant."

"I know. I'm just telling you why. And that you're not the only one who cares."

The waiter brings a bowl of pitted green olives, shining in oil. I let one melt in my mouth.

"I was supposed to be here with someone," I tell him. "This whole trip was planned for someone else."

"Right, your itineraries. I remember."

"I think I've been struggling with that a little."

"Letting that go?"

"More like how easy it's been to let it go."

"Do you miss him, this person?"

"No, I don't." Lying about this is as easy as saying nothing. "Well, maybe a little. But not as much, or in the same way that I thought I would."

"What's that?" John asks, pointing to the magazine I bought yesterday, its oversized cover still peeking out the top of my bag. He lights a rolled cigarette that I quickly learn is actually a joint.

I explain finding the issue in the bookshop, open to the pages of my drawings. He traces the lines and shadows I made with his fingers, maybe trying to figure them out. "These are lovely," he says.

"Assignments like this pay pretty well," I tell him. "Though I guess that means I might be selling out a bit."

"No, that's not it. I think you're building something," he says.

Trying to compliment Michael was always an exercise in futility. Whenever I told him I'd loved an essay he'd written or that something I'd seen or heard had reminded me of a line from one of his stories, he'd act sheepish, almost sweetly embarrassed, but he never was. Not really. I don't think I was capable of bringing that out in him. I was good enough for some things, but not others.

A few months after we met, I went to a reading he gave at a small bar in Brooklyn, its walls sponge-painted algae green. I sat at a table near the back, watching him stand behind the little podium. I remember how thrilled I was when I thought he locked eyes with me during a passage about walking the streets of Hamra as night turned back into day.

"Were you looking at me, when you read tonight?" I asked him, sitting on his roof afterward, Tribeca rising around us.

"No," he said, not unkindly. "I wasn't looking at anyone."

A group of teenagers gather around the fountain that marks the piazza at the end of the street. "Message in a Bottle" is either reverberating out of a restaurant's open door or, chosen by one of the kids, playing from a speaker or phone. It grows louder as we walk toward them.

When writing a song, you can just sing that it feels like summer, strum a guitar in the right sort of way, and people believe you. In a poem or a painting, you have to convince them.

The sound of laughter carries from a small, crowded gelato shop. People are waiting outside, children jumping up and down in anticipation.

"Do you want some?" John asks. "Looking at it, I'm suddenly starving."

We consider a long row of flavors, all of them shaped into frozen swirls to look as inviting as possible. Each one has its own prop. Mint leaves, chocolate chips, cubes of caramel: meant to be explanatory, regardless of language.

John chooses *limone*. The woman scoops some out of the tub using what looks like a palette knife. She avoids the decorative slices of lemon on top.

"That's what I wanted," I tell him, pretending to be bereft. "What do I do now?"

He catches the woman's attention and asks her for another cup, I think, but he speaks quickly and with a series of gestures I can't translate. She digs into a vat of neon-green gelato, sprinkled with pistachios coming out of their shells. Once she's finished shaping it into the little cup, she grabs a bottle of olive oil, stashed under the display case, and starts to pour. It pools on top, then starts to run down the sides.

They might be limitless—all the new and different things you can have if you know who to ask, and in the right way.

"Your dad is a bit of poet," John says as we cross the square, his face puckered a bit from the sweet and sour of the lemon.

"What do you mean?"

"I was listening to his most recent album this morning."

"*Mirror Twin?*" He wrote those songs around the time I left for college, when he was convinced my mother was about to leave him.

"Right. There was this one lyric I really liked: 'Sometimes you need someone to remind you that you are filled with light.'"

Someone has left candles on the three worn steps that lead to the door of his building. I didn't notice them on Saturday. Marking the entrance like it's some sort of sacred place.

John's keys are already in his hand. Before climbing the first step, he looks back, just to be sure I'm still behind him.

He pulls a lighter from his back pocket and clicks a flame into each one. It's just dark enough for us to see them, the shadows they make.

His neighbors are brewing coffee on their terrace. I can hear scattered bits of their conversation, smell the deep, bitter espresso—always better than the actual taste. Otherwise, the air is thick and completely quiet.

The sun is starting to set, so different from even two nights ago. Now we're enveloped by color instead of observing it from above. The pinks and oranges and purples, deepening by the minute. I'm leaning against the little counter that separates the kitchen from the rest of the apartment, sipping the last of my melted gelato from the cup, watching John watch me from the balcony.

"Will you touch yourself for me?" he asks. "Please?"

"Right here? Now?"

"Yes."

I start unbuttoning my mother's shirt.

"I want to see what it looks like when you let yourself go."

I almost make a joke, tell him I'd love to know what that looks like myself, that I don't think I've ever seen it. But I work to surrender to what I know feels good, what reliably frees me. Until, standing naked, hair hanging loose against the skin of my shoulders, legs spread in view of the window, it doesn't feel like work anymore.

It's hard, sometimes, to convince myself I deserve something. Right now it's the easiest choice, close to a fact.

When I open my eyes, he's sitting on his knees on the floor in front of me. "Fuck, that's so beautiful." He looks up at me with the simplest expression: one of reverence.

I allow myself to joyfully disappear.

My smell is everywhere: his hands and face, the sheet I'm wrapped in, the air that hangs above us, no breeze forcing it to move.

"I'm glad you decided to come here anyway. When your original plan"—he pauses for a moment—"fell through."

"Me too."

"And I'm sorry he hurt you, whoever he is. You don't deserve to be lied to, to be tossed aside like that."

"Maybe that's what upset me so much. The feeling that it was inevitable, him just passing time with me. And then seeing that confirmed."

"Honestly? It sounds like he's just an asshole."

"I know I shouldn't take it so personally. But it's hard not to think it means something else, something I wasn't or couldn't be."

"Of course you take it personally. It's personal." He says this in a way I actually believe. "But you're awfully lovable. I'd try not to worry about it too much."

Awfully lovable. I want to never forget those two words, their power in being said together, by him and to me at this precise moment.

I'm just now noticing the little aloe plant on his balcony. It's on the ground, in a generic-looking terracotta pot, pushed into a now-shaded corner, but it seems to be thriving just the same. I wonder if it came with the place or if maybe John bought it himself on a whim, something to care for. A new green leaf is curling from the center, finding its way up and out.

I see the shirt he wore on Friday hanging on a thin wire hanger—bright white linen, still smelling a little of sweat—and put it on.

He's decided to make dinner. I watch him drop anchovies in simmering butter. He stirs until they disappear, then adds black pepper. I hear the grinder make its quick, satisfying turns.

I'm starting to learn this apartment, the flow of one section into another, the emphasis on the balcony and its view. The loose knob on the cabinet above the stove, the disappearing paint on the light switch in the bathroom, worn down by so many fingers touching it in the exact same way.

What would happen if I were here with John for many nights, endless nights, instead of just three? Would we take turns making meals? Would he bring me coffee in the morning, or would we always go to the bar for espresso? Would I wake him up with sex every day, and how long until that excitement faded? Would he be quick to challenge me, retreat when I threw that focus back at him? Would I always be afraid to criticize him, my sadness for what he's been through eventually shriveling into pity? Would he, once he realized, use it as an excuse to push me away? Did he take me in so easily this time just because I admitted I was wrong?

The tomatoes he's cutting are sweet like dessert, warm from sitting in a bowl on the windowsill. He makes thick slices, sprinkles them with salt. I pick one up and eat it like an apple, one greedy bite after another. But I'm careful to roll up the sleeves of his shirt first. A little bit of juice starts to run down my arm, but I catch it just in time.

There's a little parade making its way through the neighborhood. A steady stream of people, most of them older, a few with children, move at a leisurely pace. They sing, shake tambourines, stop to say *buona sera* and *buona notte* as they pass friends sitting down to dinner.

As it grows louder, we lean out the window, look down at the street. One of the men, seemingly the ringleader, holds a guitar.

"What do you think it's all for?" I ask. "Or does this kind of thing happen here just because?"

John shakes his head. "Not sure. I remember something similar, maybe two months ago. Some kind of birthday remembrance or celebration for the guy who invented vaudeville. He was Italian, apparently. Or it might just be our usual parade." He kisses me lightly, briefly, then turns back to finish washing a dish. The faucet has been running.

After shaking his hands dry and a few taps of his finger to his phone screen, "Hungry Heart" starts to play, loud. The assault of drums right away, the manic piano, the swell of the saxophone.

I roll my eyes. "Oh, God. Bruce Springsteen? Really?"

"What? You can't be too cool for Bruce, surely." He swats my hand away when I try to press pause. "Anyway, it's a song that always makes me happy."

That broad smile is true, I can tell. I watch it take over his face. And I don't look away at the first opportunity, as I tend to do when I see such honest, uncomplicated happiness. Instead, I study the lines his past smiles have made and wonder, what does it mean to leave your life behind?

"A little later in the summer, there's a much bigger parade. They march a statue of the Virgin Mary through the streets for most of the day. People sing and throw coins as she passes by."

"That sounds nice."

"It is. They finish in a piazza not far from here, and it turns into a party. Slices of watermelon and local wine for everyone."

"Why watermelon?"

"Because it's in season, I guess." He takes a sip of wine. "And cheap."

A drop of condensation from his glass falls and hits my shoulder. It travels down my back as I look out the window, trying to find the end of the procession. His chin rests on the top of my head and he puts weight into it. I can smell garlic on his skin. The E Street Band's electric organ, played with gusto, fades in the background.

"Sometimes I think maybe I've decided to stay here so I can rot with style."

"Not rot," I tell him. "Decay, maybe."

"You're right. Decay sounds better. Much more dignified."

His body absorbs the shake of my laughter.

The singing and talking and footsteps beneath us combine to create their own kind of hum, so sustained I almost stop hearing it.

"Sure, I'm ready to die," he says. "But I'm also ready to live."

A little girl on the street below hits a pan with a wooden spoon, over and over. Squealing with delight at the sound, that she's not just permitted but encouraged to be so loud.

"Does that make sense?" he asks me.

TUESDAY

I WONDER IF I could ever know Rome the way I do New York.

Not as home, which New York will always be for me, but as another kind of shelter, maybe. Its details might become familiar, like knowing the right time to walk by Balthazar to smell the bread baking and which subway steps in my neighborhood are reliably guarded by an old man playing guitar in the evenings. All the memories and sensations and tricks I've played on myself to make me feel safe and held in an inherently dangerous, lonely place.

I wake up slowly and alone. John isn't in the bed, kitchen, bathroom, or on the balcony. In an apartment this small, there are only so many places to look. It's possible he's gone to get breakfast or taken a phone call outside or felt the need to stretch his legs for some reason.

Or could he have left me here on purpose? Did he turn over and see me this morning and feel doubt, not peace or satisfaction or the happiness I thought I sensed? With every empty minute that passes, me standing naked in his living room, no sign of him anywhere, it becomes a little more likely. Maybe last night's ease, that bit of joy I felt, didn't mean what I thought it did.

Maybe he's walking away now, to the espresso bar or some other usual place of his I've never heard of, wondering how much time he needs to allow before I show myself out. Maybe he figured it would be easier to just leave me behind, cut off the oxygen that these past few days have been. It's something he knows how to do.

But now I see he's left me a note in the kitchen, a piece of scrap paper weighed down by a lemon from the bowl on the counter.

Downstairs.

Coffee.

Come and have some?

One line stacked on top of another like a poem.

I find my clothes from yesterday, open my bag to grab my new sketchbook and a few euro coins that have fallen to the bottom. I let myself check my phone.

Mom has called twice and sent a text.

Have a safe flight. When do you leave?

Whenever Jack or I travel, she always needs the details. I think it calms her, to know when we're in the air, when we're back on her soil. Even if it's just logistics, nothing more.

The answer to her question is: *Soon.* Very soon, and growing sooner. Especially since the suitcase I imagined so seamlessly packing is in a different apartment, at least a half hour away, my clothes still strewn all over the floor. But I don't respond.

What would she do, in this situation, presented with these options? Knowing what I know? She used to love an adventure, I'm sure of that. Maybe she still loves the idea of one. I'm also sure she's weighed that against what it means to stay where she is, with all of its comforts and indignities, and decided it wasn't worth it.

The last night I spent in Hudson, she and I talked about diplomacy. A famous diplomat had recently died. He'd had a hand in every US conflict since Vietnam and helped transform foreign policy while deescalating wars and conflicts all over the world. He'd also been a nightmare of a husband and father, ultimately dying at his desk of a heart attack.

The obituaries and op-eds discussing his legacy were everywhere, as was a well-timed, sympathetic biography. Mom had bought the book, but I'm not sure if she ever read it. I see a copy of it here on John's shelf.

It was late. I sat at the edge of my parents' bed, arguing what good was a talent at tact and subtlety and peacekeeping if he had to abandon his family and his health to really use it? My mother leaned back against a pillow and shrugged.

"It's sad, yes. But not everyone is cut out to be a perfect spouse and parent. He was meant to do other important things. And besides, I'm sure the people of Bosnia are grateful to him."

Dad was brushing his teeth, filling a glass with water, finding the book he'd read a few pages of before falling asleep. I didn't think he'd been listening, but he stopped, looked at us both, and said, "You're both equal parts kind and uncompromising. It's what gives you strength. I know I'm grateful for it. You should be, too."

John reads; I sketch the breakfast belonging to the group at the next table. Two deep-brown cornetti, cut into pieces. One spread with a thick layer of Nutella, the other bursting with cream. Three espressos, one topped with foam, another with zabaglione. Orange juice, fresh squeezed and cloudy with pulp.

John pulls one of the little, flimsy napkins from the dispenser between us.

"I've never understood these." He crushes one in his hand. "It's not even that they're ineffective. They actively work against you. I think they might actually be made of plastic."

"And yet here they are, on every table."

My flight is at 5:35 p.m. When the waiter puts my espresso in front of me, it's 10:42 a.m. Fiumicino is at least half an hour away by taxi. Security and customs, another hour probably. Everything I've brought with me, except the clothes I'm wearing, is in the apartment in Monti. Nothing is packed. I'd need to allow even more time for that, more motion and energy that seem like distant concepts as I sit here.

But it's possible: John left alone on this side street, my suitcase full as I pull it over the threshold, hearing that stubborn door click behind me like it's supposed to, running through the terminal with minutes to spare. I could delay just enough, so I'm too rushed to think about anything else. There's still time for all of it to fall into place, but not much.

John knows this and says nothing. I wonder how long it's been since he got on a plane back to New York, how thoroughly he's run away from what used to be his life. When was the last time he saw his old friends, shared a meal with his parents, visited the place where his son is buried? Does he ever let himself consider what might have been?

I watch him draw a line down the margin of the page he's

just finished. It's a new paperback and doesn't want to bend, but his thumb flattens it, pries the spine open. His other hand holds the pen.

The mark isolates a paragraph in the middle of the page, opposite a photograph showing a statue of Antinous, Hadrian's lover, deified after he died young. His face is perfect, but haunting; the eyes sculpted so smooth they look plucked out. Hair bent to look like snakes.

"I like this," John says, and starts to read to me. "Popular tradition has not been wrong in regarding love always as a force of initiation, one of the points of encounter of the secret with the sacred."

"I don't know. It's beautiful, but a little simplistic, don't you think?"

"You should listen to Hadrian. He could teach you a thing or two."

"Another great man to learn from. Fantastic."

He grins as he finishes his cappuccino, tipping the cup back. "Guess you don't need any more of those, do you?"

"I think I have just enough, thanks."

"*Allora*," he says, pleasantly surprising me with the shift in his voice, the change he can make in an instant. "*Ti andrebbe un altro caffè?*"

"*Sì, certo.*"

He gets up and turns toward the open door of the café. The worn soles of his espadrilles on the tile floor, his arms leaning on the metal of the bar while he orders us more coffee and chats with whoever is making it.

I pull a fresh napkin from the dispenser and start to sketch myself as an empress, the kind of ruler ancient Rome never had. Taking inspiration from Hadrian on the cover: flowing robes, steely gaze, toga with requisite bare shoulder, finger pointed with purpose at the horizon. The napkin doesn't want to cooperate with my pen, but I press harder. Adding my long, stubbornly straight hair, one eyebrow slightly higher than the other, ugly feet, a slight smile.

I slip it inside the book, marking his place, and wait for him to come back and find it.

ACKNOWLEDGMENTS

To Susan Golomb—for recognizing Roscioli and changing my life, for believing in this story and in me as a writer.

To Karen Kosztolnyik—for a keen and thoughtful editorial eye, and for lovingly bringing this book into the world. Heartfelt thanks to Kamrun Nesa, Rachael Kelly, and everyone at Grand Central Publishing.

To Kimberly Burns—for behind-the-scenes magic and the best (R-rated) elevator pitch ever.

To Paul Beatty, Charles Bock, David Ebershoff, Sigrid Nunez, and Elissa Schappell—for sharing your brilliance, wisdom, and faith with me.

To Brian Ford—for listening always, for helping me find my voice and use it.

To Adrienne Brodeur and Lisa Taddeo—for supporting me and this novel, and for gracing its cover with your words.

To Katya Kazbek and Madelaine Lucas—for insight, encouragement, negronis, and reading with so much intelligence and care. Beautiful writers, beautiful friends.

To Kate Thorman—for reading and reading and reading again.

Thank you for seeing the note within every note, and for being just a phone call away.

To Ian Walsh and Melissa D'Agnese Walsh—for bringing "Chaos" to beautiful life and answering every Bruce Springsteen– and Leonard Cohen–related text with enthusiasm. And to Mimi Giacco Walsh for suggesting I listen to both versions of "Both Sides Now."

To Cynthia and Nelson Farris—for believing in me from the start, and for riotous living.

To Jenessa Abrams, Ali Biss, Maeve Conneighton, Bridget Good-win, Tony Rotunno, Sarah and Mike Siebold, and Hadley Smith— for true friendship, unwavering support, and so much fun. I'm beyond lucky to have you.

To Lea Carpenter—for seeing something in me, even when I couldn't. I'm blessed to call you a confidante and dear friend.

To Alex and Nick Giacco—for bringing your kindness, humor, and joy into my life. I can't imagine it without you.

And to my parents, Christine and Alex Giacco—for giving me a world full of books and possibility, for protecting and encouraging my creativity always. And for taking me to Italy. With all my love and gratitude.

ABOUT THE AUTHOR

Francesca Giacco is a graduate of Barnard College and the MFA program at Columbia University. She lives in New York. *Six Days in Rome* is her first novel.

Reading Group Guide

SIX DAYS in ROME

FRANCESCA GIACCO

QUESTIONS FOR READERS

1. In the opening chapter, Emilia insists on being addressed by her full name: "No nicknames, abbreviations, or shortcuts. Even at times when it would have been easy to settle for any of those alternatives, I've insisted, corrected people's pronunciation, written in the right spelling on class rosters and preprinted name tags." Why do you think Emilia is unwilling to compromise on the use of her given name? How does this early declaration set the stage for Emilia's journey of self-discovery and identity?

2. Writing a postcard to her parents, Emilia is comforted by the fact that, in the process of reminiscing, she "can rewrite history," i.e., keep the memories she cherishes and discard the ones that trouble her. We're often told that memory is subjective, but have you ever intentionally tried to edit a memory, to reshape an experience into something that's less jarring or embarrassing or painful to recall? Or do you believe it's important to preserve the true emotional impact of a moment?

3. Reinvention is introduced as a concept at multiple points in the novel. Like rewriting history, Emilia freely admits that she's a creative liar, adding embellishments to conversations to make

something more memorable: "There's comfort in it, knowing I can reliably become more than I am." How did this revelation make you feel? Did you appreciate her candor in this moment, or even relate to her? Or did you trust her less as a narrator? In your opinion, is Emilia's propensity to stretch the truth—or perform—an asset or a flaw?

4. When Emilia was a child, she used to pretend to be an explorer or a goddess with her father, who would also take on the persona of a larger-than-life character. How did their shared love of make-believe end up harming Emilia later in life? At what point does performance become dangerous? Do you think this led to Emilia's revelation in Rome, that "so much of what [she's] built on is crumbling"? Explain.

5. In churches across the city, Emilia would light a candle for someone in her life—from close friends and family to "lapsed friends" and strangers—for anyone who ever made her feel "nervous or hopeful or safe." Have you ever had a brief yet profound interaction with a stranger, someone you continue to think of? Why do you think your mind returns to this moment, despite the time that has passed?

6. At times, Emilia comes across as completely in control of her surroundings and her preferences. She does admit, however, that she likes feeling "confused and upended" every once in a while by the unexpected. Do you believe this is an essential component of travel? Why or why not?

7. While in Rome, Emilia tries to limit the amount of communication she has with her friends and family in New York. She hopes the solitude will help her "see more clearly," especially when it comes to her relationships with her ex-lover and her father. Do you believe Emilia achieves the clarity she was seeking over the course of the novel? How does this quote—"Today I am alone. I am in a beautiful place. I am honest, with nothing to hide. I am better off."—relate to this idea?

8. Michael tells Emilia that "the reason we love someone is because we share [the other person's] adjectives." Do you agree or disagree with this statement? Did Michael's description of love resonate with you, or did you prefer Emilia's father's interpretation, that "real love ain't the tender moments / It's the chaos in between"?

9. The line mentioned above—that "real love ain't the tender moments / It's the chaos in between"—was paraphrased by Emilia's father from a poem Emilia wrote at age seven: "Love isn't always beautiful / But chaos makes it real." This borrowing becomes a major sticking point for Emilia in adulthood, which culminates in an emotionally charged conversation with John, in which he says that her father stole something precious from her. Do you believe Emilia's father owed Emilia an apology for what he did, or do you believe that most art is inspired by the artists who come before?

10. *Six Days in Rome* is, partly, a love letter to one of the greatest cities on Earth. Did the sensory details included in the novel—descriptions of wine, pasta, music, colors, the glow of candles, the expressions on faces, the texture of window boxes—succeed in transporting you to Italy? What was your favorite scene and why? How did the book's focus on all things sensual influence your experience of it?

11. In Michael's Beirut-based novel, the main character is described as being "unmoored and feeling hopeless," until he meets a French woman who teaches at the university. "For a time, it seems she might be able to offer the happiness and security he's been seeking, could possibly save him from a life in which he's barely present." Did you see any parallels between Michael's relationship with Emilia and the Lebanese man's relationship with the French woman? If so, what? How do you think the novel Michael wrote ended?

12. Martyrdom and sainthood are two concepts that the author returns to throughout the novel: "I've never understood any of them: the selflessness and certainty, the tolerance for pain, relinquishing all their free will, ultimately their lives, for some vague, protective cloud of faith. But maybe I should be thinking about it differently, how they sought and held on to power." Did the latter half of this statement complement or upend your understanding of martyrdom and sainthood? Why? What do you think is so compelling about the mix of the sacred and the worldly?

13. At one point, Emilia observes that "Rome doesn't know what to do with a woman alone," that the "lack of a man, or anyone who might help to explain me, stands out, poses a question." Discuss society's prolonged anxiety regarding single women, and how female independence can still be stigmatized today.

14. An intrinsic part of Emilia's personality is her desire to constantly assess things, both herself and the subjects of her work. In one sense, this is positive: "Somehow, the collision of my sense of humor and endless appetite to evaluate, judge, and try to understand people has made me successful." In another, it is negative: "Checking, evaluating, assessing myself always...Wherever I go, if there's a mirror or shop window or anything that shows me some version of my reflection, I have to look in it, just to be sure. It's not a choice. If I don't, or what I see is at all wrong or embarrassing, any energy or ease I might have is gone." Where do you think this desire comes from in Emilia? Her childhood? Her parents? Societal pressure? Do you believe the perpetuation of the behavior is shame, as she suggests? Why or why not?

15. After buying cheese from a local vendor, Emilia ponders whether she should eat the cheese now or bring it back to New York with her and serve it at a dinner party with friends: "This is the cheese from Rome, I'd tell them. And they'd fall all over themselves telling me how good it was, the theatrical closed eyes as they taste it. Even the thought of it is exhausting. Or I

could enjoy it now and do my best to remember it later. Not everything has to be preserved, or even shared." What was the last thing you did just for yourself, something you chose not to share, that brought you happiness? If you had been in Emilia's shoes, what would you have done?

Q&A WITH
FRANCESCA GIACCO

Q: What inspired you to write *Six Days in Rome*?

A: I knew I wanted to capture the experience of traveling alone, and how it forces us to see the world and ourselves in a different, heightened way. We notice details we'd never stop to consider at home; we have conversations with strangers. Memories present themselves in a new light.

I was also interested in how a trip like this could be transformative for someone, maybe even revelatory. So then, the question became: What if a few days alone in a foreign city could come to encapsulate and change an entire life? The novel is my attempt to answer that question.

Q: Have you always wanted to be a writer?

A: I've been reading and writing fiction since I was very young. The sense of possibility I feel when writing or thinking about stories has always meant freedom for me, the chance to get lost in my own imagination.

Q: Do you remember the first story you ever read and the impact it had on you?

A: There were many stories I read and ones my parents read to me. Those that resonated most, and continue to, were Rudyard Kipling's *Just So Stories*. His expansive descriptions, playful and intricate use of language, and close attention to the senses have deeply influenced my own writing.

Q: **When you started writing, did any particular character feel fully formed in your mind right away? Or did personalities and motivations crystallize later on in the process?**

A: Emilia was clearest to me at first—her basic outlines and personality, at least. But she shifted and changed throughout the process, especially as other characters' motivations began to reveal themselves more and more with each draft.

While she is the central character of the novel, it was important for me to remember that the people in her life exist separately from her, with their own wants and versions of events. I think that can be one of the interesting elements of a first-person narrative like this one: How much do we trust her? How clearly do we think she sees herself and those she loves?

Q: **Did writing the novel involve any research?**

A: All Rome-related details come from my own time spent in the city, including a trip in the winter of 2019 when I was writing the first draft of the novel. I'd never been in Rome in January before, and walking much emptier streets in the cold rain gave me an appreciation for the heat that Emilia feels in July.

I also researched some elements of Catholicism and art history, especially the religious art and traditions that appear in the novel. And I spent time learning about the life of Leonard Cohen, who is the inspiration for Emilia's father.

Q: Take us through some of the significant locations in the novel. Have you personally visited all of these places? Generally speaking, how has travel informed your writing?

A: All locations in the novel are real places in Rome and New York that have some significance to me. I chose not to name most of them so readers could see each one individually and draw their own conclusions, though people who have spent time in either city may be able to guess.

It probably comes as no surprise, having written a novel like this one, that travel is hugely important to me, in writing and in life. Going somewhere new and experiencing different lives and cultures inspire creativity and curiosity like nothing else. And it's an incredible privilege to do so.

Q: The descriptions in *Six Days in Rome* are particularly transporting and lush. How do you approach sensory writing, and how did you go about perfectly capturing the taste of a vibrant wine or the texture of Italian coffee—writing these descriptions, perhaps, far away from Italy?

A: Writing sensually, with sensory details in mind, has always been what makes the most sense to me. I think it's the type of writing that's most true to life in how we experience the world, through the food we taste, the air we feel on our skin. I'm consistently paying close attention to those kinds of moments and how they create mood or shift the tone in a story.

Some of the books I love most have this focus. When sensual details are understood and deployed well, I think it makes for some of the most powerful and universal language we have.

There's a lot about being in Rome that affects me powerfully, and that I don't fully understand. It's always given me a deep feeling of calm and peace, more so than any other place. I think, in many ways, writing this story and getting as close as I could to my memories and experience of being there, was an exploration of that, trying to figure it out.

Q: Self-reflection versus external relationships—between friends, lovers, and members of one's family—push and pull Emilia's decisions throughout the novel. How did you strike a balance between these two concepts?

A: It was important to me to capture the overlap of inner and outer worlds, all our lives living within us at the same time, and how traveling alone can bring that feeling to the surface. So I was committed to reflecting that on the page, as accurately as I could.

Much of this was trial and error, reading and rereading and making sure that I was writing equal parts internally and externally, not lingering too long in a memory or scene. All with the hope that Emilia's voice would be strong and clear enough to carry these shifts and not lose the reader in the process.

Q: Describe Emilia's work as an artist and the way she satirizes

contemporary life. **What made you decide on this career path for Emilia, and play with the ideas of connection, relatability, and "accidental anthropology" through art?**

A: I knew from the start that she would be an artist (still creative, in a different way than her father), but wanted to explore what that meant in today's world. What it is to be an artist has changed significantly, with the rise of social media and all the different ways art can be appreciated and dismissed. The art world has always been status-obsessed and changeable, but there's no doubt that the internet has made it easier to both show your art to a huge audience and also feel rejected or dissatisfied by that response.

It can be challenging to write about technology, especially as it's come to touch every part of our lives. But I decided to embrace it, instead of dancing around it, and it gave me the opportunity to better understand how Emilia sees the world, what she values, what success and shame look like to her.

Q: Emilia's father is loosely based on the singer-songwriter Leonard Cohen. What about Cohen inspired you to do this, and why did you want to explore a daughter's relationship with a famous father?

A: I'd always admired Cohen's music, but didn't know much about him beyond his most popular songs. A few years after his death, his son Adam put together a book of previously unpublished poems, drawings, and lyrics, and did some interviews about the process and his relationship with his father. I listened to one, out of curiosity, and the inspiration grew from there. I'd always been interested in the children of famously artistic people, and knew I wanted to explore that dynamic in the novel—how talent and ambition are passed down, or not.

Around the same time, an exhibit on Cohen's life and music opened at the Jewish Museum, very close to my apartment in New York. I spent hours there, captivated. Not just by Cohen's work and history, but by his persona—how magnetic and maddening he must have been. It was a precious moment in the process of writing—my whole life seemed to open up to make room for the world of the novel. It felt like everything I saw and did fit in somehow.

Q: Take us through some of the choices you made while writing in terms of structure, voice, plot, and scene setting.

A: The structure was set in my mind from the beginning: telling Emilia's story within the confines of a vacation, with pressure building as time passed. I wanted her voice to mirror the way we all tend to talk to ourselves: confessional, unfiltered, sometimes sentimental, and unreliable.

The different scenes that make up the novel were a critical element. Calibrating each one, how they build on one another, and the cumulative effect they have was essential. Any resonance or power this story has relies on that foundation.

Q: What, in your opinion, are the most important elements of good writing?

A: There are so many ways to answer this question, but, to me, it's honesty, close attention to detail and language, and trust in the reader. I don't think a good story can be a good story if it's badly written.

Q: Describe your writing space and take us through your process. Do you outline or brainstorm? Do you listen to music while writing?

A: Where I write and when changes all the time. There's nothing permanent or predictable in my writing space, which I find helpful, not feeling as if I have to be at a certain desk to work. However, I am strict about writing 1,000 words a day, which holds me accountable. I find it's better than working for a particular amount of time.

I carry a notebook with me everywhere, and have for years. While I don't necessarily make outlines or plan the way a story will end, the notebooks provide structure. Notes taken at different times in my life made their way into this novel.

Music was very important when building the world of this novel in my mind. Song lyrics appear throughout and there's a reverence for the power of music that's essential to the story. While different songs influence a character's identity or how I see a scene coming together, I don't listen to music while I'm actually writing, as I find it distracts from recognizing the sentences' own rhythm.

Q: Which books or authors have most influenced your life? Have you ever read something that made you feel or think differently about fiction? Did a particular story or novel influence the way you wrote *Six Days in Rome*?

A: There are far too many to name here—different books and writers have resonated for me at different moments in my life. And there are those that have surprised me, taught me new things about what fiction is capable of. Like *A Sport and a Pastime* by James Salter, *Home Fire* by Kamila Shamsie, *Speedboat* by Renata Adler, *A Moveable Feast* by Ernest Hemingway, *Of Love and Other Demons* by Gabriel García Márquez, *The Namesake* by Jhumpa Lahiri, and *Go, Went, Gone* by Jenny Erpenbeck.

For this novel in particular, I took a lot of inspiration from *The Pleasing Hour* by Lily King. It's another novel about an American abroad, but so much more than that. It taught me a great deal about building a narrative with complexity and writing characters empathetically. It's a beautiful book.

This novel was also heavily influenced by film, specifically *Before Sunset* and *La Grande Bellezza*.

Q: What do you hope readers will take away from reading your novel?

A: I don't think I need to convince anyone of the value of travel, of how transformative it can be, but I do hope this novel explores the idea of traveling alone in a way that's interesting or unexpected or at least thought provoking.

This is a story about an observer. Emilia pays close attention to the world, to who surrounds her, and to herself. One of the lessons she keeps learning is that no one's path is fixed. People aren't necessarily what they seem, but most of us are seeking the same things—joy, acceptance, fulfillment, and love.

VISIT **GCPClubCar.com** to sign up for the **GCP Club Car** newsletter, featuring exclusive promotions, info on other **Club Car** titles, and more.

 @grandcentralpub   @grandcentralpub   @grandcentralpub

YOUR
BOOK
CLUB
RESOURCE

VISIT
GCPClubCar.com

to sign up for the **GCP Club Car** newsletter, featuring exclusive promotions, info on other **Club Car** titles, and more.

 @grandcentralpub

 @grandcentralpub

 @grandcentralpub